ChangelingPress.com

Slash/Patriot Duet

Harley Wylde

Slash/Patriot Duet

Harley Wylde

All rights reserved.
Copyright ©2021 Harley Wylde

ISBN: 9798535650791

Publisher:
Changeling Press LLC
315 N. Centre St.
Martinsburg, WV 25404
ChangelingPress.com

Printed in the U.S.A.

Editor: Crystal Esau
Cover Artist: Bryan Keller

The individual stories in this anthology have been previously released in E-Book format.

No part of this publication may be reproduced or shared by any electronic or mechanical means, including but not limited to reprinting, photocopying, or digital reproduction, without prior written permission from Changeling Press LLC.

This book contains sexually explicit scenes and adult language which some may find offensive and which is not appropriate for a young audience. Changeling Press books are for sale to adults, only, as defined by the laws of the country in which you made your purchase.

Table of Contents

Slash (Devil's Fury MC 7) 4
   Prologue 5
   Chapter One 8
   Chapter Two 22
   Chapter Three 33
   Chapter Four 44
   Chapter Five 53
   Chapter Six 68
   Chapter Seven 82
   Chapter Eight 95
   Chapter Nine 106
   Chapter Ten 117
   Chapter Eleven 128
   Chapter Twelve 139
   Chapter Thirteen 149
   Chapter Fourteen 162
Patriot (Hades Abyss MC 6) 173
   Prologue 174
   Chapter One 182
   Chapter Two 193
   Chapter Three 202
   Chapter Four 211
   Chapter Five 223
   Chapter Six 233
   Chapter Seven 243
   Chapter Eight 258
   Chapter Nine 271
   Chapter Ten 280
   Chapter Eleven 294
   Chapter Twelve 305
   Epilogue 315
Harley Wylde 319
Changeling Press E-Books 320

Slash (Devil's Fury MC 7)

Harley Wylde

Shella -- The Devil's Fury are the only family I've ever truly had. My mom was a junkie. When she died, no one wanted me. Except Grizzly. I had a home, until things went horribly wrong. I went wild, pushed too many boundaries, and overstayed my welcome. So I ran and didn't look back. Trouble always seems to find me, so it's no surprise I ended up pregnant, alone, and scared out of my mind. Then Slash shows up. Out of all the Devil's Fury brothers to come for me, why did it have to be the one I've been crushing on since I was a teenager?

Slash -- Little Shella was always a pretty girl. Spoiled. Outspoken. A complete terror. Now that she's all grown up, she's stunning. I needed to keep my hands to myself, and maybe I would have if she hadn't been adamant not to disclose the name of her baby-daddy. Only way to protect her is to give her my name. Doesn't matter I'm old enough to be her father. When I find out her secrets, and the reason she'd behaved so badly, I know I'll do whatever it takes to make her feel safe… even if it means burying a few men. I already have blood on my hands. What's a little more?

Prologue

Slash -- Two Months Ago

I heard the party at the clubhouse, the music blasting loud enough it rattled my fucking windows. Any other time, I'd have been right there with them. Of course, until the last few months, I'd also had brightly colored hair and a penchant for danger. Before I'd been staring at forty-five. My brothers at the clubhouse were mostly in their twenties and early thirties. The closer I got to fifty, the less I felt like fucking random pussy. Which was why I was at home, searching for porn so I could yank one out in the privacy of my living room, instead of taking sloppy seconds or fifths from one of the sluts who'd come to party.

I'd stumbled across a webcam site the month before and enjoyed a few of the girls. The site had boasted someone new would be on this month, and I hadn't had a chance to watch her yet. They'd kept her identity a big secret, only posting a close-up image of her eyes. Something about her had held my attention and I'd been anxious to see her show. By the time I logged in, I could see she'd already been live for a half hour. Even though I knew her show wouldn't last much longer, I clicked to enter.

My dick went rock hard.

I couldn't see her face. The man in front of her had a fistful of her hair, blocking the upper portion of her features. I could see her lips straining around his cock as he fucked her mouth. Another man tweaked her nipple as he pounded into her from behind. I'd never been one to share, but fuck that was hot! It was also the first show I'd seen that included more than just the webcam girl, at least through this particular site. I wondered if she'd do this all the time or if it was a special introductory type of show.

I grabbed the lotion off the side table and slicked my palm before gripping my cock. Using long, slow strokes, I let the tension build as I watched them make her come. She licked her lips as the one in front of her pulled out of her mouth. I imagined that pink tongue lapping at my dick and nearly came. Jesus! I hadn't even gotten a good look at her face and already I knew she'd dominate my fantasies for a while.

"Fuck, babe. You're incredible," the first man said, petting her hair.

"I'm up for more if you are." Her voice was husky and pure sex. And strangely familiar, but I pushed the thought aside. No way I knew this little goddess. I stroked a little faster, gripping my dick harder.

"Guess you better get me hard again," the man said. "Then I'm fucking your ass."

Her lips parted and I saw the pulse in her neck flutter. He'd turned her on with his suggestion. Her gaze swung to the camera and I came, right at the same time I realized I was staring at Grizzly's daughter, Shella. Holy. Fucking. Shit.

My breath sawed in and out of my lungs as I gaped at the screen. Shella was a webcam girl? And liked getting fucked by two guys at once?

Grizzly had looked everywhere for her, until deciding to give her some space. We'd thought she'd come home when she was ready. If he found out about this, it would break his damn heart. No, if he discovered I'd just jerked off to her getting fucked on video, he'd break *me*. Even if he wasn't the Pres of our club anymore, we all still respected him, and I didn't doubt for a second he could knock me to the ground with one swing.

The trio went at it again, and the show lasted another hour, with the parting shot of Shella's pussy as she fucked herself with a vibrator. The fact I'd been rock hard the entire damn time was something I'd never tell another soul. Nor would I admit to jerking off twice more as I'd watched her pleasure herself.

Even now, my balls ached with need. Knowing it was Shella made it feel all kinds of wrong, but I couldn't deny I hadn't wanted a woman this bad in months. Hell, maybe longer. Why hadn't I realized sooner she'd grown into a sexy, curvy woman?

I texted the web address to Outlaw. *Find out where the IP is located. And keep it quiet.*

He responded almost immediately. *Trouble?*

Not the kind he was thinking about. *A woman.*

I'd leave it at that. Let him think what he wanted. I needed to find Shella and bring her home. Right after I spanked her ass for fucking random men for money. She might not be out on the streets selling herself, but she'd whored herself out just the same. If her sister found out, it would break Lilian's heart. After all she'd suffered in Colombia, to have Shella do something like this was a slap in the face.

"I'm coming for you, little girl, and when I find you, there will be hell to pay."

I paid the extra to play back some of the scenes, and I took a picture with my phone of both men. If I found them, they were dead.

Chapter One

Shella

The Hades Abyss had somewhat politely asked me to stop doing the webcam show and hinted that I should go home. All right. They hadn't been polite about it at all. In fact, they'd seemed a bit concerned what would happen if my dad found out what I'd been doing. That was two months ago and now I found myself in another town, no closer to returning to the Devil's Fury. How the hell could I?

They'd hated me. Maybe not everyone, but quite a few had made it clear they weren't too impressed with me. I admitted I'd acted like a brat. Even my dad had asked me to leave for a bit. I'd left. I just hadn't gone back. I couldn't. Wouldn't. Especially after the last few mornings when I'd bolted out of bed and hung my head over the toilet.

Stupid. You're so fucking stupid. I'd let Owen and Riley fuck me for the webcam show and hadn't thought to make sure they were going to wear condoms. Owen had asked if I was clean one second and had been balls deep in my pussy the next. Since it was a live show, I couldn't exactly put up a fuss. Well, I could have but I'd have probably lost customers, and I'd needed that money to start over. Again.

I'd gone to college but hadn't finished my degree. Looking back, I wished I'd asked Dad to at least pay for me to finish online. I'd have been better off in the long run. Now I'd have even more responsibilities and going back to school would be twice as hard.

Music pulsed through the club where I worked, and the smell of sex filled the air. I wasn't taking any *extra* jobs, but some of the girls did. I didn't think badly of them or anything, but the men who came here were on the sleazy side and I really didn't want their dicks anywhere near me. Good thing too after what I'd just discovered.

Someone banged on the bathroom door and I winced as I stared at the stick on the sink. Two lines. Pregnant. Fuck my life. Owen was just a Prospect so I knew there was no way I could go crawling to him and say I was carrying his kid. He seemed nice enough, but he was still earning his spot with the Hades Abyss. If Titan was pissed to find out I'd been one of the webcam girls, I could only imagine what he'd do if he knew one of his Prospects had knocked me up.

Yeah. I wasn't going back there. Owen was better off not knowing.

But it meant I couldn't go home either. My daddy would have a fit when he found out. Not to mention, things were still a bit uncomfortable between me and Lilian. She'd forgiven me for the part I played in the fucked-up shit she went through with Dragon. I just hadn't forgiven myself yet. I'd been naïve. I wasn't exactly worldly now for that matter. I wasn't too sure Dragon had forgiven me either.

"If your ass isn't on the stage in five, you're fired," my boss yelled through the door.

Shit. I'd have to tell him. Even if I danced another month or two, eventually I'd start to show, and I wouldn't be able to strip anymore. Better get in at least one more show before I came clean. If he gave me the boot, I wanted tonight's tips to get me through another week or so. I'd been saving so I wasn't flat broke, but I wasn't rolling in cash either. As long as I found a job before rent was due, I'd be okay. Maybe.

I washed my hands, tossed the stick in the trash, and went out with a smile on my face. "Sorry, Ben. Just needed a minute."

He scowled at me as I hurried off. I went backstage and double-checked my appearance before slipping on my outfit. My music started and I rushed to the stage. On the next beat, I started strutting across the floor toward the pole. I dipped, twirled, and ran my hands down my body in time with the music. Reaching for the brass pole, I spun around it twice before leaping up and wrapping my legs around it. The men catcalled and cheered as I did my thing, slowly losing a piece of clothing at a time until I was down to my G-string.

I dropped to my knees at the edge of the stage, thighs spread, breasts thrust up and head tipped back. I arched and ran my hand down my torso. I felt the vibration and heard the thud at the same time. Jolting, I looked up and found a pair of denim-clad legs inches from my face. As my gaze lifted, I saw the bottom of a leather cut, a gray tee tucked into the jeans, but when I got to the patches everything in me went still. *Fuck.*

I jerked my gaze to his face and sucked in a breath. "Slash?"

It looked like him but it didn't. What had he done to his hair? It wasn't blue, purple, green, or any other wild color. The mohawk was gone too. He looked… normal. Or as normal as a biker could. He glowered down at me and I knew I was in big fucking trouble.

"Get the fuck up. Now," he said, his voice a low growl.

I got to my feet, my cheeks burning at the thought of him seeing me like this. How long had he been here? *Why* was he here?

The club's hired muscle rushed to the stage, but one look from Slash had both men stopping in their tracks. Couldn't blame them. The bouncers might be burly but they also didn't have a death wish. I had no doubt Slash could take them out with little effort, and it was clear they knew it.

"No one's allowed on stage," said Marcus, the younger of the two.

"I won't be on stage, just as soon as little Miss Sunshine here gets her ass backstage and covered up," Slash said. He leaned closer to me and dropped his voice. "Or I'll be spanking that ass."

I gave a yelp and rushed off the stage, knowing damn well he'd do it, and probably out there in front of everyone too. Of course, I might get more tips that way. Did I want to chance it? Nope. I raced to the dressing room with Slash right on my heels. He didn't seem to care about the naked women. Hell, I didn't think he even noticed them. He was laser-focused on me.

"What are you doing here?" I asked.

"Came for you," he said.

"Me? How did you even know where I was?"

"Took some time. Been trying to track you down for two months."

My stomach dropped. "Why? Is... Is something wrong with Dad? Lilian?"

"They're fine, which you'd know if you bothered to call them. Ever." He folded his arms. "First you have sex with men on a live show for money and now you're in this dump stripping? What the fuck, Shella?"

My stomach burned and my cheeks heated. I balled up my fists and fought hard not to take a swing at him. "What I do is none of your business, Slash. None! You don't fucking own me."

"Want to bet?"

I growled and swung anyway. He easily caught my fist, using it to yank me against him. I stumbled in my heels and crashed into his chest. Slash wrapped an arm around my waist and held on tight, no matter how much I squirmed. If he worried about the glitter now coating him, he didn't show it.

"Keep rubbing those tits all over me and see what happens," he said.

I went still, my heart racing. Slash had never spoken to me like that before. I looked up and noticed the heat burning in his eyes. Then again, he'd never *looked* at me like that before either. *Don't poke the bear!* If I mouthed off right now, what would he do? Spank me like he'd said? Something more?

I squeezed my thighs together. Shit. I was getting wet just thinking about Slash fucking me. On the upside, it wasn't like he could knock me up. I didn't think he'd find the humor in the situation, though.

"You saw my show?" I asked. "Before and… and now?"

He nodded. Slash put his lips by my ear. "Got me so fucking hot, Shella. Didn't see your face on the screen until I was coming all over my hand. Then I yanked another two out while you got yourself off. Hard as a fucking rock right now. Trying to remind myself you're Grizzly's daughter, but I'm seconds from bending you over and fucking you, and I don't give a good Goddamn who's watching."

I gripped his cut and held on, worried my legs wouldn't hold me. The Devil's Fury VP had never given me a second glance before. Always treated me like a kid. It seemed things had changed in my absence.

"What happens now?" I asked.

"I take you home."

I shook my head. "No, Slash. I can't! You don't understand."

"Wash all that glitter and shit off, put on some clothes, and we can talk about it over a burger and fries. And don't even think of trying to sneak out because I'm waiting right the fuck here."

He released me and I snatched up my clothes before darting to the small bathroom. It was really a closet with a tiny shower stall. One of the girls said Ben installed it two years ago so they could clean up before they left work. A few had kids and didn't want to go home with glitter or body oil covering them. I scrubbed quickly with the generic soap and shampoo someone had left behind, then dried off with what I seriously hoped was a clean towel and pulled on my clothes.

Slash leaned against the vanity I used when I was getting ready, arms folded and gaze locked on the bathroom door. The women eyed him like a piece of candy, and I didn't blame them one bit. He was easy on the eyes. Always had been. He also didn't look anywhere near his age. I knew he had to be around forty, but he looked closer to thirty. And at the moment, he was almost glitter free which meant he'd found a way to wipe it off or someone had helped.

My gut burned at the thought of one of the girls putting their hands on him. I wanted to scream he was mine, except he wasn't. I didn't think anyone would ever lay claim to Slash. If they did, I doubted it would be a pregnant stripper. I knew how people looked at women like me. Slash needed someone the club would respect.

I tugged on the hem of my denim skirt and fought the urge to make sure my shirt hadn't slipped down to show off my bra. Normally I wouldn't care. But I didn't typically have the VP of the Devil's Fury staring me down either. He held out his hand and I went to him, knowing it would be futile to refuse. He'd probably just toss me over his shoulder and carry me off anyway. Every last one of the bikers I knew were cavemen at heart. Sometimes they even sounded like them with unintelligible grunts instead of using words.

The dressing room door slammed open and Ben came in, something wrapped in a tissue in his hand. His face was florid, and his eyes bulged. Had someone brought drugs into the club? He might let the girls do what they wanted for cash in the back rooms, but he had a no drugs policy. He didn't want his dancers strung out on cocaine or worse. Or was it even worse and someone had left a used condom lying around? I think I'd prefer the drugs.

"Who the fuck does this belong to?" he demanded and threw something on the ground. I gasped when I saw it was my pregnancy test. The girls at my back all denied it belonging to them, and Ben's gaze bore into me. "You were in the bathroom right before your performance. Something you need to say?"

"I-I... It's mine." No point denying it. He'd find out sooner or later. Like when I started to show.

I felt Slash's reaction. The temperature in the room dropped twenty degrees and I felt like a deer being stalked by a wolf. He lifted me into his arms, grabbed my purse, and headed for the rear entrance. "She quits."

As much as I wanted to argue, there wasn't any point. Ben would have fired me anyway. Slash carried me to his bike, which I noticed was next to my car. So he'd known for sure I was here even before he saw me. Just how much had he seen before he forced me off the stage? Not that it mattered. He'd already watched the webcam show, which was way worse. I knew he was my dad's best friend, and now...

"You're going to tell my dad, aren't you?" I asked.

He eased me down beside my car and reached up to gently cup my cheek. "Baby, it's time to go home. We'll go get some food and talk, just like I said we would, but I'm not leaving you here. You can't run anymore, Shella."

I nodded and got into my car. He started up his bike and followed me out of the parking lot. He'd mentioned a burger and fries so I drove straight to the diner near my apartment. It wasn't in the best part of town, but the food was amazing, and I adored the woman who ran the place. If I'd had a grandma, I'd imagined she'd have been a lot like Ruth.

Slash took my arm and led me inside. We settled into my favorite booth and I handed Slash a menu from behind the napkin dispenser. Since I always ordered the same thing, I didn't bother with one. He skimmed over it a moment and put it back.

Ruth bustled over, a bright smile on her face. "If it isn't my favorite customer! And you finally listened to me and brought a date."

I opened my mouth to deny it was a date, but Slash reached across the table and gently squeezed my hand. "It's long overdue," he said.

I couldn't have said anything if I'd wanted to. What was he doing? Why would he pretend this was a date?

"I know she wants a sweet tea but what about you, handsome?" Ruth asked.

"The same. I think we're ready to order our food as well."

Slash rattled off his order and I managed to find my voice and told Ruth I wanted my usual. She walked off, leaving us alone again. I wasn't sure what to think or say now that we didn't have a buffer. He was right about one thing, though. I should have called home more often. It was horrible of me not to, but… I had my reasons. Mostly that I was ashamed of myself.

"What if I'm not welcome?" I asked. "What if no one wants me back? You can't sit there and tell me they weren't happy to see me go."

He squeezed my hand. "You were being a brat. Spoiled. Selfish. Can you blame everyone for being angry with you? Griz asked you to visit your half-sister with the Devil's Boneyard for a reason. He thought you needed some time to cool down, and he hoped you'd find a new perspective while you were gone. It was never his intention for you to leave and never return. I think you broke his heart."

"I caused so much trouble," I said. "My head was all over the place, and when I found out Lilian was pregnant, it just all bubbled up. I honestly thought someone had hurt her. She'd always been so hesitant around men I couldn't imagine her willingly having sex with someone."

"And after? When Griz took in those other girls, he worried you'd act out. Maybe make them feel unwelcome. You'd never been like that before."

He was a little too insightful. I wasn't ready to tell him everything. I wasn't sure I'd *ever* be ready. There were things no one knew, things I'd never share. At least, I didn't plan to. I wanted to take my secrets to the grave. What good would come of confessing anything now?

"Shella, what's going on, baby? I can tell by the look in your eyes you're hurting, but I don't know why. No one wanted you to stay gone. You have to know we all wanted you to come home."

"It's nothing," I said, looking away.

Slash reached up and gently gripped my chin, forcing me to look at him. "Talk to me. I can't help if I don't know what's going on."

"Just some stuff... from before I left. There was a reason I took off and didn't come back, and it wasn't just because I felt unwanted. Although, I did feel that way a little bit. Looking back, I understand why Dad wanted me to leave. And I can never tell Lilian enough times how sorry I am for what happened to her. If I'd kept my mouth shut, she'd have never run off."

"Baby, you can't change the past. Worrying over it won't do anyone any good." His thumb smoothed along the line of my jaw. "What made you want to leave and never come back?"

"I can't. Please, Slash. I just... I can't talk about it."

He leaned back in the booth and sighed. "Fine. Then let's talk about the baby in your belly. Whose is it? Or do you even know?"

I felt the blood drain from my face. Wow. Way to make me feel like a whore. Then again, if he'd watched my webcam show he'd seen me with Owen and Riley, and he probably thought I did stuff like that all the time. Then he found me in a strip club that offered special services on the side. I could understand why he'd think so poorly of me, since most people would, but it still hurt. If anyone could understand people doing whatever was necessary to survive, it should be the Devil's Fury.

"Doesn't matter. The baby is mine. That will have to be enough."

"He has a right to know," Slash said.

"If I tell him, it could ruin his life. I won't do that to him. He didn't ask for this."

Slash snorted. "Neither did you. Yet here you are, pregnant and alone."

He wasn't wrong. I could barely support myself much less a baby. I knew some people would say I should give the baby up for adoption, but there was no guarantee it would find a loving family. And deep down, I knew I'd miss my kid. I might not have the first clue about how to be a mom, but I knew I wanted a chance to prove I wasn't as big a fuckup as my mother had been.

"Is there even room for me at home?" I asked. "If I go with you, do I have a bedroom at Dad's house still? Or has he taken in more wayward teen girls?"

It wouldn't surprise me to hear he had a houseful. I hadn't been the first he'd adopted, and I knew I wouldn't be the last. Grizzly was a big scary-looking guy who happened to have a heart of gold. He couldn't stand to hear about a kid suffering. He wasn't my biological dad, but he'd been great to me.

Slash smiled. "Well, he definitely keeps a full house. And you know as well as I do that he only takes in those who wouldn't survive on their own. He saved you, Lilian, Adalia, and the two living in his house right now. I have a feeling he'll keep bringing home strays until the day he draws his last breath. It's just who he is."

"That didn't answer my question. Not really."

"When did you talk to him last?" he asked.

I shrugged. "A while ago. I kept it short in case he tried to trace the call."

"Your dad stepped down. He's not the President of Devil's Fury anymore. Badger is. Griz wanted to focus on the girls, and I think he was honestly tired of all the political bullshit and fighting we seem to constantly deal with."

He'd stepped down? I didn't even know what to think of that. He'd been the President of Devil's Fury since before I'd come into his life. I'd thought the club was his entire world, and he'd just walked away? Well, maybe not that exactly, but he'd given up his spot as President? I couldn't wrap my mind around it.

Ruth dropped off our drinks and food, patting my shoulder as she walked off. I'd have to remember to give her a nice tip. She'd always been so sweet to me. If I did leave, I'd miss her.

"Eat up, baby. When we're done, we'll get some sleep because in the morning we're loading your shit into your car and going home. And don't even fucking think about arguing with me."

I ate my food and tried not to worry about what would happen when I got back home. Not only did I not know where I'd stay, but I'd have to tell my dad I was pregnant. I wasn't sure it was going to be a happy family reunion. What if I got back to Blackwood Falls only to find out I didn't have a home there anymore? At least here I had my apartment for a short while longer. There I'd be alone, without a job, and no place to stay.

After we ate, Slash paid the bill and I noticed he left Ruth a fifty percent tip. It made me feel warm inside that he'd made sure to take care of her. Slash followed me to my apartment, and I heard him muttering about drug dealers and gangs as we walked up the steps. I knew it wasn't exactly the Ritz, but it had been all I could afford. I pushed open the door and went inside, Slash right on my heels. He shut and locked the door before scanning the place.

"Anything you need to do before bed?" he asked.

"No." He motioned for me to leave the room. I walked over to the bedroom, flipping on the light as I stepped into the room.

I didn't bother shutting the door. It wasn't like he hadn't already seen me mostly naked tonight. And completely naked when he'd found that damn website. I stripped out of my clothes and reached into the rickety dresser for my pajamas. After I pulled the cami over my head, I stepped into the shorts. The silky material caressed my skin and made me feel sexy.

I felt his hands at my waist and tipped my head back to look up at him.

"You like playing with fire?" he asked.

"Sometimes."

"Hope you like getting burned. Get your ass in the bed, Shella."

I turned off the light and crawled into bed, more tired than I'd realized. Sleep tugged at me almost the second my head hit the pillow. Until I heard the sounds of him removing his clothes. I leaned up on my elbow, trying to see him in the dark.

"What are you doing?" I asked.

"Going to bed."

"The couch is in the living room," I pointed out.

"So it is. Not where I plan to sleep, baby. Only way I can guarantee you won't bolt is if you sleep in my arms. You like to cuddle, right? Because if not, this is going to be an uncomfortable night."

I gaped at him, not sure what to think. Slash slid into bed and just as he'd said he would, he pulled me into his arms. The smell of him surrounded me and I fought the urge to burrow into him. Why did he have to smell so incredible? Musk, oil, and leather all rolled up together. It had always been my weakness.

"Night, Shella," he murmured, already sounding tired.

"Goodnight, Slash."

"Talon," he murmured. "My name is Talon."

Everything in me went still. Talon. A biker didn't share his name unless it meant something. I just wasn't sure *what* that might be. I liked the way I felt all warm inside that he'd trusted me with his given name. Maybe a little too much.

I'd secretly had a crush on the older man ever since I'd gone to live with the Devil's Fury. One I'd thought I'd outgrown. Until now.

Out of the frying pan and into the fire.

He was right. I was going to get burned.

Chapter Two

Slash

Waking up to an armful of Shella wasn't the worst way to start my day. Ignoring my morning wood, however, was another matter. She'd snuggled into me during the night, and in sleep, she looked sweet and angelic. Nothing like the sex goddess I'd seen on the webcam show, or the stripper I'd watched last night. So which was the real Shella? And what had sent her down this path?

I'd always trusted my instincts and right now mine were screaming that something bad had happened to her. Was it before she came to the Devil's Fury? Under our watch? Or since she'd run off? I needed to regain her trust and hoped she'd open up to me. The girl who had come to live with Grizzly had been sweet, a little shy, and independent. It was clear she still wanted to stand on her own two feet, but over the last few years she'd gone wild, and even downright mean at times.

Why hadn't I noticed the changes sooner? Or rather, I'd noticed, but why hadn't I questioned them? I ran my hand down her back, trying to figure out what could have happened. She'd seemed happy enough, always running off with her friends.

I reached down and grabbed my discarded jeans off the floor and yanked my phone from the pocket. Grizzly needed to know she was all right, and that I was bringing her home. *Found Shella. Bringing her with me.*

Straight forward and to the point. I didn't have to wait long before I got a response.

She can't stay here. I don't have the space.

What the fuck? I knew Grizzly had kept a room open for Shella. What had changed? Or was he still pissed at her? Lilian had forgiven her, and I'd thought Grizzly had too. It was possible he was hurt and angry she'd run and not come home. Still, it didn't seem quite like him.

Why not? I hit send and waited to see if he'd answer. If he was angry with her, there wasn't much I could do about it. I hoped that wasn't the case.

The dots appeared a minute before his response. *Have three girls now. Marissa, Carlotta, and Sheena.*

Who the fuck was Sheena? I knew Marissa and Carlotta had been staying with him for a while now. They'd arrived with Dagger and Guardian's woman, along with several others. But when I'd left nearly a month ago in an attempt to track down Shella, he hadn't had anyone else living there.

Griz might not be the President anymore, but I wasn't going to question him. Well, more than I already had. If he didn't have room and had three girls, then… she'd just have to come to my house. And I'd have to try really fucking hard to remember to keep my damn hands to myself. Even weeks after seeing her webcam show I still yanked one out, imagining it was her. The image of her getting herself off had burned itself into my brain. Now I'd have her little striptease from last night stuck in there too.

I eased away from her and stood next to the bed, stretching out my back as it cracked and popped. Getting old was a bitch. While Shella slept a little longer, I took my time and checked out her place, trying to get an idea of what we'd need to pack. The furniture wasn't going. No fucking way it would fit in her car, but the rest… Well, there wasn't much else to the place.

A small bookcase held about a dozen paperbacks, all romances from what I could tell. She had a picture of her and Lilian in a frame on top. The stuff in her kitchen was minimal. Her dishes and cups were cheap plastic, and her silverware looked like the stuff at the dollar store. She had one skillet, one pot, and one baking sheet. How the fuck did she make do with so little? For that matter, *why* didn't she have more?

I went back to the bedroom and checked out her dresser and closet, noting there wasn't much in either. A handful of casual clothes, stuff it looked like she wore on dates or to work, and three pairs of shoes. The most she had were pajamas, and every damn one was as sexy as what she'd put on last night.

"What have you been up to?" I muttered to myself. None of it made any sense. I knew she'd had more than this when she left home. Her car had been packed to the point of overflowing. So where was everything?

It wouldn't take long to pack all this stuff, but depending how the day went, we might have to leave tomorrow. I'd already been gone roughly four weeks. One more day wouldn't hurt anything. I'd just have to make sure Shella didn't try to run on me.

I heard the toilet flush and looked up to see her watching me. I hadn't even heard her get up, or noticed she wasn't still asleep in bed.

"We need to get some boxes," I said.

She disappeared into her closet and came back out with four flattened boxes and a roll of tape. Where the hell had she hidden those? Her closet didn't look big enough to hold boxes and her clothes. And how often had she moved around to just keep that shit handy? I'd known it wasn't easy to track her down, but

I didn't like the thought of her living her life one second to the next, never knowing where she'd be calling home later that week.

I took the boxes and tape from her, quickly putting them together. Handing her one, I held onto it a little longer, my gaze catching hers. "We need to talk, Shella."

"Not now, Slash."

"What did I say last night?" I asked, my voice going soft. I didn't like the thought of her calling me by my road name like everyone else. No matter if she was hands-off, it still felt wrong. Shella wasn't just anyone.

She flashed me a shy smile. "Talon."

Fuck but I loved hearing my name on her lips. A little too much.

"I'll start on the living room. You pack your stuff in here. I'd like to hit the road this afternoon."

She worried at her lower lip. "Will we make it in just one afternoon?"

"No. We'll stay at a hotel overnight. So keep a few things out and I can shove them in my saddlebags."

Shella shifted from foot to foot. "We could stay here tonight and just leave in the morning. Or maybe in a few days. There's no rush, right?"

I set the box aside and reached for her, tugging her closer. I cupped her cheek and forced her to hold my gaze. "Baby, what's wrong?"

She sighed and shook her head, closing her eyes. As much as I wanted to give her whatever time she needed, it was clear she didn't want to go home. I had a feeling if I hadn't come for her, she might have never come back. It had to be more than Grizzly asking her to leave for a bit.

"Changed my mind. We're having that talk now," I said. I led her over to the bed and sat, pulling her down onto my lap where I could hold onto her. Something told me she'd bolt first chance she got. "Something's wrong. Don't bother denying it. I'm thinking it went sideways a while back and no one noticed."

She took a shaky breath and leaned against me. "It's better if I don't go back."

"Why? You can't just say shit like that and think I'm going to walk away, Shella."

She burrowed closer, twisting so she could wrap her arms around my neck. I ran my hand down her hair, my imagination in overload. Not once had I ever seen her act like this. What the fuck had happened to her? If someone had hurt her, I'd gut them.

"Talk to me," I said softly.

"Everyone was always so focused on Lilian. Worried about her. I understood, but when I needed the club the most they just decided I was a problem. A bratty kid."

As much as I wanted to ask questions, I waited. It was clear she struggled to tell me whatever was weighing on her. The thought she'd been hurting all this time ate at me. She was right. The club had just thought she was being a brat. None of us had stopped to question why she was acting out of character. If she'd been hurt, we were just as much to blame as whoever had touched her.

Oh God. Surely not... I tightened my hold on her. *Please don't let her say she was raped.*

"The kids at school weren't exactly nice to me," she said. "They'd teased me from the beginning, but I didn't want Dad to worry so I kept quiet. Except they never stopped and it got worse. At first, it was just taunts and mean words. Until it wasn't."

I held her close and closed my eyes, wishing I'd known. It wasn't like I could scare the shit out of a bunch of teenagers at the high school, but I'd have done something. Anything. Shella had been so sweet, thoughtful, and downright adorable. All the signs were there. Why hadn't I seen them?

"The cheerleaders cornered me in the locker room right after gym one afternoon. School was out and the gym was deserted. I'd just gotten out of the shower and they'd hidden my clothes. The more upset I got, the meaner they became. They shoved me into the hall and into the boy's locker room."

"Naked?" I asked, fury building inside me. It burned in my veins and my jaw locked tight to the point of pain. If I ever got my hands on those little monsters, I wouldn't hold back. Didn't matter how old they were. They couldn't do shit like that and get away with it.

She nodded against me, hiding her face.

"The football team was in there. They laughed. Made fun of me. And then... then they..."

I felt her tears before I heard the first sniffle. My heart broke for her. We'd thought she was running wild. It never occurred to any of us she was acting out, that someone had hurt her in the worst possible way.

"How many?" I asked, not surprised my voice didn't sound the least bit steady.

"All the ones still there," she said softly. "Some had left already. I'd been a virgin. It felt like they ripped me apart inside. I wanted to die. It took me forever to stand, much less walk to my car. When I got home, I was going to tell Dad, but Lilian was having a bad day and freaking out. I knew if she heard what had happened to me, it would only make things worse. So I took a shower and kept quiet. Except I couldn't get clean. No matter how much I scrubbed or how many showers I took, I was still dirty."

"Jesus, Shella. I wish you'd told someone! If not Griz or Lilian, then anyone else in the club! We're your family, baby. You should have gone to the police and had every one of those fuckers arrested."

"I went to stay with a friend while Dad dealt with Lilian. Her oldest sister was in medical school and she checked me over, gave me something for the pain. She tried to talk to me into going to the hospital, but I knew they'd call the police and Dad. Lilian didn't need that right then. I managed to get tested for STDs and took the morning-after pill just in case, but it wasn't easy to do without Dad finding out." Her gaze dropped, as if she couldn't stand to look at me right then. "By the next day, the entire school was calling me a whore. It wasn't just in the hallways but on social media. I even got some text messages about it. So... I decided to prove them right. Besides, I figured it wouldn't hurt as much if they didn't have to hold me down. As screwed up as it sounds, it made me feel like I was in control. After I'd had time to heal, I became what they'd been calling me."

Didn't sound fucked up at all. I knew exactly what she meant. People could only hurt you if you let them. By not acting like the victim, it had probably thrown them off their game. They'd expected her to cry, to cower, and instead she'd embraced the names they called her and turned the tables on them.

"I want a list of every person responsible," I said. "And it's not negotiable."

"It's been a long time, Talon. I graduated two years ago," she said.

"Doesn't matter, baby. They hurt you in the worst way possible and I intend to see them pay. Even if I can't physically harm every single one, I can make their lives extremely uncomfortable. Besides, there's a chance you weren't the only one. What if some of those boys raped other girls? What if they're continuing to hurt women even now?"

She sagged against me. "I never thought of that."

I understood why she hadn't come home. She'd been hurting all that time, and none of us had paid attention. Then Griz had asked her to go visit her half-sister and get away from the Devil's Fury for a while. If he knew what she'd been through, he'd kick his own ass for doing that to her. She'd needed us and we'd turned her away. I felt sick just thinking about it.

"Now I'm going home pregnant," she said. "It's just going to reinforce all the bad things they think about me."

"You know, I've been trying to track you down for a month. No one knows I just found you last night." I knew what I was about to say could very well freak her the fuck out, but I knew it was the right thing to do. She needed me, and I'd always had a soft spot for Shella, even before I'd seen her as a woman and not a kid. Now I desired her the way a man wants a sexy, vibrant woman. "I'm claiming you. Not asking. Just telling you that's how it is. Don't have to say a word about the baby just yet. Let them think it's mine."

She pulled back and stared at me, eyes wide and lips parted. I ran my fingers over her cheek.

"That kid will be mine in every way that counts. Don't matter if we aren't blood. You ever decide to tell them I'm not their sperm donor, we'll cross that bridge then. For now, I'll be the only dad he or she knows, and the club won't be any wiser. Babies come early all the time."

"I can't let you do that, Talon. I know when you claim someone it's forever. You deserve so much better than me."

I shut her up the only way I knew how. I kissed the hell out of her. It might have started soft and sweet, but I couldn't get enough of her. Deepening the kiss, I fisted her hair in my hand, holding her still as I dominated her mouth. So fucking sweet! So damn perfect. If she hadn't left, would I have ever noticed her this way? Wanted her as bad as I did now?

When I drew back, her lips were swollen, and she looked sexy as fuck.

"Talon." My name was nearly a whisper.

"There's no one better than you, sweetheart, so I don't ever want to hear you say that shit again. Hear me?"

She nodded.

"It's time to make new memories, Shella. Start a new life. I'll be with you every step of the way. We're in this together now. Hear me?"

"I hear you, Talon." Her eyes had a soft look to them as she stared at me. "I don't know why you want to keep me. I'm not anything special, and I'll just bring trouble to your door. But... thank you. For coming to get me, for letting me tell you what happened in high school, and for accepting me despite everything."

I flipped us so she was lying on the bed and I braced myself over her. "Let's get one thing straight. You were a victim in high school, Shell. What happened to you is unforgiveable and the fact you kept going, without the support of your family, tells me you're a strong woman. The Shella I watched on the webcam show was hot as fuck and got me harder than granite. And the one I watched strip last night was like a wet dream. There's nothing to 'accept' as you put it. I'm a lucky bastard to call you mine, and I damn well know it. You're getting a man twice your age, and I won't lie, the club whores will give you shit, try to make it sound like they own me. You ready for that? Ready to fight for what's yours?"

She reached up, her touch light as she ran her fingers over the stubble on my jaw. "Are you? Mine?"

"Don't belong to anyone else, baby. Never have. Never will. I'm yours every bit as much as you're mine. Another man so much as looks at you and I'll knock his teeth down his damn throat. This sexy body is for my viewing pleasure only."

"All right," she said. "But I don't want to be just your old lady. I want a ring so that even outside the club men will know I'm taken."

I smiled down at her, then gave in and kissed the hell out of her again. "I'll give you anything you desire… within reason. And a ring sounds like a good idea. We'll get one today. Just need to ask one of the hackers to work their mojo and marry us. Preferably before Griz finds out and kicks my ass."

She worried at her lower lip. "Wizard might do it. Titan was worried about backlash on the club after he found out I'd been hired as a webcam girl."

Interesting. So the Hades Abyss Pres *had* known Shella was there and what she was up to. I'd be asking why the fuck he'd let her leave, but I'd save it for later. Right now, the woman lying under me needed all my attention. She'd been badly broken and put herself back together the only way she could. From now on, I'd see she was taken care of. Protected.

"You sure you don't want a real wedding?" I asked.

"Don't need one. I just need you."

Well, hell. When she said that, and gave me that soft look, I knew I'd do anything she asked. There was no way to make up for the past, but I could guarantee she had everything she'd want or need in the future. She was mine now, and I never gave up my possessions... especially when this one was quickly worming her way into my heart. I hadn't even realized I still had one.

Chapter Three

Shella

The last of my stuff had been packed except a change of clothes and anything else I'd need overnight and in the morning. The apartment didn't look very different. My boxes were stacked by the front door, ready to be loaded into the trunk of my car. I was going home. Just the thought of seeing my dad again made my palms sweat. Then there was the rest of the club. I was certain they didn't want me back. Didn't matter that Slash said I was welcome with the Devil's Fury. When I'd needed them, no one had been there for me. I'd acted out, doing anything to get their attention and deal with the pain I'd felt.

Slash understood now, and I could tell by the look in his eyes he hated himself for not noticing back then. I'd just been a pesky kid. Maybe if I'd told someone what happened things would have been different, but I hadn't wanted to put Lilian through that. I'd worried about her, even back then. So I'd done the opposite. Not only had I kept my shame a secret, but I decided to make my body my own again the only way I'd known how.

I toyed with the hem of my shirt as I watched Slash put a little product in his messy hair. I didn't know why he was willing to claim me, to make me his completely. He could do so much better. It wasn't like he'd ever lacked for options when it came to women. They practically threw themselves at his feet. I couldn't blame them. I'd had an insane crush on him for as long as I could remember. Those women just saw the Devil's Fury VP, but it had been something else drawing me to him like a moth to a flame. His smile, the kindness in his eyes, the way he'd dyed his hair a rainbow of colors over the years as a fuck-you to anyone who thought bikers should only look and act a certain way.

As I watched him, I realized it had been more than a crush. I'd been a little in love with him. Having him swoop in and rescue me the way he was, well… it made me fall for him a little more. I worried he'd break my heart if I gave him the chance. I couldn't let him find out how I felt. Not right now anyway. Maybe someday.

"Ready?" he asked, wiping his hands off on a towel and turning to face me.

"Sure. Where are we going?"

He lifted his chin and stared down his nose at me. "Depends. What's my wife want to eat?"

Wife. There was a flutter in my stomach. Butterflies.

"Wife?" I asked.

He gave a quick nod. "Spoke to Wizard earlier. In exchange for me not tearing their club apart with my bare hands, he hacked into the county records. According to the Bolivar County clerk's office, we're officially married. Congratulations. You're now Shella Vickers."

I chewed on my lower lip. "What if you change your mind?"

He was on me in two steps, his hand in my hair, a fierce look on his face. It seemed I'd poked the bear with my comment. Slash pressed his lips to mine and quickly bent me to his will, his mouth ravaging mine. He wasn't gentle. Didn't go slow. He took what he wanted. No, demanded my submission. When he broke the kiss, my knees trembled, and I felt like I'd fall to the floor at any moment. I'd never been with a man like him.

"Next time you utter that shit, I'm putting you over my knee and spanking your ass," he said. "You think I do things lightly? Just rush into something without considering the consequences?"

"No, Talon. I just…" I felt small with him looming over me. Fragile. I'd worked hard to build a tough exterior, but Slash blasted through those walls and left me a mess, worrying I would never be good enough for someone like him. I swallowed hard. "I'm dirty. I'm not… I'm not good enough for you."

The words were hard to say, and I ended on a near whisper. I felt vulnerable. More so than I had in a long time. This wasn't just any man. It was Slash. He'd been my ideal ever since I'd met him. No one had ever measured up to him, and I knew they never would.

His touch was gentle as he cupped my cheek, forcing me to hold his gaze. "Baby, you're not dirty. You're a survivor, and you're Goddamn beautiful. And mine."

I trembled as he leaned down and kissed me soft and slow. It was the kind of kiss I'd always dreamed of and never experienced. I whimpered, clinging to him as tears burned behind my closed eyelids. His kindness unraveled me. This big, badass biker who I knew had killed people, had left a wake of destruction in his path, treated me as if I were the most precious thing in the world.

"Come on, Shell," he said softly. "Let's go get some lunch and buy you a wedding ring. I'll get you a property cut after we're back home and I've had a chance to speak to my brothers in Church."

I worried they'd deny his request. As long as we were married, they couldn't kick me out of the compound, could they? The last thing I wanted was to come between Slash and the club. They'd been his family long before I ever came to live there. I didn't know what would happen if they didn't accept me. I'd never ask him to leave the club.

And what about his blood family? His brother was with the Dixie Reapers and his sister lived with the Devil's Boneyard. That was a lot of club members to hate me. Not to mention I'd met Tank before. I really didn't want on his bad side. Although, he wasn't nearly as bad as Demon. The Devil's Fury Sergeant-at-Arms brought new meaning to sadistic when he got pissed at someone.

He took my hand and led me out of the apartment and down to his bike. I hadn't been on one in a long time. Knowing it was Slash I'd be riding behind made me both excited and scared. He pulled a purple helmet from his saddlebag and I realized it was the one I'd used before. As a teen, I'd taken a few rides with some of the men in the club. Since Grizzly was my adopted dad, his son-in-law, Badger, had often been the one to let me ride with him. Unless Adalia was with him.

I turned it around in my hands, letting the memories wash over me. It had felt freeing to ride on the back of a motorcycle. The wind in my hair. The thrum of the bike under me. I set the helmet on my head and fastened the chin strap. Slash had already gotten on his Harley and started the engine. I swung my leg over the seat and held onto his waist. He gave me a quick glance over his shoulder before taking my hands and crossing them over his stomach. I felt the hard ridges of his abdomen and a heat flared to life inside me.

His wife. I was this gorgeous man's wife. Did that mean he planned to consummate our marriage? Preferably tonight. The sooner the better. I only hoped

I didn't disappoint him. While I'd been with a lot of guys and done some seriously wild shit the last year alone, I wasn't sure I'd be able to measure up to the women he'd been with. Besides, I hadn't cared about any of those men. They were one-night stands or quick flings. Slash was different. Even if we weren't married, it still wouldn't have been the same sleeping with him.

Slash eased the bike out of the parking space and opened her up when we got onto the road. I felt my pulse racing as he rode through town, seeming to have a destination in mind already. It wasn't a big place, and after a little while, I realized he was passing some of the same places over and over. All right. So maybe he didn't know where he was going.

"Are you lost?" I shouted, hoping he could hear me.

He gave me a quick smile over his shoulder before facing forward again. Another few minutes and he pulled into the parking lot of a Mexican restaurant. One we'd passed at least three times during our ride. I hadn't eaten here since I'd moved to town. Mostly because I couldn't afford it. I'd lived off cheap things like pasta and sandwiches. The few times I'd been to the diner, I'd still gotten whatever was on special that day. He helped me off the bike, hung our helmets on his handlebars, then took my hand, lacing our fingers together.

"This okay?" he asked, giving a nod to the restaurant.

"Yeah. You know how much I love Mexican food."

He winked. "I remember. It's why I picked this place."

We went inside and the hostess sat us at a booth near a window. I perused the menu, trying to decide what I was in the mood for. Everything sounded amazing, and I was starving. I couldn't remember the last time I'd had a meal in a place like this. My mouth watered at the scents filling the air.

A woman who looked to be in her thirties stopped by the table, setting a basket of chips and a bowl of salsa down. "I'm Terrie and I'll be your waitress today. Do you know what you'd like to drink?"

"Sweet tea," I said. It was about the only craving I had so far. I just hadn't realized it *was* a pregnancy craving at the time, but I'd definitely been drinking it way more than usual.

"I'll take a beer," Slash said. "Anything on tap is fine as long as it's not that light shit."

Terrie flashed him a smile. "I have to ask for I.D. to serve alcohol. Even if you had blue hair and a million wrinkles. State requirement."

Slash pulled out his wallet and showed her his driver's license before shoving it back into his jean's pocket. She eyed him like a prime piece of meat, making me fist my hands under the table, my nails biting into my palms.

"Sweet of you to take your daughter out for lunch," she said. Terrie reached down and placed her hand on Slash's forearm. "Not too many men like you left. I get off work in an hour if you'd like to go do something later."

Daughter? I watched Slash and noticed a tic in his jaw. He stared at the woman. Hard. Enough that she took a hasty step back, releasing her hold on him. Yeah, she'd realized he was a predator. Except if Slash stalked her, it wouldn't be to fuck her.

"I'd like another server. And the manager," he said. "But before you get either, you can apologize to my *wife*."

Her eyes went wide, and she stared from him to me and back again. When she faced me, I saw the flash of anger in her eyes and the sneer on her lips. "Sorry."

Terrie turned and stomped off, and I worried she might spit in our drinks or food. Slash watched her, his jaw set, his nostrils flaring with every breath as if he were an enraged bull about to charge. If he reacted like this to a stranger making a comment about me being his kid, what would happen if the club didn't like us being together?

"It's okay," I said, reaching over and placing my hand on top of his.

"It's not," he said. "Maybe if she'd given you a real apology I could have let it slide."

A man came over in a button-down shirt, khaki pants, and his hair sticking up like he'd been running his hands through it. Terrie stood next to him, arms crossed over her chest as she glared at me. The guy looked from Slash to me and back again, visibly swallowing and I noticed his brow was beaded with sweat.

I eyed my husband. His tee stretched tight over his biceps and chest. The cut he wore could be intimidating, especially to people who feared all bikers. Although, if they pissed off Slash, they were wise to be afraid. Especially if they'd fucked with his family. I warmed inside, realizing that included me.

"Is there a problem?" The man patted his face with a handkerchief.

"You the manager?" Slash asked.

The man nodded. "John Simpson. And yes, I manage this restaurant."

"Your waitress insulted me and my wife, came onto me, then gave a shitty apology as she glared at my woman. I want a new server and I expect that one," he said, pointing to Terrie, "to be disciplined or written up. She needs to learn better customer service."

"Terrie is one of our best," Mr. Simpson said.

"Then I suppose we should find somewhere else to eat," Slash said, standing up and towering over the plump manager. The guy took a hasty step back. "I won't sit around and let my wife be insulted."

His voice had risen just high enough the people at the surrounding tables were looking our way. A few were murmuring to one another, and two couples stood up like they were about to leave. The manager seemed to have realized what was happening. I watched as his shoulders slumped and he seemed to deflate.

"I'm sorry. We pride ourselves on good service. If you'd like another server, I'll see that you get one and your meals are on the house." He cast a quick glance at Terrie. He seemed to pale a little as he looked at her and I wondered what hold she had over him. "Terrie, I'm afraid I need you to head on home. Your shift is over for today."

Her eyes flashed and her lips thinned. "You promised me the best shifts."

"I can't have you running off customers," Mr. Simpson stammered.

Terrie snarled at him. "See if I let you fuck me again, you piece of shit."

She turned and stormed off, my jaw dropping at her declaration. I hadn't seen that one coming. The look Slash slid my way left me thinking he'd known the two were somehow involved. Did all men think with their dicks?

Slash took his seat again and reached for a chip, scooping up some salsa before he popped it into his mouth. "On the off chance your little whore did something to our drinks, I'd prefer the new server make them."

Mr. Simpson nodded and rushed off. A few minutes later, a young girl came over, her hands twisting in front of her. The way her gaze darted around the room made her look like a scared rabbit.

"I-I-I…" She licked her lips and still wouldn't look at us.

Slash leaned back in the booth. "Take a breath. I don't bite. Long as you don't say mean shit to my wife, or dismiss her, you've got nothing to worry about."

She blew out a breath and her gaze landed on him before swerving to me. She gave me a hesitant smile. "Sorry. It's my first day and Terrie was pissed when she left. She's the go-to person around here. Everyone says she has Mr. Simpson wrapped around her finger."

Oh, she had him wrapped around something, but it wasn't her finger.

"My wife wanted sweet tea and I'll take a beer."

She worried at her lower lip. "Mug or bottle?"

"Mug. Nothing light."

She nodded. "Do you know yet what you want to order? Or I can give you more time."

Slash looked over at me. "Know what you want, baby?"

"The steak chimichanga with sour cream sauce, no lettuce or tomato, and a double side of rice," I said.

"And you?" the girl asked Slash.

"Six beef tacos, rice, beans, and two chicken enchiladas on the side."

She gave a quick nod and started to take off, only to spin around, her eyes wide. "I totally forgot. My name's Bethany. If you need anything, just let me know."

After she darted off, I smiled at Slash. Women always had one of two reactions to the men in my life. Outright distaste or they fell at their feet. My dad had been no exception. Although I'd never met his wife, May, I'd heard she was his one and only. I had no doubt he wasn't exactly celibate, but I didn't think he'd ever claim another old lady or get married. He still had pictures up of May all over the house, or he had when I'd left. I'd always wanted that. To have some guy love me so hard that even in death he didn't want to let go.

I could only hope that one day Slash might come to care for me. I wasn't sure if he was capable of love. Even though I'd known him a long time, this was different. I wasn't just Grizzly's adopted daughter, a pain in the ass for the club. I was his wife, and hopefully his old lady. If the club accepted our relationship.

"You didn't think you were a little harsh with the server and manager?" I asked.

"No." He leaned forward, bracing his arms on the table. "Anyone who hurts you will answer to me. If Terrie had been a man, I'd have taken her outside and beat the shit out of her."

My eyebrows went up. "Um, correct me if I'm wrong, but if Terrie had been a man, then I'd have been the one being hit on. Unless Terrie was gay."

He snorted and a quick grin flashed across his lips before he studied me again. "Lunch. Ring shopping. Anything else you want to take care of around here before we head out in the morning? Anyone you need to say bye to?"

His hand tightened into a fist even if his face remained impassive. Was he... jealous? "Are you asking if I'm seeing someone and need to break it off?"

He shrugged a shoulder. Men were so frustrating! And endearing. I kind of liked the thought of the big and powerful Slash being jealous. No, more than that, I liked the thought of him being mine. Married. We might have not had an actual wedding, or exchanged vows, but as far as the Devil's Fury were concerned, our marriage would be one hundred percent legitimate. Same to anyone who went looking for paperwork. They'd find whatever they needed, even if Wizard had invented all of it.

Bethany returned with our drinks, topped off the salsa and chips, then rushed off again. All the while, Slash held me mesmerized. There was just something about him. When he walked in a room, everyone noticed. Especially the women. I'd never been immune to him so I could hardly blame them.

God but I loved this man. And I hoped like fucking hell he never found out. Or rather, not anytime soon. I'd be so embarrassed. And heartbroken when he couldn't say the words back.

Still fucking up, Shella. Except now you've really gone and done it.

Chapter Four

Slash

Fuck, but she was beautiful. Little Shella had grown up, had curves in all the right places, and made me hotter than hell. Even sitting across from her during lunch, I'd been hard as a steel post. Buying her a ring hadn't been as easy as I'd thought. Mostly because she wanted to fight me every step of the way.

Once again, she was browsing the plain wedding bands and I led her back to the case with sparkly rings inside. She stiffened at my side. I didn't know what she'd known about the club previously. Did she worry I couldn't afford to buy her a decent ring? Or was something else going on right now?

"Shell, you deserve the best. Would you please tell me which one you like?" I asked, waving at the case. She sighed and looked up at me. The hurt and uncertainty in her eyes nearly gutted me. What the fuck? I cupped her cheek and lowered my face, dropping my voice so only she could hear me. "Baby, what's wrong? You said you wanted a ring. Did you change your mind?"

"I don't... deserve the best. I'm nothing, Slash. Less than nothing. I don't need anything fancy. It's not like... like..." Her eyes filled with tears and she blinked them away.

"What did I say?" I asked, making my voice harder. "You're not nothing. You're sexy. Beautiful. And mine. You hear me? I want the whole fucking world to know it."

She trembled and looked seconds from more tears. I released her and looked down at the glass case. A ring in the middle caught my attention. It looked like one of those sets women get after a wedding with two diamond studded bands on either side. The center ring, which I guessed was the engagement ring, had a square cut emerald and small diamonds surrounding it.

"That one," I said, pointing it out to the salesman.

He took it from the case and set it on a black velvet display. I picked it up, noting the price, then took Shella's left hand and slipped it onto her finger. Perfect fucking fit. If that didn't mean she was fated for this ring, I didn't know what did. I took it off and handed it back to him.

"Remove the tag please? We'll take it, and she'll wear it out." He seemed hesitant so I pulled out my wallet and slapped my card down on the counter. He snatched it and ran to ring up my purchase. While he did that, I noticed Shella staring at something else. I tried to figure out what, and then it hit me. The men's rings. "Baby, you want me to wear a ring?"

She sucked in a breath and took a step back. "You don't have to."

What the hell? Why was she suddenly so timid? I waved the salesman back over and found a plain silver band that fit my finger. After I paid for everything, I slipped the ring back onto Shella's finger and led her from the shop. I didn't know what was going on in her head, or why she seemed so skittish sometimes. She had to know I wouldn't hurt her. Not on purpose.

We rode back to her apartment and went inside. She kicked off her shoes and went straight to the bedroom. I heard the shower start and ran a hand over my head. Women had never been a problem for me. They dropped their panties easily enough. Then again, I hadn't cared about them. I got off and then forgot them. Couldn't do that with Shella. Hell, ever since I'd jerked off to her webcam show I hadn't been able to stop thinking about her.

I pulled off my cut and tossed it onto the couch, then toed off my boots. By the time I reached the bathroom, I'd stripped all the way down to my skin. The frosted glass let me see my wife, and the way she leaned her head against the tiled wall, her shoulders lightly shaking, made it feel like she'd ripped my heart out. I quietly opened the shower door and stepped inside, drawing her against my chest.

"Shell, talk to me."

"S-sorry." She sniffled and rubbed her cheek against me. "I don't know what's wrong with me. I've never cared before. Did everything I could to be a bad girl, and now I'm scared to go home. I'm worried they won't accept me. Us. I don't want you to have to choose between me and the Devil's Fury."

I put my fingers under her chin and lifted her face until she held my gaze. "Shell, they wouldn't dare tell me I can't keep you. No one stands in my way when I want something."

She looked so heartbroken. So damn sad. I couldn't help myself. I leaned down and pressed my lips to hers. I'd only meant to offer her comfort, but the taste of her lit a fire inside me. I thrust my tongue between her lips and devoured her. The way she clung to me only made me want her more. I backed Shella to the wall, pressing tight against her. There was no hiding the effect she had on me.

"Slash, please…" She gripped the back of my neck, her nails biting into me. "I need you."

I pressed my forehead to hers. "I don't have any condoms with me. I'm clean, and you're already pregnant."

"I'm clean too," she said. "I had to get tested before I started working at the strip club, and I haven't been with anyone since then."

I lifted her legs around my waist and notched my cock at her opening, slowly pushing inside. Christ, but she felt fucking fantastic! Hot. Wet. Tight. I groaned, trying to hold onto my control. Bad enough our first time was in the fucking shower, but I wouldn't take her like she was a damn whore.

"So perfect," I said, kissing her again.

"Don't coddle me," she murmured against my lips. "You don't have to hold back."

I pulled my hips back, then sank into her again. Each stroke slow and deep. "You're my wife, Shell. Not a fucking club whore."

Tears glittered in her eyes. Her lips parted and I felt a tremor run through her. I reached between us and rubbed her clit. The little nub was already hard and the way her pussy fluttered around my cock I knew she was close. She felt like silk as I stroked in and out of her. Holding her gaze, I took my time, wanting to give her pleasure instead of focusing on my own.

My chest grew tight at the look of wonder on her face and when she came, calling out my name, it was the best fucking feeling in the world. No matter how badly I wanted to pound into her tight little pussy, I held back. She'd had enough men use her, treat her like shit, and I refused to be another. I held her tight as my hips jerked a little faster. My balls drew up and I knew I was going to come any second. Kissing her long and hard, I groaned as I came, filling her up.

My cock twitched inside her, and for the first time in my life, everything felt right. I'd been with countless women, but I couldn't remember a single one of them. Only Shella. Fuck, but she had me tied up like a damn pretzel. I didn't think she understood exactly how much power she held over me.

She buried her face in my chest and I felt her shaking as she cried.

"Baby, I didn't mean to upset you."

She shook her head. "You didn't. I just... I didn't know it could ever be like that."

"I can't promise it will always be soft and slow. I tend to be a rough guy, Shell. You deserve better, and I wanted to give this to you, but there will be times I can't hold back like I did just now."

She ran her fingers over the scruff on my jaw. "I don't want you to hold back, Talon. You don't have to try and be something you're not. I accept you as you are."

I smirked. "Better not say shit like that to me, baby. You'll get tied up, spanked, and fucked hard."

Her breath caught and her eyes got darker. "Maybe I'd like that. With you. I... I don't know about the tying me up part, but the rest..."

I'd find out exactly who had hurt her in high school. Might take me some time, but I'd hunt them down and make them pay. They'd broken her. She'd been a beautiful, vibrant girl. Sweet as candy. Until they took her innocence. I could turn them over to the police, but I doubted it would do any good. Even if the statute of limitations hadn't run out, since she hadn't gone to the hospital for a rape kit, and possibly had no witnesses, it would be a case of her word against theirs. And I couldn't put her through that without some hope they'd go to jail.

No, I'd handle it myself. My way.

Even those cheerleaders would pay. I might not physically hurt them, but I'd find other ways. And I'd make damn sure they knew why they were targeted.

No one was going to hurt my little butterfly and get away with it.

I helped her wash before rinsing off. We got out and I wrapped a towel around her, helping her get dry. After I sent her to the bedroom, I dried myself off and went to slide into bed next to her. It was early. We hadn't had dinner, but I wasn't done with her just yet. Now that I'd had a taste, felt her wrapped around me, I knew I needed more.

"I won't break," she said, her chin jutting out at a stubborn angle. "Unless you hold me down, then I might freak out. I won't know unless we try. I don't want to be a victim, Talon. You called me a survivor, but I don't feel like one."

"I'll help you heal, Shell. Whatever it takes."

She curled against me and I ran my fingers through her hair. She wanted the real me? I wasn't sure she could handle it. The last thing I wanted to do was scare her. I never wanted to see fear in her eyes when she looked at me. My fragile girl was stronger than she realized, but I knew she'd have limitations. Not just now but possibly forever. We'd just have to figure out where the boundaries were.

I rolled to my back, taking her with me so that she sprawled across my chest. "Ride me, pretty girl. Show me what you've got."

She placed her hands on my chest and lowered herself onto my cock. When she'd taken every inch, she wiggled a little. I watched her, waiting to see what she'd do. Determination flashed in her eyes and she raked her nails over my nipples. I bucked my hips and held onto her, my fingers digging into the soft globes of her ass.

"Tease," I said.

I smacked her ass, making her gasp and jolt. It seemed to set her free. Whatever had been going on in her head took a back seat as she raised and lowered herself, each stroke getting faster and harder, until she was riding me like I was her prize stallion. And fuck did it feel incredible.

I reached up and cupped her breast, rolling her nipple between my fingers before I pinched and tugged on it. Shella tossed her head back, her back arching. I tugged on her other nipple and worked my other hand between us, using my thumb to rub her clit.

"Talon! Oh, God. Don't stop!" Her movements became erratic and frantic as she chased her orgasm. When she came, I felt the heat of her release. I growled and toppled her to the bed, then flipped her onto her stomach. Yanking her hips up, I rammed into her.

Shella cried out and clawed at the bedding. I couldn't seem to stop, couldn't hold back. I needed to be gentle with my broken butterfly. Needed to be calm. The feel of her, the smell of her arousal, hit me like a fucking hurricane and unleashed something inside me. I slammed into her, taking her hard. I gripped her hips, keeping her still as I took what I wanted. There was a buzzing in my head, a haze settling over me. Sweat slicked my skin and I didn't stop, couldn't slow down.

I took her. Fucked her. And as I came inside her, I smacked her ass and marked her as mine. Even the red handprint wasn't enough. Some primitive part of me wanted to rub my cum all over her. I felt completely out of control. Insane. Drunk on my need for her.

"Jesus fuck." I tightened my hold on her, my cock still hard. I pulled out and turned her to her back, bending her knees and pushing her legs wide apart. I plunged into her, fucking her like a rabid beast. "Mine."

Her bed creaked and groaned, protesting the rough treatment. Every time I bottomed out into her hot little pussy, the word *mine* sounded in my head. I came again, so fucking hard I nearly blacked out. My heart pounded against my ribs and I tried to catch my breath. When I was able to focus on her face, I traced her lip with my thumb before kissing her.

"I'm sorry, baby. I didn't mean to... fuck. I don't even know what the hell just happened. It's like something inside me snapped and I needed to mark you like a fucking dog or some shit."

She wrapped her fingers around my biceps and gave me a soft smile. "It's okay, Talon. You didn't hurt me."

"You're my wife, Shell. I shouldn't have taken you like that."

"Hey." She reached for my cheek. "I told you I didn't want you to hold back. You think I haven't heard the rumors about you? The club whores aren't exactly quiet. They're catty bitches and like to spout off about the guys they've been with. I know what you're into, and as long as we can ease into things, I'll be fine. I was a webcam girl, after all. It's not like I'm all sweet and innocent."

Deep down, I knew if those fuckers hadn't raped her, she wouldn't have started screwing random guys or gone as wild as she had. She'd probably have saved herself for someone special, maybe even married them. Part of me was glad she was here, lying under me, and would soon wear my property patch. But the slightly less asshole side of me wished she'd never gone through that and could have had a normal life.

"I don't give a shit what you've heard, or what they claimed. None of them matter, Shell. I won't cheat on you. It's just you and me, baby. If I go too far, ask too much of you, all you have to do is tell me and I'll back the hell off."

"I want all of you, Talon. Everything. The good. The bad. We're in this together, right?"

I nodded. "All the way, butterfly."

A strange look crossed her face. "Why a butterfly? Because I didn't stay in one place too long?"

I smoothed her hair back. "No. I always thought of you as this vibrant, delicate butterfly when you were a teenager. Those assholes tried to break you, but you're still as amazing as ever. Even more so now that I know what you've survived on your own. So you'll always be my little butterfly."

She bit her lip so hard I worried she'd draw blood.

"Come on. Let's clean up again and figure out dinner. I want to hit the road early so we need to get a decent night's sleep."

She sighed and nodded. "All right. But if they say anything at the compound when they see me, don't get in a fight over it. I'm a big girl. Whatever they have to say, it's only words."

"Sticks and stones?" I asked, thinking of the verse I'd heard as a kid.

"Something like that."

She fucking amazed me. So beautiful. Strong.

And I was the lucky bastard who got to call her wife.

Chapter Five

Shella

I hadn't known what to expect when I got home. I'd thought maybe we'd go to Slash's house first. Instead, he stopped in front of the clubhouse and got off his bike. Great. I hadn't had time to prepare myself. I needed armor before I faced the men inside, especially my dad. Did he even know I was coming home? Did he care?

My stomach twisted as I stared at the building in front of me. Was I ready for this? It seemed I didn't have a choice. Slash approached my car and opened the door, reaching in to unbuckle me. He took my hand and helped me from the car, not releasing me as we walked up the steps and through the clubhouse doors. It was still a little early for a party to be in full swing, but there were several club whores around, music blasted from the speakers in the corners of the room, and smoke hung heavy in the air. I waved a hand in front of my face, thinking this was probably the last place I needed to be while I was pregnant.

Slash held onto me, leading me through the small crowd of people. Badger sat at the far end of the bar, a bottle of beer in front of him. He'd picked at the label and it hung halfway off, the condensation sliding down the bottle to pool on the bar top. Slash stopped next to him, waiting for Badger to acknowledge him. When he turned toward us, I saw the *President* patch on his cut. It was bittersweet. I loved Badger like a brother, but the fact my dad had stepped down left me feeling a little hollow. I knew Grizzly was getting older. It made sense he wouldn't rule this place forever, and yet it felt wrong seeing that patch on someone else's cut.

"See you found the prodigal daughter," Badger said.

"Yeah," Slash said. "Told Griz so he knows already. Need you to call Church tomorrow."

Badger's eyebrows arched. "You telling me what to do?"

Slash's hand tightened on mine. "I'm claiming Shella. Need to make it official and can't do that without taking it to the table."

Badger eyed him, then me, his gaze sliding down to our entwined fingers. He stood and tugged me away from Slash, giving me a hug. "Good to have you home, Shella."

"Thanks, Badger."

"You okay with him claiming you?" he asked.

I lifted my left hand, letting him see the wedding ring. "More than. I guess the question is whether or not the club is okay with it. I know I'm not exactly anyone's favorite person around here."

He grunted and eyed me up and down. Yeah, it was no secret the club wasn't ready to welcome me home with open arms. Slash might have been looking for me, and maybe my dad had at first, but the others? They'd moved on with their lives.

"You had some growing up to do." Badger sat again. "If Slash married you, then I guess you figured your shit out. Unless there's something else going on? You in trouble? Some reason you'd need a husband quick like?"

He saw far too much, and I hoped my expression didn't give anything away.

"Any reason you think I wouldn't want her for my own?" Slash asked.

Badger slid his gaze to Slash and didn't say anything. Great. Even my brother-in-law wasn't overly thrilled I was here. Or at least, he didn't understand why Slash would want me. If we couldn't win Badger over, how the hell would we get the club to accept us?

"We'll discuss it later," Badger said. "You can ask the club to approve her as your old lady, but we'll vote on it. Can't promise they'll be inclined to accept her. Not after the shit she pulled before."

I swallowed hard and backed up a step. It seemed not all was forgiven, even if Lilian had said she wasn't mad at me anymore. I'd known what would happen when I came here. It's why I'd stayed away for so long. I should have never let Slash talk me into this. The moment he went to sleep, I should have run and kept running.

"I shouldn't be here," I said softly. I drew back farther and briskly walked out of the clubhouse. This might have been home at one point, but it was clear it wasn't anymore.

Stupid. You were so stupid to think things would be okay.

I reached my car, yanking open the door. Before I could get in, a hand slammed against the window and the door shut. I gasped and whirled, not knowing who had followed me. Dragon glared, his eyes hard and cold. I couldn't blame him. Because of me, Lilian had nearly died. She could have lost their babies. It was clear no one had told him I was coming back.

"Why the fuck are you here?" he demanded.

"Slash brought me home."

He leaned in closer, towering over me. I pressed back against the car. I didn't think he'd hurt me, but… I'd been gone a long time. If I'd changed, surely other people here had too. And if there was one thing I'd heard about Dragon, it was that he'd do anything for Lilian. If he saw me as a threat to her or his kids…

"I'm not here to cause trouble," I said.

"Your sister may have forgiven you, but I haven't," he said. "You should have stayed gone."

My throat burned with unshed tears. So much for words not hurting me. No fucking way would I ever let him see me cry. I bit my tongue, trying to hold myself together. I waited, hoping he'd back off and let me go. He'd never been the type to hit a woman, and I didn't think he'd start now. I just couldn't be sure.

"What the fuck is going on?" a harsh voice demanded.

I whipped my head that direction and saw Demon. The moment he recognized me, a scowl crossed his face. It was clear I didn't have any friends here. Badger might have hugged me, but even he wasn't sure I'd be accepted as Slash's old lady. Now Dragon and Demon both glared at me, clearly wanting me far from here.

"Get the fuck away from my wife," Slash said, his voice a low growl as he stomped toward us. I hadn't even heard the doors to the clubhouse open.

Dragon jolted. "Wife?"

"Yeah, asshole. You're scaring the shit out of her," Slash said, coming closer. He yanked Dragon away from me and curved his arm around my waist, tugging me tight against his side.

"You married her?" Dragon asked. "Why the fuck would you do that?"

I felt the tension in Slash and knew if I didn't say or do something, he'd likely start throwing punches. For whatever reason, he felt protective of me. Even before he'd known what had happened, he'd still come for me when no one else had.

"Can we go home?" I asked softly. "Please."

His hold on me loosened and he helped me into my car, pausing to kiss my cheek. "You know where the house is. I'll be right there. Don't even think of unloading this car without me."

"All right."

He shut the door and faced off against Dragon and Demon. I backed out and turned down the road that led to his house. He wasn't far from the clubhouse. Even though he was the VP for the club, his home wasn't overly large. Or it didn't seem to be from the outside. Even though it was two stories, it wasn't as wide or deep as some of the other homes.

I parked under the double carport and went through the side door. His kitchen was a decent size, and far cleaner than I'd have expected from a bachelor. His microwave doubled as a vent over the stove. Both were a shiny black. The fridge was also jet black and looked almost new. The counters were a textured slate gray, and the cabinets were a charcoal gray. Even the floor was gray tile. The only color was on the walls. A shade of teal or blue that I couldn't quite label, they somehow fit the color scheme nicely and still made the room have a masculine feel.

A little breakfast nook was across the room, a round table and four chairs in front of a window. Another small window was over the kitchen sink. I moved farther into the house, wanting to explore my new home. The front entry had the same gray tile. The steps going to the second floor were stained black and sealed so they had a slight sheen to them. The floor in the living room was a rough wood that had a driftwood type appearance. Weathered. Pretty. He had a black leather couch and armchair. Even the wood furniture was black.

"Does he have something against color?" I mused aloud. I went past the stairs and opened a door just beyond the living room wall. The space was empty, the floor covered in a thick gray carpet. Another door was tucked under the stairway and I found a half-bath with a pedestal sink and toilet. A plain glass mirror hung over the sink.

Heading to the second floor, I opened all the doors. Two more empty rooms that I knew were supposed to be bedrooms, the same gray carpet in both, a full bath, and then the master suite. And it was definitely a suite.

I entered the room and took it all in. The bed was a huge monstrosity, hand-carved posts reaching to the ceiling. It had been stained like the stairs, and the bedding was a mix of grays, white, and black. It looked big enough for four people to comfortably lie in it, and I wondered why he needed so much space. Then decided I might not want to know.

A long dresser took up a wall, easily six feet in length. An armoire was against the wall opposite the bed, the doors slightly ajar. I pulled them open farther and saw a flat screen TV inside, as well as four drawers under it. I shut the cabinet and went to the window that looked out over the side yard. He had two comfy chairs and a small table facing the window, a book lay open on one of the chairs.

Going into the bathroom, I marveled at how large it was. A double sink with lots of drawers and cabinets underneath, the toilet was off to the side in a separate room with a door that closed. The tub looked big enough for two and had jets along the sides. I ran my fingers over the clear glass of the shower. A perfect square, I saw a small built-in bench on one wall, as well as floor-to-ceiling small shelves in one corner, most of which were empty.

Two doors drew my attention and I opened them, my jaw dropping when I realized they were his and hers closets. Not exactly huge, but plenty big enough. The rods formed an L-shape and there were built-in shelves low to the ground, most likely for shoes. Slash's closet had a bunch of jeans hanging up, as well as a few sweaters and two button-down shirts. He had at least three different types of Harley Davidson boots in the bottom, and a dressier pair of ankle boots, although I had a hard time picturing him wearing those. He had two black leather jackets, and several hoodies on the rack as well.

"Find what you're looking for?"

I squealed and spun to face him. "I didn't hear you come in."

He smirked. "Obviously."

"I was just checking everything out. If this is going to be my home, I thought I should know where everything was." I folded my arms, feeling defensive. Yes, I'd been snooping, but if we were married could it *really* be considered being nosy?

"I brought up two of your boxes. I'll get the other two if you want to put some things away. There are several empty drawers in the dresser and I'm sure you found your closet."

I looked around again before focusing on him. "Do you have something against color? Nearly everything is monochromatic."

"I'm not that great at matching shit. Anything you don't like, you can change. Want to paint the walls? Let me know. I'm not going to let my pregnant wife wield a paintbrush, but I can take you out somewhere and have a Prospect paint the place."

"What about a soft aqua in the bedroom?" I asked. "If you don't want it on all the walls, maybe at least an accent wall?"

He tugged me against him, placing his hands at my waist. "Whatever you want, Shell. This is your home now. You can make any changes you'd like."

I worried at my lower lip. "Will it be my home if they don't accept me as your old lady? Or will I be asked to leave the compound?"

He gripped my chin. "Baby, they're going to accept you just fine. You let me handle it."

"Are you going to tell them?" I asked. "About what happened. Before."

His thumb lightly rubbed my skin. "Yeah, baby. I'm going to tell them. They need to know. For one, we all fucked up. The fact you were hurting and none of us fucking saw it? You bet your ass I'm letting them know. Your behavior was a cry for help, and we were all fucking deaf and blind to it."

"I don't want their pity."

He kissed me, his lips soft against mine. "My beautiful butterfly. No one will pity you, although they're going to be pissed at themselves for not realizing you needed help. Especially your dad."

I clung to him, cuddling against his chest. He made me feel safe. Wanted. It had been so long since I'd felt those things. I hoped he was right. If I had to give him up, the one man I'd always wanted, it would tear me apart. But I refused to come between him and the club.

"Go put your things away, butterfly. I'll get the other two boxes and we can check out the kitchen. I'll need to clean out the fridge since I've been gone for a bit, tracking you down. We'll need to make a list. I'm sure you aren't up for a grocery run so I'll get a Prospect to pick up everything."

I opened and shut my mouth, blinking at him. "Are you telling me that you're going to send someone to gather the items we want, or that you're going to do a grocery pick-up like a soccer mom?"

He snorted. "I'm not completely uncivilized, butterfly. I'll use the app on my phone to place my order and ask Matt to pick it up. He's done it before."

I wasn't sure what to make of Slash. Badass biker. VP of the club. Sometimes tender lover. And he used an app to buy his groceries? He was a conundrum, but hopefully, I'd have the rest of my life to figure him out. Knowing we were married filled me with a warmth I'd never felt before. My crush had turned to full-blown love, and only he had the power to destroy me. He just didn't know it.

I went around him and back into the bedroom, seeing my boxes on the floor by the bed. I opened the first one and started unpacking my clothes. It only took a moment to find the empty dresser drawers. My underthings and pajamas all fit into one drawer. It was a bit sad. At one point, I'd had a ton of clothes and shoes. Over the years I'd been gone, I'd lost them all. The things I had now were cheap and most had come from secondhand stores. Except the shoes. Or bras and panties. I refused to buy any of those items used. But even those came from the discount store.

Slash placed his hands on my hips, his chest against my back. "What happened to all your belongings, Shell? I know you had a crap ton when you left."

I shrugged a shoulder. "Most were stolen. My places were broken into a few times in the various towns I stopped in. Another time I forgot to lock my car, and someone took anything I had left of value. Oddly, they didn't want the car itself. Or maybe they thought it was a higher risk of getting caught."

"If you know your sizes, we can shop online later and have some stuff delivered to the compound. You need more clothes, and a sturdy pair of boots. Not that I want you on my bike all that often right now, with you being pregnant, but eventually you'll ride with me more frequently."

I turned to face him. "And how are you going to explain not wanting your new wife on your bike? They'll know we weren't together long enough for me to know I'm pregnant."

He leaned down, his nose brushing mine. "Then I'll have to tell them I'm doing my damnedest to knock you up and don't want to take any chances."

He kissed me again. Another soft, slow brush of his lips that left me tingling.

I reached for him, grabbing onto his cut and holding on. He groaned and I felt his fingers brush my belly as he unfastened my jeans. He tugged them down my thighs before yanking my panties down too. I managed to kick off my shoes and step out of my clothes before tugging my shirt over my head.

I heard the clink of his buckle as his lips ravaged mine. Soon, he gripped my hips and lifted me, pressing my back to the wall as my legs went around his waist. He thrust deep, filling me up and making me cry out in pleasure.

"Yes!" I held on tighter.

He growled and slammed into me again and again, like he'd been possessed. He took me hard, fast, and deep. I nearly saw stars when I came, the breath leaving my lungs. My nails bit into him. When he came, he roared out like some wild beast, his hips jerking as the hot splashes of his cum filled me.

"Fuck," he muttered. "I did it again. Lost complete fucking control."

"I liked it," I admitted. "In case you hadn't noticed."

I wiggled where he'd pinned me to the wall, my breath catching when I realized he was still hard. Like, really hard. I hadn't known men his age could have such a quick rebound, but I certainly wasn't going to complain. I squirmed again and he pulled me away from the wall, walking into the bedroom.

He slid free of my body and before I could say a word, he'd spun me around and bent me over the side of the bed. Slash fisted my hair, tipping my head so he could hold my gaze. I felt his cock press against me before he thrust forward.

"Give me your wrists," he said.

His voice had gone dark and deep, with a rasp to it that drove me wild. My hands shook a little as I crossed my wrists behind my back.

It's just Slash. Just Slash. He won't hurt you. I repeated the words over and over as his hand closed around my wrists in a tight grip. He released my hair, putting his other hand at my hip. He had me pinned to the bed, holding me still, and panic welled inside me. I pushed it down, not wanting to freak out on him.

When he started fucking me, it was raw and savage. Gone was the gentle touch and soft words. Even in the bathroom, he hadn't been like this. My heart raced and I watched him over my shoulder. My eyes slid shut as he hammered into me harder.

A sharp slap to my ass made me yelp and open my eyes again.

"Focus on me, Shell. Just you and me," he said. His voice was more growl than anything else. I'd heard the old ladies laugh and say their men went all caveman on them, and I'd never understood. Until now.

He worked his hand between me and the bed and rubbed my clit. It didn't take long before I was coming, screaming out his name. His hips slapped against my ass as he came, not slowing even after I felt the heat of his release.

Slash's breathing was ragged. He leaned over me, pressing his lips to my shoulder blade, then biting down on my shoulder. I gave a little yelp and he licked the spot he'd bitten. Was he... marking me? Like some sort of animal?

I'd read enough werewolf romances the thought wasn't exactly abhorrent. If anything, I tried to lift my ass and silently beg for more. His weight pressed me down onto the bed. He released my wrists but they remained pinned between us. When he started stroking in and out of me again, my body lit up. Whatever he was doing, it was more than working for me. He caged me between his forearms, his chest to my back.

"That's it, pretty butterfly. Take it. Take everything I give you."

"More," I begged. "Please, Talon."

My nipples were so hard they ached and my clit pulsed. I wanted his hands on me. His mouth. Anything. Everything.

He leaned down putting his lips by my ear. "You ever let someone fuck your ass?"

Heat zinged through me. "N-No. Almost. Once."

"You're about to." I bit my lip as he pulled free of my body and lifted his weight off me. "Keep those wrists right there. Don't you fucking move, butterfly."

He shoved two fingers into my pussy, then spread my ass cheeks wide. Using his cum, he toyed with the forbidden spot I'd never let anyone play with much less fuck. Slash took his time, working one finger into my ass, then a second. I squirmed. It burned and felt strange, and yet, I wanted more.

His fingers eased from my body and he held me open. I felt the head of his cock as he pressed against me. The cry that fell from my lips couldn't be held back as he pushed into me. I scrunched my eyes shut tight and fought to breathe through it.

"Hurts, Talon." I whimpered. "Too much. I can't..."

"Oh, you can and you will, butterfly. Just need you to want it as much as I do."

He worked his hand past my hip and over the lips of my pussy. He toyed with my clit, rubbing and pinching until the pain began to ebb and all I felt was this insane need. As he stroked in and out of me, his fingers danced over my clit.

"Talon."

"That's it, butterfly. Let go."

A keening sound filled the air and I realized it was from me. The most intense orgasm I'd ever had ripped through me, leaving me shaken. Slash growled and pinned me down. He rode me hard, taking what he wanted.

"Gonna fill this tight little ass up with my cum. You want it, don't you?" he asked.

"Y-yes. Please!"

My nipples rubbed against the bedding with every stroke of his cock and I came as I felt the heat of his release. When he was finished, he held still, his cock twitching inside me. I felt... I didn't know what I felt. A million emotions and sensations overwhelmed me.

"My perfect little butterfly," he murmured, kissing my neck and shoulder.

He withdrew from my body and helped me stand. His cum ran down my thighs and heat flared in his eyes as he watched. "Get dressed. Don't even think of cleaning any of that off you."

He reached out to tweak my nipple and my body responded instantly.

Then he winked, fastened his pants, and left the room. Either he didn't care if he cleaned up, or he planned to take care of it downstairs. Being a man, he had the luxury of rinsing off in the sink. I heard his steps on the stairs and figured he was checking the kitchen like he'd said he would.

My heart slammed against my ribs as I tried to figure out what the hell had just happened. I put my panties and jeans back on, leaving his cum on my body as he'd demanded. Then on shaky legs, I finished putting my things away. After I was done, I went downstairs to find him. I saw him toss a half-gallon of milk into the trash as well as what looked like rotten veggies.

He had a pad on the counter with a pen and I saw he'd been making a list of what he needed to replace. While he cleaned out the fridge, I worked on the cabinets, checking to see what he had in them. Things I knew I liked, I added to the list, like graham crackers and oatmeal cookies. Then we sat down and discussed meal options for the week and finished off the list together. After he ordered everything through the app on his phone, and paid, he messaged Matt with the pick-up time and order number.

"So, what now?" I asked.

He wrapped an arm around my waist and pulled me closer until we were hip to hip. It wasn't fair. All he had to do was look at me and I wanted him. And when he touched me... It felt like I was going up in flames. It wasn't fair for a man to be so damn sexy.

"Now, I'm going to cuddle with my wife on the couch and watch whatever movie she picks."

I narrowed my eyes at him. He'd fucked me like a demon had possessed him. Now he just wanted to watch TV? I still felt raw and like part of my soul had left my body. Not Slash. He was completely calm.

"What if I want to watch a chick flick?" I asked.

"Then that's what we'll watch."

"Did someone sneak in and hit you over the head while I was still upstairs?" I asked. "Because you aren't acting like you. The Slash I know isn't this agreeable."

"Maybe I'm luring you in, showing you my nice side, and when you least expect it, I'll strike. Besides, if we don't watch a movie in the living room, I'll just toss you over my shoulder and carry you upstairs. I think we both know what will happen then."

I licked my lips. "Maybe I'm okay with that."

His eyes went dark and he growled before lifting me into his arms. He slung me over his shoulder, smacking my ass, then took the steps to the second floor. It looked like I was about to get my wish. I just wasn't sure which Slash I'd end up with. The one who'd just blown my mind, or the sweeter version from my apartment?

Chapter Six

Slash

I shouldn't be doing this. Regardless of what she thought, Shella was fragile. I needed to handle her with care, show her not all men were assholes. Truth of the matter was that I *was* an asshole. Just not with her. Or at least, I didn't want to be an asshole when it came to her. My beautiful butterfly was special. For one, I'd never once been tempted to keep a woman. I may have told her I was doing it for her benefit, to keep her safe, give her and her baby a home. Deep down, I knew I was full of shit. She'd fascinated me. I'd wanted her, so I'd made her mine.

Before I'd gone downstairs, I'd completely lost control. I'd taken her rough, demanded things I shouldn't have. I'd seen the moment she almost came unraveled, when I'd gripped her wrists and held her down. I'd been a total dick and made her push through it. Then I'd fucked her ass and treated her like the whore I kept saying she wasn't. What the fuck was wrong with me?

I kicked the bedroom door shut and eased her down until her feet touched the floor. I made quick work of stripping both of us, then yanked the covers to the foot of the bed. She'd said she couldn't handle being held down, but my body had pinned her to the mattress, and I'd held her wrists without too much of a fuss. I wondered if she'd do okay being tied to the bed. Or handcuffed. As much as I didn't want to push her too far, I didn't like the idea of her past haunting her forever. I remembered Dingo once saying something about Meiling needing him to push her, make her realize what happened to her couldn't hurt her anymore. Did I need to do that with Shella?

"You're thinking too hard," she said.

"I want to tie you to the bed, but I'm worried you'll freak out. I know it was touch and go when I grabbed your wrists earlier."

She pushed her hair back and I noticed her hand shook. Yeah, probably didn't need to tie her up right now. Too much too soon. I decided to forgo the rope for now, or any other restraints. We hadn't been together long, so there was plenty of time for us to explore one another and push her boundaries.

"Too soon," I said. "Don't ever feel like you have to give in to me, Shell. Not in the bedroom. Outside this house, or in company, is another matter. But when it's just us and sex is involved, you can set the pace."

She came closer, pressing a kiss to the center of my chest. "I'm sorry I'm so screwed up. I've had sex with plenty of guys since it happened. I just never let them pin me down, or tie me up. You already managed to get more out of me than anyone else ever has, and it's because I trust you. If you want to tie me up, I'll let you."

"Then let's see what you can handle, with or without being tied down." I lifted her and tossed her onto the bed, making her giggle. Her breasts bounced and fuck if I didn't get even harder. Her eyes were bright, and a sweet smile curved her lips. "My beautiful butterfly. Not sure I deserve you, but I'll never let you go."

I felt like a Goddamn teenager. I couldn't remember the last time I'd been able to go again so quick. I'd already taken her three times, and now, not even an hour later, I was ready for more. No one had made me feel like this. Ever. Only my sweet butterfly. Fuck, but I wanted her more than air.

I crawled onto the bed, hovering over her. Bracing my arms on either side of her, I leaned down and rubbed my whiskers against her neck and collarbone, making her squeal. I hadn't had a full beard in a while, although, if she wanted me to grow it back, I gladly would. Shaving wasn't my favorite thing, so I only did it every three days.

"Gonna mark you as mine."

I nipped the side of her neck, then sucked at the skin along her shoulder, leaving little love bites. Her nipples were so fucking hard I couldn't resist them. I licked and gently bit them, making her writhe and moan under me. I slipped a hand between our bodies and stroked her pussy, loving that she was already soaked. Even though I wondered if at least some of it wasn't the cum I'd told her not to wash away. I felt where it had hardened on her thighs. It seemed my wife was not only sexy, but wanted me as much as I wanted her.

I trailed kisses down her stomach and left little bites along her hips before settling between her splayed thighs. I pushed them wider apart. So pretty and pink. Parting the lips of her pussy, I flicked her clit with my tongue. Her legs tightened against me, squeezing me, as I sucked the hard bud into my mouth. Shella cried out, arching her back. I slid my hand under her ass, holding her still as I ravaged her slick folds with my lips and tongue.

Slicking my finger in her wet pussy, I used it as lube and worked my finger into her ass. I grinned, feeling my cum still inside her as I stroked my finger in and out of her tight little ass while I sucked on her clit. I bit the hard bud, then licked away the sting.

I made her come twice before I settled over her and sank into her tight pussy. She gripped my cock like she was made for me.

"So Goddamn perfect, butterfly. And all mine." Her eyes went wide, and I hesitated only a second. "Cleaned up downstairs, baby. I promise. Not taking chances with you getting an infection or something."

I may have always used condoms, but I knew better than to fuck her ass, then stick my dick in her pussy without washing up first. And yeah, I'd fucked more than one club whore in the ass over the years. Far safer than risking getting one pregnant. But with Shella, it was totally different. She was mine, and *only* mine. Even if she hadn't been a virgin when I'd claimed her, I'd still been the first to fuck her ass.

Bracing my weight with one hand, I gripped her hip tight with the other and drove into her. Each stroke harder and deeper than the last. Her nails bit into me as I fucked her. The way she looked at me, the flush riding her cheeks, unleashed my primitive side. I pounded into her, taking what I wanted, what I needed. When she screamed out my name, her pussy tightening, I knew I couldn't hold back. I groaned as I filled her with my cum, not stopping until the last drop had been wrung from my balls.

"Fuck!" My chest heaved as I tried to catch my breath. And the stunning woman under me gave me the sweetest smile. "You okay?"

She nodded. "Perfect."

I kissed her, my cock still hard and twitching. At forty-five, it had been a while since I'd been able to go again so soon. Only Shella seemed to bring out this side of me. Any other woman, I'd have come and been done for the rest of the night. With her, I couldn't seem to get enough.

"What the fuck is going on?" someone roared from the bedroom doorway.

I jolted, yanking the covers over Shella before facing an enraged Grizzly. His face had started to turn purple, and he'd fisted his hands at his side.

"Griz. You don't knock anymore?" I asked, standing and reaching for my underwear. I pulled them on before facing him. No fucking way I'd give him a clear shot at removing my dick since he'd just found me balls-deep in his daughter. Probably a good thing I hadn't pulled out any toys, like the nipple clamps I couldn't wait to use on her.

"I did knock." He snarled at me. "You said you were bringing her home. You didn't say a fucking word about treating her like a Goddamn whore!"

I lifted my hands, hoping to placate him. "Griz, it's not what you think. And I'd never treat her like a whore."

The ex-Pres took a swing at me, his fist connecting with my jaw hard enough I saw stars. I shook it off and blocked the next blow, but he landed a solid hit to my ribs. "She's my daughter! I ought to kill you."

"Dad, stop!" Shella stumbled from the bed, the sheet wrapped around her. She stood at my side and I reached for her, putting my arm around her waist, ready to move her if Griz came at me again. I knew he wouldn't hit her, but I didn't want her getting between us.

He let out another roar and charged me. I pushed Shella out of the way right before her dad hit me with the full force of his weight. I went down to the floor and tried to block most of his blows. The fist to my stomach knocked the wind out of me for a moment, and he clocked me along my jaw again. I knew I'd be bruised as fuck later, but I understood. He needed this.

Shella screamed and I saw tears streaming down her face. I needed to end this. Griz had his shot at me, got to feel like he was protecting his kid, but I'd never fucking hurt her.

"I'd never treat Shella like a whore," I said, my voice calmer. "She's my wife, Griz. I married her."

He stood and staggered back a step, seeming to deflate as he looked at her uncertainly. "You married Slash?"

She nodded. "Yeah, I did. And he's been great to me."

Griz glowered at me, not bothering to help me up. "You didn't say anything about marrying her."

I stood and winced at how tender my ribs felt. I reached for Shella and pulled her against my side again. If Griz lost it, I'd shove her out of the way, but I hoped he was calm enough to be reasoned with. And maybe I should have given him a heads-up before now.

"Dad, you know I used to have a crush on Slash. Is it any wonder I'd want to marry him someday?" Shella asked.

She'd had a crush on me? I didn't dare look at her. If I did, I might give away how I felt hearing those words. It made me feel ten feet tall, knowing she'd always had a thing for me.

"He didn't force you?" Griz asked, focusing on his daughter. "Or did he do the caveman thing and just tell you to marry him?"

"I want to be with him," she said softly, leaning her head against my arm. "Please, Dad. Don't hurt him."

"Fine." Griz swung his gaze to me. "Welcome to the family. You hurt her, I'll fucking bury you."

"I'd never hurt her," I said. "In fact, I'm doing my best to knock her up. You ready to be a grandpa again?"

A smile ticked up one corner of his mouth before he scowled at me again. "She's just a kid herself. Only twenty! She has plenty of time to start a family."

"Maybe. But I don't. I know I'm twenty-five years older than her, and maybe you have an issue with that, but I will protect her with my life. I want a family with Shell, and I hope you can learn to accept that."

Griz sighed and ran a hand through his hair. "Fine. You have my blessing, as long as she's happy. The second she comes crying to me about you fucking up, we're going to revisit this. And I won't hold back."

I wouldn't expect anything less. I ushered Griz from the room so Shella could get dressed, stopping only long enough to grab my jeans. I slipped them on and went downstairs with him. He didn't seem quite so agitated now, even though I'd hardly say he was calm. It had to be a shock to find me fucking his kid. If I'd walked in on some guy with my daughter, I'd have wanted blood.

Griz sat in the living room and I sprawled in the chair by the couch. He scanned the room, looking everywhere but at me. Couldn't blame him. He'd just seen far more of me than he ever wanted to. I only hoped he didn't get too big an eyeful of Shella. I heard her racing down the stairs and I shot up, hurrying over to her.

"Slow down! What if you tripped and fell?" I asked, reaching for her. I held her hand as she walked down the last three steps, then led her into the living room. I should have let her sit by her dad. Instead, I tugged her down onto my lap in the chair.

"You're already coddling her," Grizzly said. "I was the same way with May, even from the beginning. It's clear you have feelings for my daughter, and this wasn't just out of the blue."

The way he eyed me made it clear he wondered exactly when I'd started noticing Shella. As much as I wanted to set him at ease, if I wanted everyone to believe this baby was mine, the less I said the better. I simply held his stare until he shook his head and looked away.

"You talked to your sisters yet?" Grizzly asked her.

"No. I don't even know if they realize I'm home. I saw Badger when we first got here, so it's possible he told Adalia," Shella said. "And Dragon..."

She trailed off and I knew she didn't want to finish that sentence. Dragon hadn't reacted well to seeing her again. I'd had a talk with him, and I'd hit him hard enough he'd eaten dirt. I could only hope I'd made a big enough impression he'd back the fuck down.

"No doubt. He doesn't keep anything from her, unless he thinks it will upset her. She's pregnant again, and after losing two babies Badger's ready to tear into anyone who so much as breathes too heavy around her," Grizzly said. "We honestly thought she couldn't get pregnant again. It's what the doctor said. Seems he was wrong."

"Did he say she *couldn't* have another baby or *shouldn't*?" Shella asked.

Griz rubbed his beard. "Maybe it was the second one, in which case, Badger is probably going to come unglued until the baby gets here."

Just what we needed. Our Pres focused on his pregnant woman. Shit. It meant I'd probably have to take up the slack, except with Shella under my roof, I knew I'd be distracted too. With so many of my brothers starting families, it was a wonder the club hadn't fallen apart. We were turning into a bunch of pussywhipped men.

"I'll call her tomorrow," Shella said. "I think I just want to get settled into my new home tonight. Besides, I don't think a lot of people will be happy to see me. The ones at the clubhouse weren't thrilled I was back."

Grizzly twisted his wedding band. He'd never taken it off, even all the years after May's death. I could tell something was weighing on him and I hoped like hell he wasn't about to ask why she'd been so bratty before she'd taken off. It wasn't a conversation I thought she'd be up for right now.

"You were a bit wild before you left," Griz said. "I never intended for you to stay gone, Shella. I loved you. Still do. You might not be my blood, but you're my daughter just the same."

"Dad, I know I screwed up. It's why I stayed gone. I figured no one really wanted me around here. Thought it best if I kept my distance," she said.

I tightened my hold on her, knowing she was thinking about *why* she'd been acting out. Griz would find out soon enough. The entire club would. There was no fucking way I'd let them treat her like shit, or make her feel bad, when it was us who'd failed her. I knew the moment I told them what she'd been through, it would be like setting off a bomb in the middle of Church.

I still needed to find out the names of the boys who hurt her. Then I'd have Outlaw figure out if they still lived in the area. Their lives were about to be hell. Whatever was left of them, because I had no intention of letting any of them live. Once I got my hands on them, it was only a matter of time before they drew their last breath.

The doorbell rang, and then I heard the door open. "Slash? I've got your grocery order."

"Then get in here and put the shit in the kitchen," I said.

He peered around the door, saw Shella in my lap and Griz on my couch. He gave them a slight wave, then darted toward the kitchen with a handful of sacks. It took him two more trips to get everything into the house, and I heard him putting it away.

"You need anything?" Grizzly asked, looking at Shella.

"I'll be buying her some new stuff. She's not your financial responsibility anymore, Griz. She's my wife and I'll see she's taken care of," I said.

"Not trying to step on your toes, Slash. She's my daughter, even if she's married to you. Do you honestly think I don't still buy shit for Adalia and Lilian? Because I do."

"Just sayin', I can take care of my woman." I patted her thigh and she stood up. I leaned forward, holding his gaze. "She's my wife, Griz. I have no idea if the club will accept her as my old lady. You want to do something for her? Make sure they vote yes when I take it to the table. She's worried they'll ask her to leave."

Grizzly puffed up. "They better not fucking dare."

I just stared at him until he nodded. With him on my side, there was a better chance of Shella being accepted. Even before I told everyone how badly we'd fucked up. Whatever it took, she was staying right here with me. Now that I had her under my roof, and in my bed, I wasn't letting her go. Not now. Not fucking ever.

"Then let's get it over with now," Griz said. He pulled out his phone and sent a message to someone. Badger most likely. Within two minutes, my phone chimed.

Church in five.

"Let's go," Griz said. "Why don't you ask Matt to stick around in case Shella needs anything while we're gone?"

"I'll meet you at the clubhouse." Griz hugged Shella, then left. I pulled her into my arms, kissing her. I could feel the tension in her body and knew she was scared. "It's going to be fine, butterfly. You'll see."

I kissed her once more, then went to tell Matt he needed to stick around. If Shella didn't want him in the house, he could sit on the porch. Either way, I'd feel better knowing he was here. After I had everything arranged, I got on my bike and went to the clubhouse, ready to do battle for my woman.

I was one of the last ones in the door and took my seat. Badger looked tired as fuck, rubbing his eyes. Several other brothers didn't look too happy to be here either. Mostly the ones with families. Seemed I wasn't the only one with other plans for tonight. After the last of us had taken our seats and the doors to Church had closed, Badger slammed his fist on the table.

"We're meeting for one reason only. Slash brought Shella back to the compound," Badger said.

A few men groaned, and I wanted to pound them into the fucking ground.

"He wants to claim her as his old lady, so we're going to take it to a vote," Badger said.

"No fucking way," Dragon said. "Not after the shit she pulled with Lilian. My woman may have forgiven her, but I sure the fuck don't."

"I'd have to agree," Cobra said. "She's trouble."

I leaned over to whisper in Badger's ear. "There's something the club needs to know. It's not pretty and Griz is going to flip the fuck out when he hears what I have to say."

Badger eyed me. "About Shella?"

I nodded. He waved for me to say whatever needed saying. I stood and looked at each of my brothers.

"I know Shella caused problems when she was here before, but I have a question for you. Most of you remember when she came here. How sweet and shy she was. Then it seemed like overnight she went wild. Anyone ever ask her why? Or wonder about the change in her?" I asked.

Grizzly tensed, his gaze laser-focused on me. Yeah, he knew I was about to say something that would change everything. I could almost see the gears grinding in his head as he tried to figure it out.

"Are you saying something happened to make her act like that?" Outlaw asked.

"Yeah. It's exactly what I'm saying, and every last one of us fucking failed her. We didn't notice, or didn't bother to ask *why* she'd changed. Myself included. Before you decide she's not worthy of being my old lady, or being part of this club, you need to hear what happened," I said.

I glanced at Badger and he gave me a nod, then stood and went around to Grizzly, standing just behind his chair. I knew when the old man went ballistic, Badger would keep him under control. Best he could at any rate.

"When Shella was in high school, something happened. Something bad." I swallowed hard, my hands fisting at my sides as I remembered what she'd told me. "She was gang-raped. They held her down and took turns. When she came home, Lilian had been having a bad day. Shella didn't tell anyone because she didn't want to upset her sister even more. She cleaned herself up, went to stay with a friend, and kept it to herself."

Grizzly roared like the bear he'd been named after, his fists pounding on the table. I heard the wood crack and his chair fell as he stood. Badger tried to hold him back, and two other brothers jumped up to help.

"It was our job to keep her safe. We failed." I looked at each of them. "If you don't accept her as my old lady, I'll walk. I can't be part of a brotherhood who would turn their back on my wife after all she's suffered. You can do whatever the fuck you want with me, but I won't stay if she can't."

Badger held my gaze. "No vote. None needed. Congratulations, Slash. You have an old lady. I'll have a property cut made for her. And for what it's worth. I'm sorry. Should have fucking noticed something was off."

Grizzly openly wept, the big man falling to his knees. I'd known it would hit him hard. It's why I hadn't wanted to say anything in front of Shella. The last thing she needed was seeing her dad fall apart.

Dragon came to me, his head hung. "I'm sorry, Slash. So fucking sorry. I had no idea. None of us did."

I rammed my fist into his jaw, knocking him to the ground. He worked his jaw back and forth and stood up, accepting the hit.

"I know you're sorry. Just think before you open your mouth around her. She's strong, but inside she's still a bit broken. Your words hurt her more than you realize. She didn't want to come back. I had to force her. She knew damn well no one wanted her here."

He nodded and walked off. The others gave me a wide berth, but I saw the looks on their faces. Each pitied Shella and felt sick over not realizing she'd been hurt. It would take time for them to accept their part in all this, just like I'd have to learn to accept mine. I left Badger to deal with Grizzly and went home to my woman. It was time to give her the good news. I'd just leave out the part of how the club reacted when I told them what she'd suffered. Some things were better left unsaid.

Chapter Seven

Shella -- Two Weeks Later

Lilian sipped some tea and eyed me over the rim of her cup. "I'm glad you came home. And I'm sorry I haven't been by to see you before now. The babies haven't been sleeping well, which means I'm not either."

"It's fine. I've been trying to get my bearings around here anyway."

Lilian spun the cup on the table. "So. Dragon told me what happened. In high school. I'm sorry you felt like you couldn't tell anyone because of me. And for the record, I'm glad Slash punched him for being an idiot. I'd have done the same. In fact, when he told me and admitted what he'd said to you when you arrived, I threw a plate at him."

I tried not to laugh at the image of her throwing dishes at Dragon. "It's not your fault, Lil. I never blamed you."

"Maybe not, but..." She shrugged. "You needed help. Our support. Instead, you dealt with it on your own. I don't know how you survived that, or healed without anyone being wiser about what happened. You're stronger than me, Shella."

I took a swallow of my sweet tea, then nearly gagged before it went all the way down. With my hand clamped over my mouth, I bolted upright and ran from the kitchen, heading for the half bath. I hit my knees and threw up in the toilet, something I'd done every day for the last week. Thankfully, no one had witnessed it. Until now.

If there'd been any doubt that little test stick had been right, there wasn't now. Morning sickness was a bitch.

Lilian hurried after me and gasped in the bathroom doorway. "Shella, are you all right? Should I get Slash? Take you to the doctor?"

I flushed and stood. I rinsed my mouth at the sink, then splashed some water on my face. "I'm fine. I don't need a doctor."

Her eyes went comically wide. "Are you pregnant? Because I can't think of another reason you'd puke your guts up and not want to see the doctor."

Shit. I wasn't ready to tell anyone yet. I'd only been with Slash less than three weeks. Of course, as far as the club knew, we could have been together the month he'd been gone when he'd searched for me. I nodded, knowing I couldn't lie to my sister. "Yeah, I'm pregnant."

She squealed and bounced on her toes. "Does Slash know?"

"He knows, but we wanted to keep it quiet a while longer."

The excitement dimmed in her eyes. "Why don't you want anyone to know?"

I hated lying to her, but I couldn't exactly tell her the truth either. The last thing I wanted to do was hurt Lilian. If I told her what I'd done, how I'd hooked up with random men as a way to prove to myself I was in charge of my body, she'd never understand. And then she'd wonder who the father of my baby was, instead of accepting Slash was the dad. I needed to think fast and give her a plausible reason.

"What if I can't carry the baby to term?" I asked, thinking of Adalia. "Besides, I haven't been to the doctor. A home test and an upset stomach doesn't mean I'm pregnant for sure. Those things give false positives all the time, right?"

Lilian sighed. "All right. I won't say anything. Just promise you'll see the doctor soon. If you are pregnant, you'll need prenatal vitamins. You should also restrict your caffeine intake and watch what you eat."

I rolled my eyes and smiled at her. "Okay, Mom. I get the point. I'll talk to Slash about setting an appointment soon. I don't know if I'm on his insurance or not. I know Dad got the club a health plan when he took in Adalia, but I figured he'd dropped me after I left and didn't come back. We haven't discussed it."

Once I knew my stomach was settled, we went back to the kitchen. I pulled down a box of crackers from the cabinet and nibbled on them while I sipped some water. I wondered if Dragon had told Lilian about what had happened in high school, did that mean Badger had told Adalia? Or would he have kept it to himself, not wanting to stress her out while she was pregnant?

I didn't like leaving the house because I saw the way the club eyed me. Like I was something broken they needed to fix, and at the same time they didn't know how to act around me. Most avoided me. I'd known they wouldn't see me the same way. It was only a part of why I hadn't wanted Slash to tell them. The other... well, honestly, I was hurt they'd been willing to accept my behavior as a way to lash out after the rape, but if it had just been surging hormones, or me being a bitch they wouldn't have forgiven me? It made me feel like shit, and like I hadn't been good enough to be part of their family until they realized I'd been hurt.

"Shella, what's wrong?" Lilian asked, reaching for my hand. "You got quiet and have this look on your face."

"I don't belong here," I said. "I shouldn't have listened to Slash. He wanted me to come home, but... this place isn't home. A home is where you're accepted, where you go when you've hit your lowest point."

"You're accepted," she said, squeezing my hand.

I shook my head and pulled my hand free. "I wasn't. Not until Slash told them about the rape. After that, suddenly it was okay to forgive my behavior, to welcome me back. Until then, they wanted me gone. Especially Dragon."

Slash hadn't planned to tell me. In fact, he *hadn't* told me. I'd overheard him talking to someone. No way he'd have ever let me find out. He'd known it would hurt me. He still didn't know I'd listened to his conversation. It had been hard as hell to pretend I didn't know how the club felt.

Lilian paled and chewed at her lower lip. I didn't want to upset her. I should have just kept my mouth shut. If she went home crying, Dragon would show up and want to rip into me. Then I'd have to tell Slash I knew everything.

I stood. I didn't know where I was going, but I needed to leave. Taking off for the front door, I stopped long enough to grab my purse and keys. I got in my car and slammed the door. My hands shook as I turned the key in the ignition and backed down the driveway. When I approached the gates, the Prospect standing guard let me through. I turned toward town and cruised through the streets with no destination in mind. The diner drew my eye like a beacon, and I pulled up in front and parked.

I stepped through the glass door and the bell overhead chimed. I'd missed this place. The red vinyl seats, the fifties-style uniforms, even the black-and-white checkered floor, all of it made me feel like I was home, more than being at the compound. I'd spent a lot of time here before I'd left.

I took a seat by the window and looked over the menu, smiling when I realized it hadn't changed. Well, the diner may not have, but the staff certainly had. Then again, they got a lot of turnover here. A young girl, probably still in high school, stopped by the table, her blonde ponytail swinging behind her.

"Hi! I'm Molly and I'll be your server today. Have you had a chance to look at the menu?"

"I have and I'll take the loaded cheeseburger with fries and a glass of water."

She flashed me a smile and hurried off. While I waited, I twisted the saltshaker, needing something to keep my hands occupied. It wasn't until the conversation from the booth behind me filled my ears that I realized exactly who was in the diner with me. My entire body locked up and it felt like I couldn't breathe.

"She's just as hot as she was in high school," the voice said, full of venom and that cocky arrogance only assholes seem to have. "Maybe we need a repeat."

The other guy laughed. "Oh yeah. I'd love to have me some of that again. Won't be as good as virgin pussy, but I bet she's still a screamer."

My blood turned to ice and everything around me blurred. I knew those voices. Would never forget them. JJ and Mike. Two of the Blackwood Falls High football team members a little over two years ago. And two of the boys who'd held me down and raped me. I tried to stand but I wasn't sure my knees would hold me. I needed to leave, to get far away from this place. From them.

"Everything okay?" Molly asked, coming over with my water.

"N-no. N-n-need to... to..." I couldn't even get my tongue to work right.

"Rick," I heard Molly yell out. "We need you out here."

"Think she's still wild?" Mike asked. He didn't even bother to keep his voice down.

"Oh, I bet she is. I think we need to find out," JJ said.

"Fuck yeah. I'm hard just remembering that day," Mike said.

When two large hands settled on my arms, I screamed and lashed out. I was locked in a nightmare and couldn't break free. "No! No! You won't hurt me again!"

I heard two men laughing and just knew it was JJ and Mike. Everything slowly came into focus, and I gulped in a lungful of air. My gaze settled on a man with a concerned look in his eyes, and I noticed his name tag. *Rick -- Manager.*

"You all right?" he asked.

I gave a quick nod, then shook my head. No, I was far from all right. With those two so close to me, I wasn't sure I'd ever be *all right*. If they were still here, roaming free, what would stop them from hurting me again? It sounded like they were already making plans.

I heard the heavy tread of boots and yanked my head in that direction, relaxing a little when I saw Steel. He reached for me, tugging me against his chest.

"You all right, Shella?" he asked.

"I-I..."

"She was fine before. Then I brought her water and it was like she was in a trance or something,"

Molly said. "She freaked out when Rick tried to help her."

"He touched me," I murmured. "His hands... I thought..."

Rick backed up. "Whoa. I didn't touch her in any way that would be considered inappropriate. I only grabbed her arms because it looked like she might pass out."

"I've got her," Steel said. "Can you get her order to go and put it with mine? I'll see she gets home safe."

Rick nodded and hurried off. Molly stood nearby wringing her hands.

"Shella, can you tell me what happened?" Steel asked, his voice low.

I glanced over my shoulder to where Mike and JJ sat. They had the audacity to sneer at me. They knew exactly why I'd freaked out, and they were getting off on it. My stomach churned and I held onto Steel a little tighter. His gaze followed mine and I felt his body tense as he stared at the two guys who'd hurt me.

"Who are they?" he asked.

I looked up at him, hoping he'd figure it out without me having to say it. Mike and JJ had gotten quiet with Steel here now. Everyone at school had known I lived with the Devil's Fury. Even they weren't stupid enough to fuck with the bikers. It made me wonder if they'd known back then that I wouldn't say anything. If Lilian hadn't been spiraling that day, I would have told someone what happened. Steel pulled out his phone and put it to his ear. "VP, need you at the diner in town. Now."

He hung up and curved his arm around my back, holding me close. Knowing Slash was on the way made me feel a little better, until I remembered why I'd left the compound to begin with. Mike and JJ still talked to one another, too low for me to make out their words, but I could just imagine. They were plotting. Planning to get me alone again so they could hurt me some more.

I could hear the pipes on several bikes before Slash came into view with Dingo and Wolf. He came inside, heading straight for me, and tugged me from Steel's arms.

"You all right, butterfly?" he asked.

I shook my head and buried my face in his chest, just breathing him in. I knew he would keep me safe, but I hated those two had this kind of power over me still. Instead of getting mad and lashing out at them, I'd turned into a frightened rabbit who had wanted to hide. No, worse. I'd frozen.

I heard Steel murmuring to him, most likely telling him about JJ and Mike. Except, Steel didn't know for sure what they'd done to me. I hadn't said anything. Unless he'd heard them earlier. Even when Slash had asked who had hurt me before, I hadn't given him any names. I knew he could handle them without going to jail, but it didn't mean I wanted him to have to.

"Shell, who are they?" he asked.

"Guys from school." He growled and tightened his hold on me. "I just want to leave. Please, Slash."

"Find out everything you can about them," he said to Wolf. "And I mean everything."

He lifted me into his arms and carried me out of the diner. I looked over his shoulder at JJ and Mike. JJ was making the motion of jerking himself off with a leer on his face. With everyone focused on Slash, I knew the Devil's Fury hadn't seen him. And he knew it too. If I ran into them again, and I was alone, they'd not stop with just words. Steel was on Slash's heels and set my food on the passenger seat of my car. Slash let me slide down his body before he opened the driver's side door.

"Go slow. I'm going to be right behind you, butterfly." He pressed a kiss to my forehead. "Straight to the house. Hear me?"

I nodded and got into the car. I drove slow, like he'd said, and pulled through the gates a few minutes later. When I stopped in front of the house, I sat in the car, not sure I could stand just yet. I was still rattled from hearing JJ and Mike. Out of all the places they'd had to eat today, why the diner? I'd known there was a good chance I'd run into people I'd known in high school and college. Didn't prepare me for the reality of it.

My door opened and Slash reached in, shutting off the car, then helping me out. He led me inside, sat me down at the small table in the kitchen before disappearing outside again. When he came back, he set my food down in front of me and claimed the seat next to mine.

"Those two of the boys who hurt you?" he asked.

"Yeah. JJ and Mike. I hadn't noticed them when I sat down. They started talking. About me. It brought it all back and I guess I had a panic attack or something."

Whatever had happened to me, I didn't want to experience it again. If I froze next time, I'd pay the price. Of that I had no doubt. Those two wouldn't hesitate to hurt me.

"Thought you were meeting Lilian this morning," he said.

"I did. It didn't go so well, and I felt the need to escape. The diner brought back good memories. Until…" I bit my lip.

"We'll get what we can on them, and I promise I'll handle it. They won't hurt you again, Shell. I won't let them." He ran his fingers through my hair. "What happened with Lilian?"

"She knows I'm pregnant. I got sick while she was here, but I hate keeping secrets from her. I had to lie so she wouldn't go tell everyone. There's still no guarantee she won't say something to Dragon. What if they figure it out?" I asked.

He pressed his hand to my still flat belly. "This baby is mine, butterfly. Told you before. I don't care if the DNA says otherwise. I'm raising this kid, and that makes him, or her, mine. Just like you're mine."

"I'm sorry I ran."

"Why did you? It has to be something other than Lilian figuring out you're pregnant."

I sighed and dropped my head to the table, pressing my forehead against the cool surface. "They know. They all know what happened that day, and they don't know how to react around me. I heard you. I know you told them, and the only reason they accepted me was because they feel guilty. They didn't want me here, Talon. They hated me."

He gently lifted my head and leaned in, kissing me. The taste of him made me feel warm inside and I moved closer to him. Even as hurt as I'd been, knowing the club didn't truly want me here, I wasn't sure I could walk away from Slash. He was my everything. I hadn't told him how I felt, and I wasn't sure when or if I ever would. He already had too much power over me.

"My beautiful butterfly," he murmured before kissing me some more. "You're precious to me, Shell. Don't ever fucking leave. If you do, I'll come for you. You belong here, with me, in my house. My bed. Lying in my arms every night. Nothing will stop me from tracking you to the ends of the earth, not even a fucking bullet."

"It makes you sound like a stalker," I said.

He cocked his head, somehow managing to look both sexy and arrogant at the same time. "You're the only one I want to stalk, butterfly. I found you, didn't I? Even when you were hiding."

"Yeah, you found me. No one else even bothered looking."

He cupped my cheek. "Not true, butterfly. Griz asked Outlaw to find you, but you disappeared. We kept track of you for a bit. Until we couldn't. The few phone calls you made to Griz gave him hope you'd come home someday. Then I saw you on that fucking webcam show and tracked you to the Hades Abyss in Mississippi. I still owe Titan a right hook for letting you do that shit."

"He didn't. The second he knew who I was he fired me. Told the woman running the business to send me packing. So I left."

"And became a stripper. I think that was a unilateral move," he said. "Nothing wrong with stripping, or being a webcam girl. I'm sure both jobs are very lucrative. Just don't try it again. Now that you're mine, no one is allowed to see you naked except me. Otherwise, the bodies will start piling up around here."

"You saying you'll kill any guy who sees me naked?"

"That's what I'm saying, butterfly, and it won't be an easy death. I'll make them suffer first."

I smiled and leaned into his touch. "I think I like the bloodthirsty side of you. Possessive men might be a turnoff for a lot of women, but I guess having been around the club for a few years, I know it's just your way. You'd never knowingly hurt me, Talon. And I know you'd protect me with your life."

He nodded. "I would. I will."

"My knight in black leather."

Slash grinned. "You know it, butterfly."

He nudged the food container closer and I opened it, lifting the burger out. I took a big bite and moaned at how fantastic it was. I hadn't realized exactly how hungry I was until now. Devouring the burger and fries, I felt so full I wanted to pop.

"Promise me something?" I asked.

"You know I'd give you the world if I could," Slash said.

"You already have, Talon. But I want you to promise that if you ever fall in love, if you find someone you can't live without, you'll tell me. I don't want to stand between you and happiness."

He ran his finger down my nose. "My silly butterfly. Don't you know?"

"Know what?" I asked softly.

"That you're the one I can't live without." He pressed his lips to mine. "You. Only you, butterfly. No one could ever compare."

My heart melted and tears misted my eyes. He might not have outright said he loved me, but it was probably as close as he'd ever get to it. I didn't know why a man like Slash would feel that way about me. He was so strong, powerful, and completely beyond my reach. Or so I'd thought. And here he was telling me I was it for him.

"I love you, Talon. I didn't mean to, but my crush turned into more."

He kissed me so hard and deep my toes curled, and my panties were soaked. Without a word, he lifted me and carried me to our bedroom. I already knew he was a man of few words, especially when it came to his emotions. If he never said the words, I'd be okay with that. As long as he kept *showing* me how he felt. It would be enough.

It had to be.

Chapter Eight

Slash

It wasn't easy letting Wolf take point on finding out what he could about the men at the diner. The two had hurt my butterfly and I'd make them pay, but I knew there had been others. She'd said the entire team wasn't there that day, but I wasn't sure even she knew exactly how many of the boys had raped her. How the fuck she survived, much less got herself home, I didn't know. It was a fucking miracle. I wanted them all. Every last fucker who'd been part of it, even the cheerleaders, would suffer. I'd toy with them, drag things out, and when they least expected it, I'd end their miserable lives. At least the boys. I wouldn't kill the girls. But they might wish they were dead when I was finished with them. Right after I told them why I'd done it. I wanted them to know, to see their fear, and finally their acceptance that their lives were over.

I sat at the bar in the clubhouse, sipping a beer as I contemplated my next move. Lilian knew about the pregnancy, which meant Dragon probably knew by now. It wouldn't take long to get through the club. I didn't know shit about babies. Was it too soon for the baby to be considered mine? The club hadn't wanted to welcome Shella back. I could only imagine what they'd think of her being pregnant with someone else's kid. Especially since she wouldn't say who the baby's father was, assuming she knew. She'd mentioned ruining his life if he found out, so she must have some idea. Considering the timing, I had to wonder if it wasn't one of the two men who had been in her webcam show. Then again, if she'd been hanging around the Hades Abyss compound, there was a chance she'd been to the parties, meaning it could be anyone's kid.

It made me want to burn their entire fucking compound to the ground.

I tapped the bottle against the bar before I drained it and flagged down Beau for another. He popped the top and set it in front of me. When he didn't move on right away, I knew he had something on his mind. I just wanted to see if he'd get the guts to spit it out. He'd been a Prospect for a while, and probably would have patched in by now, except he'd lost the club's trust when we found out about Meiling. Dingo's woman had lived in hell. Beau had left her, didn't say a fucking word to any of us about a young girl in need of help, so he had to make up for it. Meiling had forgiven him, but I wasn't sure if Dingo ever would.

I wasn't too proud of the part I'd played that day either. She'd come to us for help, and I'd treated her like she was auditioning to be a club whore. We all had. There'd been a reason for it, but that didn't mean I felt good about it. She'd been scared. Abused. And I'd been just another asshole trying to use her.

The other two Prospects who'd joined when Beau did had been patched in a month ago. Simon now went by Romeo and Henry was Ripper. Wouldn't be long before we needed to patch in a few more. Couldn't leave them hanging forever. Although, the more we patched in, the more new Prospects we'd need. Unless Badger decided we had more than enough brothers. The club had grown a lot over the years. Sooner or later, we'd run out of room around here. Not to mention, with more of us settling down, the Devil's Fury were quickly becoming more family-oriented. Or as much as men like us could be.

Beau cleared his throat, reminding me he was still standing there. I stared him down, waiting on him to get the balls to speak his mind, or ask whatever the fuck he wanted to know. He was a good kid, for the most part, but there were times he was a little too timid in my opinion. Not that we needed a bunch of sadistic bastards like Demon running around this place. Balance was a good thing.

"What the fuck is it, Prospect?"

"I heard something. About Shella." His gaze darted around the room and he lowered his voice. "Heard some whispers that she was a webcam girl. A few of your brothers saw her show. Either it's still up on that site, or they caught it before it was removed. They don't think she told you the truth about being raped, saying a victim wouldn't turn into a whore like that."

I squeezed the beer bottle so hard it broke in my hand, bits of glass digging into my palm. Beau backed up and paled a little. I wouldn't shoot the messenger, but I did want to know who exactly had seen that show and been running their fucking mouths. Then I'd make sure they learned a lesson. A harsh one.

"Who?" I demanded.

Beau licked his lips. "I don't want to be a rat. If I ever want to patch in…"

Yeah, yeah. I got it. If he told me who'd said what, when it came time to vote him in, there was a chance some of the brothers wouldn't want him in the club. If there was one thing we didn't like, it was a rat. Still, I needed to know who was saying shit about my woman.

"Trisha was sitting with them," Beau said.

Now there was an in if ever I heard one. A club whore had heard it all? The club might not want to take her word against our brothers, however, I damn sure would in this instance. I scanned the room and saw her in the back corner with Gina. I motioned for Beau to give me another beer and he handed over a bottle, along with two shots of tequila.

"They've only had a few drinks. Figured another might loosen their tongues," Beau said.

It was early in the day for club whores to be hanging out. Then again, unless the Pres declared the clubhouse off-limits, there were usually one or two lurking in case a brother needed to blow off some steam. Most of the girls had lives outside the club, but some were so hopeful they'd land a brother they stuck around as much as possible. And these two were favorites. Not that I'd ever sampled either one. They'd only been here about four months, which meant they came here after I'd stopped using the club whores.

I set the shots down on their table, kicked out a chair, and sat to face them. Their eyes went wide. Yeah, it wasn't common for me to seek any of them out. Which meant they knew I likely wanted something, seeing as how I'd made it no secret I had a wife now. Some clubs might not offer fidelity to their old ladies and wives, but I sure the fuck did and so did the other brothers here who'd found their other halves.

"Anything either of you want to tell me?" I asked after they downed their shots.

Trisha shared a look with Gina, which told me she'd likely said something to the other woman. I knew the girls gossiped. In this case, it might be beneficial.

"We know what happens when we cause trouble," Gina said, eyeing me. "Heard about Demon branding a club whore."

Well, fuck my life. I'd known it would come back to bite us in the ass at some point. Demon had wanted to put the fear of God into the women, keep them from causing issues. They'd put our women in danger one time too many. I couldn't blame him. If one of these bitches had caused Shella to get hurt, I'd want their blood, even if they were women. They were on our turf, in our clubhouse, and the rules were different here. Wouldn't matter. Right now, I needed them to be more afraid of me than Demon. I had to know what my brothers had said about Shella.

"A little birdy told me you might know something," I said, looking at Trisha. "Something that was said about my wife. I take any threat to her seriously, even if it comes from a brother."

The women stared at one another, seeming to communicate silently. After a moment, Gina shook her head and Trisha shrugged, chewing her bottom lip. It was clear they were conflicted. Or rather Trisha was. I had a feeling she wanted to confess what she's heard, but Gina worried it would be dangerous for them.

"I won't let Demon hurt either of you," I said. "Or anyone else. They touch you, they'll answer to me. I need to know if my woman is in danger."

Trisha opened and shut her mouth a few times. "They were drunk. I'm sure they didn't mean anything."

So there was something. I needed to know who had said it and what exactly they'd said. I could understand Beau not wanting to speak up. Not if he ever wanted to patch into the club. He was right to be cautious. And the fact he'd warned me would go a long way to me voting yes when it was his time.

"It was Hot Shot and Cobra," Gina said.

"Thought it wasn't safe to talk," Trisha mumbled.

"He's right. If his wife is in danger, he needs to know. I think it's sweet he wants to protect her. Wish I had a guy watching out for me sometimes," Gina said.

Trisha blew out a breath and nodded. "So, they were both drunk. Like seriously almost falling-down drunk. Hot Shot saw your wife when she was a webcam girl. Or said it looked just like her. Then he started running his mouth about how a rape victim would never do something like that. Called her a whore and…"

"He said she'd probably asked for it in high school," Gina said, her voice lowering.

"It made me uncomfortable," Trisha said. "I didn't stick around much longer, but Hot Shot was trying to convince Cobra to get Shella to confess to everything. The way he made it sound… it wasn't good. I know you guys typically don't hurt women, which is why I love hanging out here, but they seemed really pissed you'd married her and wanted to accept her back into the club."

Jesus. What the fuck was wrong with those two? I ran a hand through my hair and tried to think of how best to approach this. I could confront them straight on, except they'd want to know where I heard it. Then I'd have to either throw Beau under the bus or the girls.

"I'm going to talk to the Pres and see how he wants this handled. He might ask to speak to both of you. Hear firsthand what you heard."

They nodded, but I saw the fear lurking in their eyes. Badger was unpredictable at best, and with Adalia pregnant again, the man would lop off heads first and ask questions later. They had every right to be scared.

I finished my beer and left the clubhouse, knowing I'd find Badger at home. Last time Adalia had been pregnant, he'd hardly left her side. It had driven her crazy, but she was his entire world and if anything happened to her, I didn't know if he'd survive. Much like Griz had loved May, Adalia was Badger's one and only. He'd gone to prison for her, and I damn well knew he'd die for her.

I rode my bike to his house, parking in the driveway. Both his bike and Adalia's car were under the carport, so I knew they were home. I knocked on the door, trying not to be too loud in case Gunner was napping. Badger answered, a scowl on his face.

"We need to talk," I said.

He tipped his head and stepped back, waiting for me to enter. I saw Adalia on their living room couch, and she gave me a little wave. I didn't see Gunner and figured he must be in his room. Following Badger into the kitchen, I took a seat and waited while he got two sodas from the fridge. I smiled as I popped the top on mine and wondered if I'd soon be stocking soda instead of beer. He'd cut back on how often he drank at home since Gunner had been born.

"What's so important you had to come here to talk?" Badger asked.

"Heard that Hot Shot and Cobra were talking about Shella," I said, getting right to the point. "She was a webcam girl for a short time, and they found her show online. Said she couldn't have been raped like she claimed since she'd been such a whore."

Badger snarled. Yeah, I'd forgotten for a moment she was his sister-in-law. He wouldn't take too kindly to someone calling Shella a whore. Or a liar. Even if he didn't like the way she'd acted before, Adalia loved her so that made her important to Badger.

"Trisha said they were talking about forcing her to tell the truth. I don't know if they'll hurt her or not, but Pres, she *did* tell the truth. Just ask Steel. He saw her reaction to seeing two of the guys who raped her. I have Wolf looking into it."

Badger swore and got up, pacing the room. "What the fuck are those two idiots thinking? I swear to Christ if they touch one hair on her head, I'll lose my shit. Adalia doesn't need this kind of stress, and Shella is her sister."

"I haven't confronted them," I said. "After I heard what Trisha had to say, I came here. She's scared, Pres, worried this will blow back on her. And as much as I hate to admit this, Beau heard them talking too. He didn't want to come forward and jeopardize any votes when it's time for him to patch in, but he couldn't stand back and do nothing either. He's the one who told me to talk to Trisha."

Badger nodded. "Beau is more than making up for what he did, and I'm sure Meiling would agree. Won't be long before he's patched into the club. But for now... I need to figure out the best way to handle this shit. I expected better of Cobra. And Hot Shot, well, he's hotheaded at the best of times. Probably just running off at the mouth."

"She said they were falling-down drunk," I said. "Maybe nothing will come of it, but I don't like the thought of my brothers calling my wife a liar, or possibly hurting her because they don't believe her story."

"For now, if you leave your house, send Shella over here. Even if I'm not home, no one would dare try anything with Adalia around. They know I'll bust their fucking heads if they upset her. Safest place for Shella. No one would dare start shit."

I nodded. He had a point. Anything happened to Adalia, and Badger would kill the person responsible. It meant everyone in the club walked on eggshells around her. So yeah, if Shella came here, no one would try anything if Adalia was present. Perfect plan. I just had to get Shella to agree.

"When I find out everything I need to know about her rapists, I'm handling it," I said. "I want those fuckers to suffer."

"Do what you need to do. Whatever it takes to make her feel safe and give her some peace," Badger said. He gazed off toward the living room. "I'd go to prison all over again for killing the bastard who raped Adalia. I only wished I'd gotten there before he'd hurt her."

I understood. Knowing Shella had been hurt and I hadn't been there to save her ate at me. None of us had bothered to ask why she'd suddenly started acting out. Maybe we could have resolved the issue sooner and things would have turned out different. If we'd known then what we knew now, would she have still left? Or would she have stayed?

"What about Hot Shot and Cobra?" I asked.

"I'll handle it. They don't have to know who said something. For all those fuckers know, I have the entire clubhouse wired and can hear everything."

I stared at him a moment, wondering if he really did have cameras and mics hidden around the clubhouse. Wouldn't surprise me. Badger didn't like to take chances with his family. He was the sort to do what was necessary and didn't give a fuck if people didn't like the way he handled things. Since he was now the club's President, his word was law. The rest of us just fell in line or paid the consequences.

"What about Grizzly?" I asked. "You going to tell him?"

"No. He feels bad enough about what happened. Knowing the club was trying to start shit would just make it worse. I'll handle it. Besides, he's got enough on his plate with those three girls in his house. I don't think I could handle all that drama."

I smirked. "You know damn well if you had three girls, you'd be just as happy as you are now. You'd love those girls and threaten to kill anyone who looked their way."

"You aren't wrong." He grinned. "Adalia wants to be surprised with this one. Honestly, as long as both baby and momma are healthy, I don't give a shit about anything else. Girl. Boy. Doesn't matter."

I lowered my voice so Adalia wouldn't hear me. "I thought y'all were being careful since the doctor said she shouldn't have more kids."

He sighed and cracked his neck. "We were. I don't know how the fuck it happened, and now I'm scared shitless I'll lose both of them."

"And after this one?"

"The second we found out she was pregnant I had a vasectomy. I'm not taking any more chances. Adalia fucking cried because she wants a big family, but I'm not risking her life to have a houseful of kids."

"Why didn't you adopt one or two of the kids we rescued from Miss Humes?" I asked.

"Thought about it. Probably should have, but I wasn't sure Adalia was ready. But there's plenty of kids out there who need a home, right? Never too late to adopt. Once we get through this pregnancy, and the baby is a little older, we can talk about adding to our family."

"Shella's pregnant," I said. "We aren't telling anyone right now. She hasn't been to the doctor yet, but she's sick in the mornings and she's late. I think Adalia's miscarriages have her worried she won't carry to term. She wants to wait a bit before we tell everyone, but Lilian found out so I'm sure Dragon knows. It might spread and I didn't want y'all to find out last. Not sure how Adalia will handle it."

"Fuck," he muttered. "She's not exactly a weak woman, but when she's pregnant her emotions are all over the place. And stress isn't good for her or the baby. I'll wait until the time is right and talk to her about it. I'll make sure she knows you want to keep it quiet, and I'll have a talk with Dragon. Make sure he knows that shit stays in the family."

Chapter Nine

Shella

I hated that the boys from my past could still make me scared to leave my house. Granted, they weren't boys anymore. They were adult men, and even scarier than before. Seeing two of them at the diner had given me nightmares the last four nights and brought back every second of that horrible day. Knowing they were still in town, I hadn't wanted to leave the compound. I knew I couldn't hide forever, but I wasn't ready to face them. If two were here, what if the others were too? If all of them found me at the same time, I knew I'd never be able to fight them off. Just like last time.

I eyed my car keys on the counter. I'd pulled them out of my purse, even managed to shower and dress, but now I'd lost my nerve. I knew if I said I wanted to go somewhere, Slash would either come with me or send a bodyguard. It would just mean pulling them away from whatever they were doing right now for the club. I hated being needy. Weak. Pathetic. I was sure they had plenty of ways to describe me around here. The last thing I wanted was to give them another reason to dislike me.

Even though I hadn't been to the doctor yet, I knew I was pregnant. Even if the little stick hadn't told me as much before I'd run into Slash again, it had been long enough I should have at least started feeling cramps. I hadn't had so much as a twinge. Lilian had mentioned prenatal vitamins and I'd looked online. I just wasn't sure which ones were the best out of what I could get over the counter. Instead of having it delivered to the house, I thought it would be better to go the store and talk to the pharmacist. Now I was second-guessing myself.

I scrolled through the app on my phone and decided to just order some online and take my chances. At this rate, I'd never leave the compound. Or the house. I didn't like venturing out where everyone could stare at me. Slash assured me the club accepted me, but I had this unsettled feeling when I left the house. It was safer in here. Badger had apparently decreed that I was to stay with Adalia at their home whenever Slash left. I'd gotten out of it today because she hadn't been feeling well.

Now I was alone. Although, there was probably someone outside keeping watch. I doubted Slash would go off without making sure I was safe. Something was going on, but he wouldn't talk to me about it. He seemed more tense than usual. I didn't know if it was club business or something to do with me.

I placed my order on my phone and decided to browse baby items. I'd need to buy stuff sooner or later. Slash had given me access to his accounts, since I wasn't working, but I didn't want to spend a fortune either. Not knowing if I was having a girl or boy limited my options. I didn't want a bunch of white, yellow, or green stuff. If I had a girl, I wanted to dress her in cute frilly things. Although, some of the boy outfits were downright adorable too.

I rubbed my stomach, wondering how much longer before I could find out what I was having. I really didn't know anything about being pregnant. Well, except morning sickness. I'd heard about it and experienced it. The rest was a mystery. I closed out the app and pulled up a web browser so I could do a little research.

It wasn't that I thought I'd learn everything about pregnancy on my phone. I knew not all websites were accurate. I just figured knowing at least something about this pregnancy was better than the big fat nothing I knew right now. I still needed to schedule a doctor's appointment. Slash had already said he wanted to go with me so I was waiting to see when would be a good time for him. As the VP of the club, I knew he was busy with stuff that didn't pertain to me. I loved spending time with him. But I knew it wasn't realistic to think he could spend every waking moment with me. Honestly, I wouldn't want him to.

A knock at the door startled me bad enough I dropped my phone. It clattered on the tile and I winced, hoping it hadn't cracked the screen. I went to the front door, put my hand on the lock, then hesitated. Theoretically, I was in the safest place ever. Except I knew I hadn't received a warm welcome.

"Who's there?" I called out.

"Colorado."

I chewed on my lower lip. He'd never been mean to me. Still... I wasn't sure if I wanted to take the chance and open the door. I had no doubt if anyone in the club hurt me, Slash would tear them apart. It didn't mean I wanted to cause problems, though.

"Shella, I know you're scared. I'd cut off my arm before I hurt you. Wizard needs you to look at some pictures. Outlaw asked for his help, but he's tied up right now. He gave me a tablet with the images. You don't even have to let me in the house."

I flicked the lock and opened the door, peering out at him. "What pictures?"

"Slash had Wolf, Outlaw, and just about all of us trying to track down the guys who hurt you in high school. And Outlaw called Wizard. We know about the two at the diner, but Wizard wants you to verify if these other men were in on it too. Don't want Slash gutting the wrong person."

Maybe I should have been horrified my husband planned to kill my rapists. Another woman might have been. I was far from what I considered normal. Having been raised around the club for the formative part of my teen years, what I considered an everyday occurrence would horrify most people. Yeah, Griz had tried to keep all that from me and Lilian, but we'd still heard stuff.

I took the tablet from him, bracing myself as the images loaded. The first two were the men I'd seen at the diner. A cold sweat broke out across my brow and a chill skittered down my spine. I flipped through five more images.

"This one," I said, pointing to one of them. "He was part of it."

"And the others?" Colorado asked.

I flipped back an image. "This one too."

"Not the other two?" he asked.

I shook my head. I didn't recognize either of them. If I'd gone to high school with them, they'd changed too much for me to know who they were. I couldn't even be certain how many there'd been that day. One of them had slammed my head against the cement floor a few times and left me dazed. I mostly remembered pain.

I swallowed hard and handed the tablet back to Colorado, my hand shaking so bad I nearly dropped the device. He grabbed it from me, then tugged me against his chest, holding me tight.

"You're okay, Shella," he murmured. "We won't let those sick fucks hurt you ever again. I only wish you'd told us when it happened."

Woulda. Shoulda. Coulda. It was in the past, which is where I'd wanted it to stay. Coming back to Blackwood Falls had been a mistake. If I'd kept running, I might have been able to leave it all behind me. Eventually. Being here brought it all back and had me scared to venture outside the house. Yes, I had Slash, but at what price?

"I'm glad you don't hate me," I said.

I felt him tense before he backed away. "What the fuck? Why would anyone hate you?"

"I know everyone would have been happier if I'd stayed gone. You don't have to pretend otherwise. Dragon made it clear what he thought about me coming back. I know there are others who aren't happy about it either."

He reached out and tipped my chin up. "You listen and you listen good. Every last man in this club would never condone what happened to you. And it fucking happened on *our* watch. You should have been safe. You weren't. To make matters worse, Griz asked you to leave for a while and not one of us tried to stop you. If anyone says shit to you that makes you feel bad about being you, you come tell me. I'll lay them the fuck out."

I fought back a smile. "Thanks, Colorado. I appreciate it."

"Surprised Slash left you here alone, though," he said.

"I figured someone was outside the door, lurking or whatever." I looked around. "Guess not."

His brows lowered as he scanned the area. He pulled his phone from his pocket and tapped on the screen. When it dinged a few minutes later, his eyes flashed with anger.

"Slash *did* leave someone here. You remember the Prospect called Simon? He's patched in now. Goes by Romeo. He was supposed to be on guard duty." Colorado started tapping again.

"I'm sure it's fine. Maybe Badger called him away for something, not realizing Slash asked him to be here."

"Motherfucker," Colorado muttered. "Hot Shot called him away. Slash is going to be fucking pissed. Go back inside and lock the door. I'll wait here until either Slash comes or sends someone else."

Something didn't seem right. "What's going on? And don't tell me club business because it's obviously not."

"That's for Slash to tell you. Ask him. I'm not about to get my ass handed to me because I mouthed off when I shouldn't have. Go inside, Shella. I need to keep you safe."

Yeah, but from what? Or who?

I shut the door and locked it. After I checked my phone, which had cracked as I'd feared, I tried to busy myself in the kitchen. If Slash did come home, he might be hungry. And I knew I was supposed to be eating three meals a day. The baby needed me to stay healthy. I rubbed my belly as I looked through the cabinets and fridge. The butterflied pork chops looked amazing.

I rinsed them, seasoned them, and popped them into the oven. It would take a good forty minutes for them to cook, maybe longer since they were so thick. Plenty of time to make some mashed potatoes and maybe some squash with onion. I set the pot of water on the stove to boil while I peeled and sliced the potatoes. I added a dash of salt to the water before I dumped them in.

Someone had brought us farm-fresh squash yesterday. I washed it and sliced it up. I melted some butter in a skillet while I sliced up a sweet onion, then put both the squash and the onion into the skillet and cooked them until they were soft. When everything was finished, Slash still hadn't come home and I wondered if I'd made a big meal for nothing. I went ahead and fixed him a plate, then slid it into the microwave. Fixing my own, I sat down and took a bite, the flavors bursting on my tongue.

My mouth watered and I realized I'd been hungrier than I'd thought. I'd made it halfway through my meal when I heard the front door open. Knowing I'd locked it, I wasn't too worried. Although, there were several guys in the club who could pick a lock. I set my fork down and watched the doorway. If it wasn't Slash, I'd have the option of running out the back door.

I heard the thud of boots as the steps grew closer, then my husband appeared in the doorway, staring down at his phone with his brow furrowed and his lips turned down. My shoulders relaxed and I picked up the fork again, shoveling another bite of food into my mouth.

"Lunch is in the microwave if you want it," I said.

He looked up and smiled. "You made lunch?"

I nodded. "Got hungry. Colorado made it sound like maybe you'd come home, so I decided to make enough for two. If you didn't eat it today, I could have always put it away for tomorrow."

Slash came farther into the room and leaned down, pressing a kiss to the top of my head. "Thanks, butterfly. I'm starving."

"He wouldn't tell me what's going on. I know it has to do with me. Is the club pissed I'm here? Do they want me to leave?" I asked.

"You're not going anywhere. You're my wife, and the cut you have hanging in the closet says you're my old lady. If anyone here has an issue with it, I'll handle it."

"Why would Hot Shot tell Romeo to leave his post?" I asked.

Slash cracked his neck and sat down with his plate. "Because he's a fucking idiot. The fact I knocked him out cold for his stupidity should put an end to it. Badger took a turn with him too. If that doesn't, Colorado was ready to light him up. You have plenty of people who want you here, butterfly."

Right. Plenty but not all. Which meant Hot Shot probably was one of the ones who wished I'd leave. I couldn't change the past, couldn't go back and not be such a bitch to everyone. If I could, I would.

"Thought you said once they found out what happened to me everyone was fine with me being here," I said.

"I didn't want to talk about this shit with you, Shell. I don't want you stressing out." He set his fork down and leaned forward, bracing his arms on the table. "Look. Hot Shot and one other brother decided you might be lying about being raped. They saw your webcam show and said a rape victim would never do something like that. I think I put an end to their way of thinking. If I didn't, Colorado telling them he worried you'd pass the fuck out when you were pointing out your attackers should have done it."

"I don't know if that was all of them," I said softly. "Honestly, it seemed like there were more. What if there are others? What if you take out the ones I know were there and someone else decides to get even? I have a baby to think about, Slash. I don't want to bring more trouble to the doorstep."

"I'm not about to let them get away with it, Shell. They'll pay for what they did. End of story. You don't get a fucking say. I can't get you to leave the damn house because you're scared. You think I'm going to let you live the rest of your life like that? Fuck no!"

I sighed and nodded, knowing I wouldn't win. Once he made up his mind, that was it. Part of me loved how protective he was. The other half wanted to be able to fight my own battles. I knew Lilian had trained with Dragon to learn some self-defense. Maybe I needed to learn a few moves too. Although, probably not right now. What if I was hit in the stomach or fell hard and lost the baby?

"Wolf, Colorado, and Steel are rounding up the men who hurt you," he said. "I'll be taking care of them soon enough. And if there were others, I'll get their names."

"You're bringing them here?" I asked.

"Beneath the clubhouse. I don't want you anywhere near them, you hear me? Not unless I know they're restrained good enough they can't hurt you."

"I don't know if I could face them anyway."

"You should," he said softly. "If you need that for closure, to say your piece to them, I'll make it work. I just won't take a chance with your safety, butterfly. There will be several brothers down there with us, and those men won't have a snowball's chance in hell of getting their hands on you."

"I'll think about it," I said.

He winked. "Lunch is great by the way. Best damn pork chop I've ever had. And whatever you did to the squash is fan-fucking-tastic."

My cheeks warmed. I wasn't the best cook in the world, but I did well enough. It made me happy that he enjoyed the food I made. Maybe if I had some recipe books, I could learn to make more stuff. I didn't want to serve him the same sort of meals week after week. Although, he sent someone to pick up take-out at least three times a week. I'd thought he wasn't too crazy about my cooking but it seemed I was wrong.

"I like cooking for you," I said.

I'd never thought I'd be all domestic and crap, but here I was. Married. Baby on the way. And I liked cooking for my husband. Hell, I didn't even mind the cleaning. I'd been so focused on survival since I'd left here, I hadn't had a chance to really settle anywhere. Now that I was back home, and Slash seemed intent on keeping me here, I could relax a little and make the house into a home. We hadn't painted anywhere yet, but I'd added some personal touches to the house. It felt a little cozier than it had before.

I definitely wanted to paint the baby's room, after I knew what we were having. If what I'd read was correct, I had a little bit to go still. I thought I was only around two months pregnant, or close to it. Assuming the time on the webcam show when Owen hadn't used a condom was when I'd gotten pregnant. Condoms weren't exactly fail proof.

"Thank you, Talon," I said.

"For what?"

"Being you." I reached over and placed my hand on his. "As scared as I was to come back here, I had nowhere else to go. You heard them fire me at the strip club. I'd have lost my apartment, starved, and not even had money for gas. It was like Fate threw you into my path again at exactly the right time, even if I didn't want to admit it."

"Anytime, butterfly." He reached out and ran a finger down my cheek. "I'd do anything for you."

I wanted to sigh in contentment, but I held it back. This wasn't some sappy romance movie. Slash hadn't said a word about loving me, even though it was clear he felt something. I might not get the fairy-tale ending, but this was close enough.

Chapter Ten

Slash

JJ Pierce, Mike Stratton, Billy Simms, and Joe Fredrick sat tied to chairs, sullen expressions on their faces as they eyed me. Fuckers had no idea yet why they were here, but they'd learn soon enough. And my fun was only beginning. Wolf had made sure I knew which was which. I remembered seeing JJ and Mike at the diner, and knew they were the ones who'd scared the shit out of Shella when she'd gone for a burger.

"You boys know why you're here?" I asked.

"We're not boys," JJ said, spitting on the floor. "We're grown-ass men and you need to let us go before we send the cops after you."

"Isn't that cute?" I asked Wolf. "They think they're men. Last I checked only little bitches gang-raped girls. Probably couldn't get laid any other way."

JJ snarled and fought against the ropes holding him down. I just laughed in his fucking face, then took my booted foot and shoved his chest until he fell over backward, chair and all. He still struggled and cussed a blue streak, but I switched my attention to Mike.

"In case you haven't figured it out, I know the four of you raped Shella in high school. In fact, I know two of you had rape charges filed against you since then but the cases somehow fell apart. No worries. Those girls will get justice." I smiled. "Now, before we get started, anyone want to tell me who else was there that day? I already know some cheerleaders shoved her into that locker room. But I want to know if you four were the only ones who hurt her."

"Fuck you," Mike said.

Joe stared straight ahead, his jaw tight as he remained mute. Sooner or later he'd talk, or at the very least scream.

Billy had paled a little and his gaze skittered around the room. Sweat beaded his brow and I decided he was the weakest link. He also hadn't had any other girls pointing a finger at him claiming he'd raped them. Unlike JJ and Mike. I held my hand out to Wolf and he slapped a large knife against my palm. I curled my fingers around it, brandishing the blade in front of Billy's face. The stench of urine filled the air as he pissed himself. Definitely the weakest.

"Anything you'd like to say, Billy?" I asked.

"It wasn't just us," he blurted. "There were three others."

Seven. Seven of these fucking assholes had raped Shella. A red haze settled over my vision and I snarled, wanting to rip the fuckers apart. I wanted to bathe in their blood, dance in their entrails. I wanted their heads on spikes and to piss on their bones after I sent them straight to hell.

"Shut the fuck up," JJ said where he still lay on the floor.

Steel walked over and yanked him upright, the chair teetering for a moment before settling on all four legs again. Then he hauled back his arm and slammed his fist into the asshole's face, breaking his nose. "That's for scaring the shit out of that sweet girl in the diner the other day."

"Oh, God. Oh, God." Billy looked like he might piss himself again. "I'll tell you whatever you want to know. Just don't kill me!"

"Shut. Up," JJ said. "They don't have shit on us, you moron. Stop talking!"

"Shella identified the four of you as part of the group of boys who raped her," I said. "Whether you talk or not, you're not leaving this room alive. The question is how much you suffer before you die. The more you give me, the easier I'll be on you."

"Which cheerleaders were in on it?" Wolf asked.

"Lauren, Faith, Erin, and Carrie," Billy said. "They were in on it. Said Shella needed to learn her place."

I leaned into Billy's space, the knife still clutched in my hand. "And how many times did you rape her?"

The blood completely drained from his face and his eyes went wide. He shook his head back and forth, not wanting to answer. I slammed the knife down, embedding the blade into his thigh, and he squealed like a little pig.

"Once!" he yelled out. "Just once. I-I didn't want to, but JJ said..."

"Shut. Up," JJ yelled.

"It was one time too fucking many," I said. "Give me the names of the others, Billy, and I won't make you hurt as much as the others."

He rattled off more names and I saw Wolf tapping on his phone. I knew he'd be sending the info to Outlaw to see what he could find on them. Sooner or later, they'd be in this room too, and none of them were getting out of here alive. The cheerleaders I'd deal with another way, but it would still leave a lasting impression.

"Now, Billy. We're going to play a little. For each cut, you're going to give me another piece of information. When I'm satisfied you've told me everything you can, I'll end your suffering." I yanked the blade free of his thigh, making him scream again. I made a slice along his bicep. "That's one. Give me something. How many times did JJ over there hurt my girl?"

"F-four," Billy stammered.

Fire burned in my gut and I knew JJ wasn't dying anytime soon. No. He'd suffer greatly before I was finished with him. I made another cut and got another detail from Billy. When he didn't seem to have anything left to say, I sliced his throat and let him bleed out.

"What now?" Wolf asked, standing back, arms folded over his chest.

"Now I'm going to play with these three a little, then get cleaned up and go see my wife. The club can come down here anytime they want, but I want these fuckers alive. No one gets to take them out except me. Not even Grizzly or Badger."

"Might want to ask Badger to save his brand of justice until the end," Wolf said. "Doubt he'll leave you much."

He wasn't wrong. There was a reason the club Pres had gotten the name Badger. Fucker was mean as one, and vicious when he was crossed. Except where Adalia was concerned. She was the only one who ever saw his softer side. But hell, he'd gone to prison for her. He'd more than proven he'd do anything for his woman.

I made the other three bleed. JJ refused to break, but I knew he would eventually. The other two seemed to have accepted their fate, or at least they weren't as mouthy as JJ. Their screams were music to my ears as I tortured them. It wasn't enough. Would never be enough. They'd violated Shella, stolen her innocence, and treated her like trash. Death was too good for them, but I wouldn't let them roam the earth anymore. The justice system was too flawed to guarantee they'd never come for her again. They'd hurt the woman who meant everything to me, and I'd see them in hell for it.

When I'd had my fun for the day, Wolf stepped in to take a turn. I went upstairs and washed off in one of the showers and changed into a clean set of clothes. Shella hadn't known why I was coming to the clubhouse, so I'd made sure I had the exact same color shirt to change into. Last thing I wanted to tell her was I only had some of the people who'd hurt her. I wouldn't say a damn word to her until I had them all. Even the names of the cheerleaders so I could start getting my revenge on them too. Billy had given me four names, but what if there were others? I wouldn't stop until I knew for sure, and had exacted my revenge on all of them.

Hot Shot leaned against the wall outside the bathroom when I stepped out. I eyed him and waited to hear what he had to say. I noticed quite a few bruises on his face and arms. The way he winced when he moved told me there were likely more under his clothes. He ran a hand through his hair and seemed to struggle to find the words.

"I'm sorry," he said. "I was drunk and let my mouth run off. I shouldn't have called your woman a whore. I sure the fuck shouldn't have left her unprotected when I called the Prospect away from your house. And I should have believed you when you said she was raped. I was an asshole."

"Yeah, you were."

He nodded. "I'm sorry, VP. Won't happen again."

"And Cobra?" I asked.

Hot Shot winced. "Um, Grizzly found out what we'd said. He cornered Cobra. Dude had to get his jaw wired shut when Griz broke it in several places. I got off light in comparison."

"So are you apologizing because you admit you were wrong, or because you're worried Grizzly will tear into you again?" I asked.

"I know I was wrong. Now. And I told Outlaw where to find that webcam video. Someone must have hacked the site and downloaded a bootleg. He's making sure it's taken down everywhere so no one will ever see it again. I'm sorry, Slash. Really. I mean it."

"Fine. Keep the fuck away from my wife. You have to earn my respect again, because right now I wouldn't piss on you if you were on fire."

He gave a quick nod and walked off.

Looked like the two in-house issues had been resolved. For now. I knew Badger and Grizzly would help me keep anyone in line who decided to say shit about Shella. It pissed me off that men I called brothers, men I trusted to have my back, hadn't believed me when I'd told them what happened to Shella. Even worse, they'd mouthed off about it in the clubhouse where the club whores and Prospects could hear. That shit was far from all right, and I planned to make sure everyone knew it.

I made my way through the main part of the clubhouse and outside to my bike. Shella was waiting at home with Colorado standing guard. Now that I knew Hot Shot and Cobra weren't an issue, I wouldn't worry quite so much. Unless there were others who just hadn't spoken up within earshot of anyone. Might not be a bad idea to leave someone watching over her anytime I left, as long as I knew I could trust them. Like Colorado and Beau.

Definitely needed to talk to Badger about patching the kid in. He'd proven himself by coming forward about Hot Shot and Cobra, even though he'd feared losing his chance to ever officially be a member of the Devil's Fury. His loyalty to me and to Shella went a long way to mend his past mistakes. I knew if I asked Meiling and Dingo, they'd feel the same way.

"Got a minute?" Doolittle asked, approaching as I swung my leg over my bike.

"Just on my way home. Is this club business or something else?"

"Something else," he said.

"Follow me home? I need to relieve Colorado of guard duty and check on Shella. Unless you don't want her to hear whatever you need to say?"

He shook his head. "It's fine. I'll meet you there. Just need to tell Steel something real quick. Heard he was here. Then I need to grab something from home. Won't take long."

"He's downstairs," I said.

I backed my bike away from the front of the clubhouse, then pulled down the winding road that led to my house. Shella's little car was still under the carport, where it had remained since her run-in at the diner with JJ and Mike. She'd been too scared to go out since then. It wouldn't be long before she'd feel safe leaving again. I'd make sure I made an impression on the cheerleaders, since they'd be the only ones from that day who were still breathing when this was over. Anyone else who had a hand in the incident would pay the ultimate price.

I parked next to her car and shut off the bike, putting down the kickstand before I got off. Colorado stood not too far from the front door and gave me a nod as I got closer.

"You can head out," I said. "I don't plan to leave again anytime soon. If I have to go anywhere, I'll get Beau to come watch her for a bit."

"You know I'm happy to help," Colorado said. "I've been kind of a dick in the past. Consider this my way of making up for past deeds."

I smirked knowing he'd already paid for that transgression. The woman in question had kneed him in the nuts. He'd been livid, but whatever had been going through his head at the time, he'd sorted it out.

I went inside but didn't shut the door since I saw Doolittle coming down the road. I checked the living room and smiled when I saw Shella passed out on the couch with a movie playing. She looked so damn innocent right now. Hell, despite all that she'd done, she really was innocent. Yeah, she'd been with two guys at once, been a stripper, and a webcam girl, but those had been her cry for help, her way of being something she wasn't. When I looked into her eyes, they weren't hard and jaded. She still had a sweetness to her.

Doolittle stepped into the house and shut the door. The moment I realized he had what looked like a baby sling strapped to him, I was more than a little intrigued.

"Knock someone up?" I asked.

He snorted and tugged the material down until two long ears poked out. "Sorry. Bestiality isn't my thing."

I lifted Shella into my arms and sat. She murmured in her sleep and only snuggled closer to me before sighing and getting quiet again. Doolittle grinned at her as he sat in the chair I normally used.

"So why are you here with a rabbit?" I asked. "I'm assuming that's what you went to get."

He nodded. "It is. This is Tinker. She's a Jersey Wooly and needs someone with a gentle touch."

"Uh-huh." I had a feeling Shella and I were about to become parents to a rabbit, especially if she woke up and saw it.

"She's been bottle-fed and is now weaned. I got her from a breeder who decided to retire. Tinker's mom died. The lady was able to sell all but Tinker and one other. The little boy already went to a home, but Tinker hasn't had any takers, even though I've asked a few people who came through the clinic."

"Where's her stuff?" I asked.

Doolittle smirked. "Knew you were a softie."

I just stared him down.

"All right. I get it. Big bad VP and all. You really going to take her in?" he asked.

"Shella will fall in love with Tinker the second she meets her. You knew damn well she'd want that rabbit, and that's why it's now in my living room. Strapped to your chest like a baby, I might add."

Doolittle shrugged. "She's a calm bunny. It's part of the charm of her breed. But I've noticed she isn't as stressed when she's strapped to me like this. Didn't even seem to mind the bike ride over here."

"Why not bring your truck with all her shit?"

"Because I wasn't entirely certain you'd let her stay. She's litter-box trained so she won't mess on the floor the short time it will take me to head back to the house for her stuff. Or I can close her in a bathroom if you'd prefer."

Shella mumbled again and stirred, rubbing at her eyes. "Talon?"

Doolittle's eyes went comically wide at her use of my name. Since I knew damn well she wasn't aware anyone else was here, I couldn't exactly reprimand her for it.

"Butterfly, we have company."

She bolted upright and tensed. "Oh my God. I'm sorry!"

I ran my hand down her hair. "You get in a good nap?"

She nodded and eyed Doolittle, or more specifically the baby sling. "What's in there?"

"Our new kid," I said. "It seems I have *sucker* written across my forehead."

Shella stood and approached Doolittle. When he tugged the fabric down and she saw the little bunny, she gasped and reached out, plucking it from the sling and cradling it against her.

"Aren't you just the cutest thing ever?" she cooed to the bunny.

"Her name is Tinker," Doolittle said, removing the sling and handing it to Shella. "She likes being carried in this when she feels stressed. Tinker was bottle-raised, but she's fully weaned now. I'm going to run home for her stuff and bring it over. Told Slash she's litter-trained, but if you're not going to supervise her, you'll want to put her in her cage so she'll be safe."

Shella nodded, not looking away from the rabbit for a second. Yep. She was in love with Tinker already. Lucky fucking rabbit. Couldn't think of anything better than being loved by a woman like her.

"I'll bring over her food, treats, hay, a cage, toys, anything else you'll need to get you started," Doolittle said. "She's already had a check-up, but bring her to the clinic if she gets sick. I'd like to see her in about six months just to weigh her and make sure everything still looks good."

"She's beautiful," Shella said, stroking Tinker between the ears.

"I knew I made the right choice bringing her here." Doolittle smiled and let himself out.

"Guess we better figure out where we're putting her cage. I'm thinking it would be better to keep her downstairs. Might need a gate or something across the stairs if you want her to run free when you're down here," I said.

"We have that room down the hall that's empty. What if we put her cage and stuff in there with a litter box? It could be her area. If we put a baby gate across the door, then she could run around there sometimes if I can't watch her."

I shrugged not knowing much about rabbits. "Guess it would be fine. You can check with Doolittle when he comes back. I'm thinking we'll have to rabbit-proof the house."

Shella rubbed her face against the rabbit, a smile spread across her lips.

How the fuck I went from torturing her rapists to owning a rabbit was anyone's guess. No, I knew exactly how it happened. I'd do anything for Shella, and the second I'd seen the bunny I'd known she'd love it. I wanted to see her smile, to forget about the pain of her past. Maybe having the bunny to cuddle would help in some way.

Chapter Eleven

Shella

I stared at the local newspaper and bit down on my lip so I wouldn't laugh. Lauren Brewer, one of the girls who'd shoved me into the boy's locker room, was front page and not exactly looking her best. I skimmed the article and saw the now bald woman had experienced a string of misfortune over the last week, the latest of which had been her hair falling completely out.

Tinker sniffed my foot and I reached down to pick her up, cradling her on my lap. It seemed Lauren and her best friend, Faith Marx, had been run off the road a week ago. Since then, both ladies had one bad thing after another happen to them. Someone had put sugar in Lauren's gas tank, and all four of Faith's tires had been flattened. Both ladies claimed to have a rotten stench in their homes, a smell no one could locate. The grass in their yards had died almost overnight. Each had received pictures proving their husbands were cheating on them -- with each other. And somehow, both ladies had been covered in poison oak even though they claimed to have not stepped foot near any.

"Tinker, it couldn't have happened to anyone better. They're getting what they deserve."

Slash leaned over my shoulder and snorted when he saw the paper. "Oh, butterfly, I'm only just beginning."

I shoved the paper away and stared at him. "Talon, are you trying to say you're responsible for all this?"

"And then some. Wait until their bank accounts are suddenly drained and closed. Not to mention, they'll never find the smell in their homes. There's raw shellfish in their air ducts. The poison oak wasn't easy, though. I had Nox and Dax sneak in while they were sleeping and rub the plant over any exposed skin. Except Nox took it further. Did you notice Lauren is scratching her ass in the photo?"

I gasped. "He didn't!"

"Oh yeah. He rubbed it all over her ass and between her legs. Apparently, she sleeps like the dead, not to mention naked, and didn't so much as twitch. He waited until her husband was off screwing someone else."

"And them being run off the road?" I asked.

"Just scaring them a bit. They didn't hit anything or wreck. Probably got close to having a heart attack."

I reached up and snagged his leather cut, pulling him down. Pressing my lips to his, I kissed him long and hard. "I love you."

"Erin Rogers and Carrie Worth both moved away. Outlaw is fucking with them as much as he can from here, but they're getting off light compared to the other two. We've rounded up the seven guys who raped you. They won't hurt you, or anyone else, ever again."

"Is that where you kept running off to all week?" I asked.

He nodded. "I've had JJ, Mike, and Joe for about eight days. Billy got a quick death since he gave me the information I wanted. Parker, Aaron, and Eddie were a little harder to find since they don't live here anymore. Sent some men after them and they're secure for now. Soon enough, they'll be dead."

It should bother me he spoke of killing them so easily, without the slightest bit of remorse. Honestly, I couldn't find even a little sympathy for them. After what they'd done to me, I hoped he made them suffer.

"Can I see them?" I asked.

"Butterfly, you don't have to put yourself through that."

I took a breath and let it out. "I think I need to."

He nodded. "All right. Put Miss Tinker back in her cage and change clothes. But I have to warn you, JJ, Mike, and Joe aren't looking so great. Billy's already dead and buried. I haven't had a chance to work much on the other three."

I held Tinker against my chest and carried her to her room. I put her in the cage and made sure it was locked before heading upstairs to change. What was I supposed to wear? I'd never been down to the secret room that really wasn't so secret. Everyone in the club knew about it, including the old ladies.

I pulled on a black shirt and dark jeans, with the boots Slash had bought me. Lifting my property cut off the hanger, I slid it over my shoulders. I ran a brush through my hair and made quick work of braiding it. The woman staring back at me seemed more confident. I'd still been scared my attackers could be out there, watching and waiting, but I'd ventured out into the compound a bit more the last week.

No one whispered when I passed them, or made me feel bad. Colorado and Doolittle always greeted me with a hug, and my sisters had been extremely supportive. I'd even met the three girls currently staying with my dad. They seemed sweet and I was glad he'd been here to help them.

I rode on the back of Slash's bike. Even though I was pregnant, as long as he went slow, I was still allowed to go on short rides. When I started to show, I knew that would change. His protective instincts would kick in and he'd make me ride in the car. He parked out in front of the clubhouse and I saw a few bikes, as well as a car I didn't recognize.

Slash took my hand and led me inside. Wolf stood at the bar with a petite Hispanic woman. Tears streaked her cheeks, and he seemed to be doing his best to comfort her. I wondered if she was one of the ladies who'd arrived with two of the girls living with my dad.

"Wolf and Franny have been seeing each other off and on since she came here," Slash murmured in my ear. "He didn't like her moving out, but she's a determined little thing."

We walked past them and down the hall. Slash led me down to the area where they held anyone they needed to question, or kill. I saw six men tied to chairs, although three of them were barely recognizable as human. My hand trembled in his as I stared at them. These were the boys who'd hurt me? They didn't seem so scary right now.

JJ's eyes looked like the skin around them had been burned and the vacant way he looked around the room made me think he was blind. He was missing half his fingers, and I saw burns, cuts, and bruises covering almost every inch of him. They were all naked and I made sure I took in every inch of their bodies. That day, I'd been terrified and in pain. Now, not so much.

I approached JJ first. He'd hurt me the most. "What happened to him?"

He tensed at my voice. Slash's hand landed at my waist and I felt the heat of his body against my back. "You really want to know?"

I nodded. "I think I need to."

"Badger held hot pokers close enough to his eyes it burned the skin and cost him his sight. Then used those pokers to leave burn marks all over his body. The cuts are from me. Wolf worked him over with his fists. Steel knocked him around a bit and removed three of his fingers. I took the others." His hand tightened on me, as if he expected me to run.

I eyed JJ's crotch. "You finished with him?"

"He's all yours, butterfly," Slash said, taking a step back.

I went over to the table where they'd laid out all the things they'd used to torture the men. An ice pick drew my attention and I picked it up, the handle fitting easily in my hand. I approached JJ and stared at him.

"I was scared of you for so long. Let you haunt my nightmares. Let's see how you like having things shoved into you." I brought the ice pick down straight through his scrotum. He screamed and squealed before passing out.

"Damn, butterfly. Looks like you drove that right through his testicle. Remind me to keep sharp things away if I piss you off."

"If he doesn't die from it, can someone kill him?" I asked.

"That's the plan. None of these men are leaving here alive," Slash said.

I approached Mike next. His jaw jutted and there was defiance in his eyes, along with a hint of fear when he looked over my shoulder at Slash. He didn't look quite as rough as JJ, but dried blood crusted his skin. Someone had pulled out his fingernails and burned off his eyebrows and hair. His scalp was blistered from whatever they'd used.

"Did he tell you what he did? What he said?" I asked.

"He hasn't spoken much," Slash said.

"He called his friends and asked if they wanted to have some fun. Told them he had a little whore they could use, put their dicks anywhere they wanted. He took pictures of me naked and held down. Sent them to his buddies."

I heard a roar and crash, spinning to see Slash breathing heavy and a metal chair now mangled on the floor. Slash picked up something off the table and shoved me to the side, then drove a knife straight into Mike's heart. The guy's eyes went wide and blood dripped from his mouth before his head slumped.

It probably should have scared me, the violence inside Slash, but I knew he'd done it to protect me. Sometimes, people were so rotten, there was no saving them, and I knew Mike was one of them. If he'd gone to prison, he'd have eventually gotten out and been just as bad if not worse.

"Outlaw will find those pictures," Slash said. "If they're still out there, he'll track every single photo and wipe it from existence."

The others looked a little less intimidating. I remembered them. When it had been Billy's turn, Parker had held my wrists while Joe and Eddie each held my legs. Aaron had taken his turn too, egged on by his friends. Flashes of that day came back to me in technicolor and my palms started to sweat. My pulse raced and I felt like I might throw up at any moment. I told Slash what they'd done, then turned and walked out.

I knew he'd end their lives, and I hoped they'd suffer horribly.

Wolf and Franny weren't at the bar anymore. Dagger and Guardian sat in the corner. It looked like they were deep in conversation so I left them alone. Blades sat kicked back in a chair across the room with a bottle of beer in his hand. I hadn't had a chance to get to know him all that well, since he mostly spent his downtime with China and Meiling. I moved closer, noting the moment he saw me coming. He didn't give me any *fuck off* vibes so I pulled out a chair next to him and sat.

"Your man finally ending those bastards downstairs?" he asked.

"I think so. I put an ice pick through JJ's balls, though."

Blades spewed the beer he'd just drank and belted out a laugh. "Didn't think you had it in you. Good for you, Shella."

I knew China and Meiling had suffered greatly at the hands of men. For me, I'd only suffered through one day of being raped. Not even a full day. But they'd spent years in that situation. I didn't know how they'd coped. There had been times I'd felt like I was coming apart.

"Do you think Meiling or China would talk to me?" I asked. "About what happened, I mean. They just seem so…"

Blades put all four chair legs back on the ground and reached over to cover my hand with his. "Shella, you're stronger than you think. Your sisters wouldn't let men near them after what happened. Adalia didn't so much as kiss anyone until Badger came back from prison. And Lilian hid from the world until she finally let Dragon get close. Everyone heals differently and deals with shit in their own way. Just because it's taking you longer than you think it should doesn't mean you aren't healing, or that you're going about it the wrong way."

"You don't think I'm a whore for sleeping around after what happened?" I asked.

He squeezed my hand. "No. You needed to regain control and that's how you did it. I'm not about to look down on you for it, and neither will my woman or my daughter. You ever want to talk to them, you just come on by. China doesn't like interacting much when it comes to large groups, but she's okay in smaller gatherings. She's not doing as well as you think. Still feels dirty when she thinks about what happened to her, and what she did to survive until I found her."

"Wish everyone felt the way you do," I said.

"You thinking of Hot Shot and Cobra? Because your daddy handled that situation. Neither one will say a bad word about you ever again. Hell, if Cobra doesn't heal right, he might not be saying shit period."

"I never asked him to hurt anyone in the club. I wish he could have brought them around a different way. Is it going to cause any problems?" I asked.

Blades shrugged. "The ex-Pres defending his kid? Not likely. Besides, Badger already saw them, and your dad is still roaming free. If anything, I think your brother-in-law agreed with his methods. There are some things we don't tolerate around here and talking shit about someone's old lady is one of them. Since you're officially the property of Slash, anyone defending you would get a free pass for hitting a brother."

"You ever going to claim China?" I asked.

He flashed a grin and shook his head. "That stubborn woman isn't having any of it. I've tried, but she doesn't feel worthy of the position. Far as I'm concerned, she's mine anyway. We live together, have a kid together. Don't really need anything else. I know how she feels about me and that's enough. This club considers her my woman even if she doesn't wear my patch."

I looked over my shoulder back down the hall. Slash hadn't come up yet. I didn't know if he wanted me to wait for him or find a ride home. He hadn't said anything about finishing things right this minute.

"I want to do something," I said. "I'd like the club to be involved, but I'm not sure how to even get started."

"Something doesn't narrow it down much," Blades said.

"I didn't have anywhere to go after I was raped. If I'd gone to the hospital, they'd have called Dad before treating me. And the police. Lilian would have fallen apart even more, and Dad would have been entirely focused on me when she needed him too. I'd called a friend and she knew someone who was able to treat me. Not everyone has a friend like that in their lives."

Blades motioned for me to continue.

"What if we set up a counseling line where people could call in anonymously? I know there's something already in place nationwide, but it's not well-known. I was thinking smaller scale, like for our town or county?"

Blades ran a hand down his beard. "What if we set up a clinic of sorts? Something under the radar. A no questions asked sort of place? Probably illegal as hell, but it would have given you a place to go for treatment without having to get creative about it. If you had that issue, I'm sure others have too, and maybe they weren't as lucky as you."

"You think we could do that?" I asked.

"Well, we'd need a location, and it would have to look legit if anyone came nosing around. Doesn't mean we couldn't treat some rape victims on the sly, long as it didn't bring the law to our doors. We'd also need volunteers."

"Maybe I'll mention it to Badger, and he can decide if he wants the club involved. I'd like a way for other girls to feel safe coming forward without worrying about repercussions. If I'd had something like that, and maybe some counseling, things might have turned out different for me."

Blades shot a look over my shoulder. "Seems to have turned out fine. Might have been a rough road, but you're right where you're meant to be."

I turned and saw Slash coming out of the bathroom, shirtless with blood splattered across his jeans. He'd pulled his cut back on, and I had to admit he looked sexy as hell like that. I licked my lips and my cheeks warmed at the smirk he gave me. Yeah, I might not have gotten here the easy way, but being with Slash was the highlight of my life.

He stalked toward me, holding out his hand. I took it and let him haul me to my feet. Without any warning, he yanked me against him and kissed me hard. I felt the bulge in his jeans press against me and had no doubt we were about to go home and get naked. Not that I would complain. Slash made me burn, and I hoped it was always like this.

"Ready, butterfly?" he asked, drawing back a little.

"Yeah." I hesitated a moment. "Are they gone?"

He nodded. "The club will dispose of them. As for the women, I don't think they pose a physical threat to you. We'll toy with them a bit more. They're overdue for some bad luck. Can't stand stuck-up bitches who think their shit doesn't stink."

"Thank you, Slash. For everything, but mostly for coming to get me. Blades is right. I'm exactly where I'm meant to be. It took you chasing me down and forcing me to come home to realize that."

"I'd have gone to the ends of the earth for you, butterfly. Now that's settled, let's head home. I need a shower, and then I'm going to get my sexy wife very dirty."

He swatted my ass and led me out to his bike.

My toes curled in my boots. I was anxious to get home and get him naked. I couldn't wait to put my hands all over him. Maybe my mouth too. With Slash, sex was beyond amazing, and I had to wonder if it was because I loved him. Whatever the reason, I hoped the fire burning inside us never died out.

Chapter Twelve

Slash

It had been a month since I'd ended the miserable lives of the men who'd hurt my butterfly, and while it had helped soothe some of the rage inside me, I'd spent a considerable amount of time making sure the women involved were living in hell. Far as I was concerned, their turn of fortune needed to continue until they hit rock bottom. Already one of them, Lauren Brewer, had applied for a job at the strip club we'd bought back when Meiling had joined us.

It had changed names a few times. Currently, it was going by The Inferno. Seemed like a good name for a strip joint owned by the Devil's Fury. Since most men in this town were scared shitless of us, it meant the dancers could do their job without being afraid of the customers. Although, I'd willingly pay the bouncers extra to look away if someone wanted to get a little handsy with Lauren. I'd never let them take it too far, but it would do her good to get a taste of what she'd put Shella through by shoving her into that locker room.

I was an asshole and I could admit it. When it came to Shella, I'd do anything to protect her. Lauren was a bitch who deserved what she got. I'd made sure she'd fallen so far, she'd have one hell of a time climbing up out of the gutter. The others weren't in much better shape.

I'd taken care of my club business for the day and I was more than ready to spend some time with my butterfly. She'd gotten closer to her sisters and their husbands over the last few weeks. We'd also told the club about her pregnancy, and just left off the part about me not being the baby's biological father. Didn't matter to me. That kid was mine whether we shared DNA or not. I'd be the only dad they would know. I still wanted to know if we were having a son or daughter, but when I'd finally taken Shella to the doctor, they'd said it was too soon to tell. Other than confirming she was pregnant, and taking her vital signs, they hadn't done much else.

Entering the house, the first thing I noticed was the quiet. The TV was off. I didn't hear Shella in the kitchen, and it seemed Tinker was in her room. Which meant my woman was upstairs, unless one of her sisters had come to kidnap her. I checked my phone and didn't have any missed texts or calls from her, so that wasn't likely. She knew better than to leave without letting me know.

I took the stairs two at a time and went to our room. The shower was running, and I knew exactly what I was about to do. I stripped off my clothes and boots, then padded into the bathroom as silently as I could. Shella stood in the shower, water streaming down her, as she tilted her head back. Her eyes were closed and if she knew I was here, she hadn't let on yet.

I opened the shower door and stepped inside before quietly shutting it. I slid my hands around her waist and tugged her back against my chest. The smile that curved her lips made me happier than I could say. Even though she hadn't known I was heading home, it hadn't startled her to have a man put his hands on her. She'd trusted she was safe here. It had taken us a little time to reach this point, but I was happy to see her adjusting better.

"Missed you," I murmured and kissed the side of her neck.

"I missed you too. You home for the day?"

"Unless the sky falls, or something blows up. Barring any emergencies, yeah, I'm home for the rest of the day. You have something in mind? A way to pass the time?"

She turned to face me, her hands going to my chest. "I may."

Shella tugged my head down and kissed me. She'd become a greedy little thing, always wanting more orgasms, and never getting enough of my cock. I loved every fucking second of it.

"What did you do today?" I asked when she backed off.

"Went shopping with the girls."

My eyebrows arched. "I don't recall getting a message or call saying you were leaving the compound. Unless you shopped online?"

She shook her head. "We went into town. It's a surprise. Besides, Dragon and Dingo knew. Badger knew too because Adalia stayed behind to watch the kids with China. We had Colorado and Beau with us."

"Someone is getting a spanking," I said. "In fact, I think you need one right now."

I spun the two of us until I could sit on the small built-in bench and I yanked her down across my lap. She squealed and grabbed onto my leg, her ass in the air. Since her skin was wet, the spanking would sound even louder, and burn more. Oh yeah, my butterfly was about to have a red ass.

I brought my hand down on one cheek, then the other with a loud *crack* with each swat. She cried out and squirmed, but I held her down by placing my arm across her back.

"You fight me, it's going to hurt more," I warned.

"It already hurts!"

I brought my hand down harder. *Smack*.

She squealed and thrashed on my lap. Fuck if I was going to let up. She hadn't told me where she was going, or let me know she'd left the compound. What if something had happened to her? I spanked her until her ass was cherry red and I could feel the heat coming off it. Wouldn't surprise me if she bruised a little. She'd think about her actions having consequences every time she sat down for the next day or two.

I spread the lips of her pussy and shoved two fingers inside, drawing a moan from her. "Can't complain too much. Seems this pussy is nice and slick. You can scream all you want, but you like it when I punish you."

I felt her body tense and the vibration of her moan. Oh yeah, my butterfly had liked getting a spanking, no matter how much she claimed otherwise. I worked my fingers in and out, feeling her pussy flutter as she got close to coming. Not yet. I wasn't ready to reward her. I eased my fingers from her and gave her ass a light slap.

I flipped her over and kissed her soft and slow. Fuck, but this woman turned me inside out. I'd never wanted anyone as much as I wanted Shella. It wasn't just the sex, even though it was amazing. No, it was *her*. I loved her smile, her laugh, her strength. Everything.

"Love you, butterfly. So fucking much."

"I love you too," she murmured before pressing her lips to mine again.

"Come on. Let's get out and you can show me what was so important for you to leave the compound and not tell me. What if I'd come home early and you'd been gone?"

She worried at her bottom lip. "I didn't want you to be concerned, Talon. But I don't like feeling like I'm a prisoner either."

"I'm not your jailer, Shell. I want to keep you safe. If something happens when you're outside the compound, I can get to you faster if I know where you were going."

"I guess that makes sense. I'm sorry, Talon. I promise I won't leave without telling you." She kissed my cheek, then stood up.

It would have to do. Something told me Shella was going to be tough to wrangle, but it was part of her charm. A docile, biddable woman would be boring as fuck. She'd keep me on my toes, and I'd punish her every time she ran off without telling me.

I shut off the water, dried off, and went into the bedroom. She'd pulled a sack from somewhere and started laying things out on the bed. Nipple clamps, a vibrator, a butt plug, padded handcuffs, and a flogger? Where the hell had she gone shopping? And what had prompted her to buy all this stuff?

I had plenty of things tucked away, unused toys I'd been eager to try with Shella, but the timing had never seemed right. It seemed she was going to take matters into her own hands.

"Shell, something you need to tell me?" I asked.

"We may have been talking before we decided to go shop. Zoe wanted to spice things up with Dagger and Guardian, so Meiling suggested the adult store in town. It seemed like fun so I picked up some things. We don't have to use them all. Or any of them."

"Oh, butterfly. We're definitely using these things just not all at once." I picked up the handcuffs. "You really ready for this?"

"You've held me down several times now, using your body, and I was all right. I know it's you here with me and that you won't hurt me."

I cupped her cheek. "You have no idea what it means to me, knowing you trust me."

"Of course, I trust you, Talon. You came for me when no one else did. Claimed me. And you love me. Who better to trust than you?" she asked.

"When you put it like that..." I smiled and kissed her again. "But we're definitely using the nipple clamps. Hope they came with batteries and don't need to charge."

"I-I don't know." Her eyes were wide and full of excitement.

I helped her open the toys and clean them. The nipple clamps did use batteries. I made sure they worked and set them aside. The handcuffs joined them on the bedside table, as well as the vibrator. The other stuff could wait.

I slipped my hand between her thighs and felt how wet she was. Toppling her to the bed, I reached for the handcuffs and shackled her to the headboard. She tugged at them but didn't seem like she was going to freak out. If anything, she gave me a shy smile.

My jaw was rough with stubble and I rubbed it against her neck and across the tops of her breasts. Not only did I like marking her, but my sweet butterfly liked it too. She always arched into me and made the sexiest sounds.

I cupped her breasts and licked one of her nipples before sucking it into my mouth. It hardened against my tongue and I gently bit down. Shella cried out and her hips bucked. I took my time teasing her and making sure her nipples were nice and hard. Reaching over to the bedside table, I grabbed the nipple clamps and clipped them in place. With the press of a button, they turned on and she sucked in a breath.

"Oh, God. Talon! It feels so good."

"That's what I want to hear. I'll be making you feel even better." I settled between her thighs and spread them wide. "Time to make you beg, Shell."

I spread her pussy open and gave her a long, slow lick. So fucking sweet! I lapped at her, not touching the one spot she wanted me to the most. I worked around her clit before giving it a light bite. She squealed and her body tensed, but she was so fucking wet I knew she'd liked it.

"More!" she demanded.

I brought her close twice and backed off each time. No matter how much she wanted to come, I wasn't ready to let her. The more I teased her, the harder she'd orgasm when I finally allowed it.

I grabbed the vibrator off the bedside table and turned it on. Slipping it into her wet pussy, I didn't stop until she'd taken it all. The toy wasn't as big as me, but it wasn't exactly small either. I licked, sucked, and nibbled on her clit while the vibrator buzzed inside her.

"Talon! I need more. Please! Fuck me!"

I barely moved the toy, only withdrawing it an inch or two before easing it back inside her. When she cried out in frustration and squeezed me with her thighs, I chuckled and gave her another slow lick. Her cries of frustration finally made me relent. I worked her pussy with the vibrator and sucked her clit hard until she came, screaming out my name.

She shuddered and panted. I shut off the toy and set it aside before settling my body over hers. The dazed look in her eyes made me smile as I brushed her hair back from her face. "So beautiful."

I reached for her thigh and hiked her leg over my hip, opening her to me. I went slow, filling her with my cock, and fought for control. Hot. Wet. Perfect. Next time, I'd flip her over, work her ass with that vibrator while I pounded her pussy, and make her scream. But this time I wanted to give her something more.

I'd fucked women since I'd been sixteen. With Shella, I wanted to make love to her. I went slow, making her come twice as I kissed her. Gripping her hip, I drove into her harder. Every stroke was like heaven. I groaned as I came inside her.

"What was that?" she asked, sounding dazed.

"That was me making love to my wife," I said, kissing her again.

"I liked it." She smiled. "But I also like it when you take what you want."

I reached up and tugged on one of the nipple clamps. "That right? Because I'd thought about flipping you over and using the vibrator to fuck your ass."

Her eyes dilated and knew she was intrigued. Oh yeah, my little butterfly was fucking perfect for me. I adjusted the cuffs so I could turn her over. I had lube in the drawer and grabbed it along with the vibrator. After I got her ass nice and slick, I turned the toy on and let it buzz against her tight little hole. Shella squirmed and whimpered, clearly wanting more.

I took my time, easing the toy inside her. I gave her a few short strokes until I knew she could handle more. My dick was already hard as granite. I plunged deep into her pussy and gripped her hip with one hand while I fucked her ass with the toy. Fuck! The vibrator was just fat enough that it made her pussy feel even more incredible. Not to mention how the vibrations felt along my cock.

I pushed the vibrator in deep before grabbing her hips with both hands. I leaned over her a little, holding the toy in place as I fucked her. I rode her hard, taking what I wanted, what I needed. No, what we both needed. My hips slapped against her ass. I leaned back a little and looked down, watching as I stroked in and out of her. The sight alone was nearly enough to make me come.

"Don't stop, Talon! Please don't stop."

I slipped my hand down between her legs and rubbed her clit. Her pussy clenched down as she came, and I couldn't hold back another second. I came inside her, my cock twitching. I stayed buried inside her, running my hand up and down her back. If I were younger, I'd fuck her all night long. Even though I'd already come twice, and could possibly go one more round, I also didn't want to be too rough with Shella. Not while she was pregnant.

I eased out of her, thrust the toy in and out of her ass a few more times, then pulled it out. After I released her from the handcuffs, I lifted her into my arms and carried her to the bathroom. I'd wash my butterfly before I cleaned the toys and put them away. I let the shower get nice and hot before I carried her into the glassed-in stall.

I took my time soaping her skin. She cuddled against me and swayed slightly on her feet. I'd worn her out. Hell, I felt pretty wiped out myself. I cleaned up and dried us off. I tucked Shella into bed, where she promptly closed her eyes and gave a soft sigh. I cleaned the toys and left them in the bathroom to dry, and I crawled into bed next to my wife, holding her close.

"Get some rest, butterfly. We'll take a nap, and then I'll order some dinner for us."

She mumbled something I didn't quite understand and I knew she was asleep. I couldn't remember a time I'd felt more content. The men who'd hurt her were gone. The women had been punished. There wasn't anything standing in our way.

Chapter Thirteen

Shella

I gripped Slash's hand tight as I stared at the machine. I didn't know the exact date of my webcam show, but I thought I was only about three and a half months pregnant, but the doctor wanted to get a better idea of the date I conceived. I'd hoped the ultrasound would tell us if we were having a boy or girl. I had another few weeks to go before that could happen, but at least we'd know our baby was healthy.

Slash stared at the screen as the image became a little clearer. My eyes misted with tears as I stared at the baby. Then the technician moved the wand and I couldn't stifle my gasp. "There's two?"

The tech grinned. "Congratulations! You're having twins."

Twins. Two babies. I didn't know how to take care of one, and now he was telling me there was another one? I felt the panic welling up inside me and Slash dropped to his knees next to me. He forced my gaze on him and gave me a smile.

"Easy, butterfly. I know you're worried, but you're going to be the best mom to these kids. And I'll be there every step of the way."

I reached over to cup his cheek. "It's like you can read my mind sometimes."

He grinned. "You're easy to read. It looked like you were about to bolt off the table and make a run for it. Just so you know, I'd find you."

He'd already proven that when he'd dragged me back home two months ago. I stared at the screen again. Two! They didn't look very big. The tech was moving the wand around, taking measurements of each baby, and even printed off a few pictures. It was surreal. Even though I knew I was pregnant, realizing there were two tiny humans in my belly was beyond amazing, and terrifying.

"It looks like one of your babies is a little smaller than the other. They seem healthy, but you definitely need to watch what you eat. Make sure you're getting plenty of nutrients not just for you but for them too."

"So you can't tell when she conceived?" Slash asked, eyeing the tech.

"Based off her first missed period, and the larger of the two babies, not to mention their rate of development, I'm going to say you're around four months. Let's see if we can get the bigger baby positioned right and see if we can tell the sex yet. Usually, the doctor likes to wait until you're twenty weeks. He'll be in here for that visit. He likes giving happy news."

She pushed on my belly and tried to turn the baby. After a few minutes, she huffed out a breath and shook her head. "Stubborn little thing. I'm sorry. I'd hoped maybe we could tell the sex of at least one of them."

"Just knowing they're healthy is enough," Slash said.

I didn't know how he could be so calm. Four months? Granted, it was only about two weeks off from what I'd thought, but when it came to babies, what would normally be a small amount of time made a huge difference. There was no way we'd convince everyone the babies were his. I'd already started gaining weight and had a little pouch. Slash had promised to take me shopping for maternity clothes after this appointment. As long as I didn't wear my jeans, my clothes were fine. Just a little snug. But my breasts were getting huge already. I spilled out of my current bras and needed a few new ones to get me through the pregnancy. If they kept growing, they'd be so big they'd enter a room two minutes before me.

"We'll see you back in a month to do another ultrasound," the tech said. "I think the doctor was calling in a prescription for prenatal vitamins. The over-the-counter ones aren't as strong, and with two babies, you'll need the extra oomph. If you have any questions, or start to feel any discomfort, notice any spotting or bleeding, call us immediately."

She wiped the goo from my stomach and pulled the paper shirt down. After she left the room, Slash helped me dress and we went out front. He set my appointment and added it to the calendar on his phone. Taking my hand, he led me from the doctor's office and to the truck at the curb. He'd bought it last week, saying he'd need something when the baby got here. Except now he'd be driving two babies around. Good thing it had a large back seat.

Slash helped me into the truck, then leaned across and buckled me. I got a wink and the flash of a smile before he shut the door and walked around the front of the vehicle. I didn't know where he planned to take me. It wasn't like I'd bought maternity clothes before, or gone shopping with anyone who else who had. When he stopped in front of a small store with a stork on the front window, I glanced his way, wondering how he'd known this was here.

He leaned closer and softly kissed me. "You're cute when you're trying to figure out who I've brought here before. And don't deny you were thinking it. Adalia told me about this place. Said they had better stuff than the shops in the mall, so I thought we'd start here."

My cheeks warmed. "I wasn't jealous."

"Sure you weren't, butterfly. You know what? I like it when you get a little jealous." He grinned. "Even if you have nothing to worry about. You're it for me, butterfly. No other woman could ever compare."

"Talon, what we are going to tell everyone? They're going to realize the babies aren't yours."

He narrowed his gaze at me and I pressed my lips together. He hated it when I said they weren't his. As far as he was concerned, the babies were his kids. He didn't care if he was their biological dad or not. It wasn't that I was trying to make him feel like they weren't his babies. I just worried how the club would react. They hadn't taken it well when I'd returned with him. They might accept me now, but would it all change when they realized I'd already been pregnant when he found me?

He placed his hand on my belly and the slight bump. "These kids are mine. No one else's. You hear me? If anyone questions how far along you are, I'll tell them I found you faster than I claimed. We'd discussed that before. Instead of padding it a week or two, we'll make it a month. I wanted time with you, convinced you to marry me, but I knocked you up right after I found you. They don't have to know I'd been searching for you nearly a month before I saw you in that strip club."

"I'm sorry. I love you, and I don't want you to feel like…"

He smoothed his thumb over my lip. "I know, butterfly. I understand what you're struggling with. We'll make it work, all right?"

"I don't like lying to everyone, but I don't want them to hate me again either."

"No one will hate you, Shella. Grizzly has how many kids that aren't his biologically? Think anyone would dare say you aren't his daughter? Or the others either? Dagger and Guardian adopted Luis. Steel adopted Coral. I dare you to tell any of them those aren't their kids."

He was right. I was worrying again for no reason. I needed to let the past go. The club had, and Slash had seen that anyone who'd hurt me paid the price. It was time to move forward with my life and stop looking behind me. What I'd been through, and the way the club had reacted, couldn't be changed. It was time I forgave them, and maybe forgave myself too.

"All right. I'll do better."

"Come on, butterfly. Let's find you some pretty things, and some jeans that won't squeeze our kids to death. You might not be riding on my bike anytime soon, but that doesn't mean you can't still dress like an old lady if you want to."

I nodded. Right. T-shirts and jeans. Lots of them.

Slash was surprisingly patient while I shopped. No matter how many times I picked something up, put it back, then circled back around to it again, he didn't make a sound of complaint. He'd sprawled in a chair along the wall and played a game on his phone while he waited. I'd tease him later for playing Candy Crush in a maternity store. It completely ruined his bad boy biker image.

I ended up with five pairs of jeans, twice as many shirts, and a few dresses. When I'd told him I was ready to checkout, he'd tossed a few long-sleeve tops onto the pile. Since I was always hot lately, I didn't think I'd need them anytime soon, but it wouldn't hurt to have them just in case.

"There's one more stop we need to make," he said, as he put my bags into the back seat.

Since he hadn't said anything before now, I wondered if it was club business. Although, it wasn't likely he'd want me tagging along for something like that. So where was he taking me? I could ask, but it didn't mean he'd tell me. I'd learned that Slash only gave me the information he wanted me to have. The rest I had to wait and discover when he was good and ready.

He parked in front of a small storefront. The large glass window sat empty except for some cobwebs. I got out and peered inside, thinking it didn't seem very large compared to the other shops on either side.

"What's this place?" I asked.

"This is where your dream is going to come true," he said. He pulled some keys from his pocket and opened the shop door, ushering me inside. I went in, sneezing at the dust motes that filled the air. "After a lot of scrubbing, this place should do nicely."

"For what exactly?"

"Well, out here will appear to be a used bookstore. Rachel and Elena have offered to help set it up. Any proceeds will help fund the behind-the-scenes part of the shop."

He took my hand and led me through the back door. My jaw dropped a little. There was a desk near the rear entrance and it looked like employee bathrooms as well as two other rooms on either side of the back entrance.

Slash waved a hand to the room on the left. "We're going to set up a small exam room in there. We've already put out some feelers for nurses or doctors who might want to help, all under the table since it won't exactly be legal. It's not like the club doesn't know how to get their hands on whatever medication will be needed."

"An exam room?"

He grinned. "You wanted a place rape victims could go if they were too scared to go to the ER. You're right. If they went untreated, they could die if their injuries were severe enough, or contract an STD, maybe end up pregnant. We'll get the word out to a few key people who can help steer them in our direction. If they need a morning-after pill, we'll get it. STD screening, and anything they might need to heal from their assault. Including the number of a counselor."

"Talon, I…" My eyes filled with tears. "You're really doing this?"

"Blades told us about your idea. The club agrees there's a need for a place like this. The other empty room will be split between book stock and medical supplies. We'll have a sign there are no public bathrooms so we don't have to worry about someone coming back here and discovering what we're up to."

"I don't know what to say."

"It's not going to get up and running right off. We need to clean this place really well, find the medical workers we need, and come up with a better plan. But it's a start, Shella. And as long as it isn't too tiring for you, I'd like you to be a part of it. Behind the scenes, because I don't want you dealing with any of this in person."

"There's no greater present anyone could have given me. Thank you!" I threw my arms around him and hugged him tight. "I love you, so much. You're the most amazing man I've ever known."

"I'll remind you of that the next time I have to spank your ass for disobeying me," he said dryly.

My cheeks burned, but we both knew I liked those spankings. No matter how much I said otherwise, I got wet every time he yanked me over his knee and turned my ass red. Although now that I was showing, he'd changed things up a little. Last time, he'd had me kneel on the bed, ass in the air, and he'd gripped my hair with one hand to hold me still while he'd spanked me.

He smirked. "Or maybe you want me to find a reason to spank you. I'm sure I can come up with a reason to punish you, butterfly. Just not here. This place is too filthy for the things I'd like to do to you."

"Is sex always on your mind?" I asked.

"Oh, please. On *my* mind? Baby, for the last month, all I have to do is look your way and you want to climb me like a damn tree. All I did was tell you good morning yesterday and you had my zipper down before I'd even processed what you were doing."

"You complaining?" I asked.

"Not even a little." He slid his hand down my back and squeezed my ass. "I like that you love my cock so much you can't get enough. I bet if this floor were clean, all I'd have to do is tell you I'm hard and you'd drop to your knees and suck me off."

I gasped and half-heartedly tried to pull away. He wasn't wrong. I was completely addicted to him. I loved the taste of him, the way he stretched me, and even liked the burn of him fucking my ass. There wasn't a single thing we'd done in the bedroom I hadn't enjoyed.

"Maybe we need to go home," I suggested.

"You going to worship my cock when we get there?"

"Unless you find a private spot before then. I'll be happy to show my appreciation in the truck." I licked my lips so he wouldn't miss my meaning.

Heat flared in his eyes as he took my hand and practically ran back to the front of the shop. He locked up and helped me into the truck. The tires squealed a little as he pulled out of the parking spot and I couldn't help but smile. It seemed he was overly eager. Honestly, he wasn't the only one.

Slash pulled off the road before we reached the compound, the truck bouncing down a dirt path that led into the trees. When he put it into park, I unfastened my seatbelt and shoved the armrest up out of the way. Slash had already started to unfasten his belt and jeans.

"If you're going to be this hot for me during the entire pregnancy, we might have to start having sex right before we leave the house. Not sure I can find enough secluded places to satisfy your needs when we aren't home."

"*My* needs?"

"All right. Both our needs. You saying you don't want to wrap your lips around this?" he asked, waving a hand at his hard cock.

Nope. I wasn't saying that at all. Not even a little. I wet my lips and got onto my knees on the seat. Leaning over, I gripped his cock at the base before I lapped at the head, licking off the pre-cum. Slash groaned and sifted his fingers through my hair. His grip tightened and he used my hair to guide me.

He thrust deep, making me take all of him into my mouth. I gagged a moment and my eyes watered.

"Fuck, butterfly. So hot!"

He pushed deep again, gagging me once more. By the fourth stroke, I'd adjusted and took him easily.

He grunted as his hips thrust up and he brought my head down. He used me, taking what he wanted. Instead of being a turnoff, all it did was make me burn hotter for him. I felt my pussy grow slick and I squeezed my thighs together.

"That's it, Shell. Suck me."

He started thrusting faster, his motion erratic. I knew he was close to coming. My clit pulsed and I moaned around his cock.

"Fuck! Fuck, fuck, fuck." His cum filled my mouth and I swallowed as much as I could, but felt some leak from the corners and down my chin. He released me and I wiped the mess off my face, my lips feeling swollen from him fucking my mouth.

I squirmed on the seat, wanting to come so bad a little whine escaped me before I could stop it. His chest heaved as he stared at me, his eyes heavy-lidded and dark with hunger. Slash reclined his seat until he lay nearly flat, then motioned for me to come closer.

"Take your pants off, Shell. Get up here so I can lick that pretty pussy."

His words alone nearly made me come. I struggled to get my pants and panties off, then climbed on top of him. Slash helped position me so that I could brace myself on the back seat, my thighs splayed and my pussy hovering over his mouth. He tugged me down until I felt the wet heat of his tongue as he lapped at me.

"Talon!"

"That's it, butterfly. Scream all you want. Let me hear how much you enjoy this."

He spread the lips of my pussy and flicked my clit with his tongue. Little cries escaped me as he teased me. My thighs trembled and had he not been holding onto me, I wouldn't have been able to hold my position. He sucked at my clit and I jolted, jerking my hips. I reached up and grabbed onto the handle over the side window, lifting myself a little. It gave me just enough leverage I was able to rock my hips.

"God, Talon! Don't stop. Make me come!"

He worked my pussy while I rode his face, so close to an orgasm yet not quite there. He dipped his finger into my pussy, using short, slow thrusts while his tongue and lips tortured my clit. When he pulled his finger free and pressed it between my ass cheeks, a keening sound escaped me as I rocked against him. He worked his finger inside me, stroking it in and out while his mouth did sinful things to my pussy.

I came, screaming out his name, riding him harder. A roaring filled my ears and I forgot to breathe as sparks shot along my nerve-endings. Trembling, I sucked in a breath and looked down to make sure I hadn't suffocated him. He winked and kept working my pussy and fucking my ass with his finger. It didn't take him long to get me off again. Still I craved more. It was like something had been unleashed inside me and I wanted to demand orgasm after orgasm.

I slid down his body, but he wouldn't let me go back to my seat. Instead, he maneuvered us so that I lay on the driver's seat while he hovered over me. Slash reached for my thigh, lifting it over his hip, and I felt the prod of his hard cock against my pussy. I moaned and my eyes slid shut as I lifted my hips, wanting him as much as he seemed to want me.

"Need you, butterfly. But you're not getting off easy. When we get home, I'm going to wear you out. Fuck you so good you'll lose your voice from all the screaming you'll be doing."

My nipples hardened and I reached up to grab onto him. "Just fuck me, Talon. I need it. Need *you*."

He thrust into me, not taking his time. The slam of his cock over and over had the truck rocking and had me begging to come. He twisted his hips on the next stroke so that he rubbed across my clit and I saw stars as I came. My body twitched as I rode the wave of my orgasm.

"That's it, butterfly. Fuck but you look beautiful when you come."

I felt the heat of his release as he came inside me, grunting on the last two strokes. I wished we weren't in the truck on some random piece of land. If we were home, he wouldn't have to pull out right away. I ran my nails down his back and pressed him tighter against me.

"When we get home, I'm going to use the toys to make you come multiple times," he said. "Then I'm fucking your ass."

He kissed me hard and deep before withdrawing from my body. I whimpered at the loss and hoped the cum I felt sliding out of me wasn't going to ruin his truck seats. Not that I thought he'd care. More than likely, he'd decided it was some sort of badge proving how awesome he was.

He helped me back over to my side, and I pulled on my panties and pants. Slash put his seat back into the upright position and zipped up his pants. He turned the truck around and headed back to the road that would take us to the compound. Stopping just this side of the tree line, he gave me a heated look.

"Need something to hold me over until we get home."

I arched my eyebrows. "Again? I just sucked you off *and* you fucked me."

"Not what I meant." He smirked. "I see those hard nipples poking through your shirt. Show me."

I lifted my shirt and Slash reached over, pulling the cups of my bra down. He kneaded my breast and tugged on my nipple.

"Give me the other side, butterfly."

I twisted so he could reach. Even though I'd just come several times, my pussy already throbbed, wanting more. He worked my nipples, rolling them between his fingers, pinching down, and tugging on them. It was almost enough to make me come.

"Talon, I can't wait much longer. You've got me all hot and achy again."

He leaned over and sucked a nipple into his mouth, giving it a gentle bite before helping me right my clothes. "Hold on, butterfly. We'll be home soon."

Not soon enough!

I didn't know if I'd always feel this crazy need for him, but I hoped so. I never wanted the day to come that I wouldn't crave his hands on my body, need him more than my next breath. Slash might have come to take me home two months ago, but I'd been home the second he'd decided I was his. It didn't matter if we lived at the compound or somewhere else. As long as he was with me, that's all that mattered.

Chapter Fourteen

Slash

I stared at the clock on the wall and only half-listened to what Badger was saying. In the last five weeks, Shella's project had made great strides. Rachel and Elena already had several boxes of donated books to help get the store open. Except no one could settle on a name for the damn place. I drummed my fingers on the table, wondering how much longer this would take.

"Butterflies and Books," I said.

"Where the fuck are we putting butterflies in there?" Demon asked.

"They don't have to be actual ones, asshole." I glared at him. "Shella's been making all sorts of things lately. Keychains and bookmarks seem to be her favorites. If the club chipped in for the stuff she needs, she could make butterfly- and book-themed items to sell at the front counter. Maybe get some paper bookmarks printed off with the shop's info to give out for free with the purchase of three or more books."

"This isn't about real butterflies, is it?" Blades asked. "I've heard you call Shella that. Your butterfly."

I shrugged a shoulder. "She was broken but still beautiful, and I knew she'd eventually fly again."

"So the butterflies are partly for Shella and also a reminder of what we're accomplishing in the back rooms?" Badger asked.

"Right," I said.

"Then Butterflies and Books it is," Badger said. "Any other orders of business for today?"

I cleared my throat. "Not business, but there's something I'd like to tell everyone. As you know, at the last doctor appointment, we found out we're having twins. Shella went back two days ago. One of the babies refused to cooperate, but the bigger one is definitely a boy. They said we could try to see the sex of Baby Two another time if we wanted. There's just no guarantee it would yield any results."

"Smaller one is stubborn like her momma," Grizzly said with a grin.

"Yep. And I'm telling her you said that," I said. "Just so she doesn't broadside you, she wants to name the boy John."

Griz cleared his throat and nodded, but I could tell it meant a lot to him.

A loud bang had several club members jumping to their feet, and when the doors of Church flew open, even Badger stood. Everyone but me, since I knew exactly who'd decided to show up. My half-brother, Tank, strolled through the doors like he owned the place, a Cheshire grin on his face.

"Don't start the party without me," he said.

"Motherfucker," Badger muttered. "I should gut you for barging into Church uninvited."

"Technically, I had an invitation from your VP, and I come bearing gifts." He reached behind him and yanked a young woman into the room. "Meet Glory."

"We don't allow club whores in Church," Demon said.

Tank winced and Glory's face turned red. Not in an embarrassed sort of way, but more in an *I will rip off your balls* way. She jabbed her finger in Demon's direction and snarled.

"I'm not a fucking club whore. You try to put your dick anywhere near me, I'll rip it off."

Badger sat and leaned back in his chair, apparently settling for the show. Our other brothers reclaimed their seats, eyeing Demon and Glory. The Sergeant-at-Arms stared down his nose at her.

"First off, I have a woman so I wouldn't *want* my dick anywhere near you. Second, you point at me again, and I'll --"

Badger cleared his throat and shook his head giving Demon the *shut up* look. The Sergeant-at-Arms clamped his lips shut and glared at Glory. The cute blonde didn't seem the least bit intimidated.

"Introduce Glory, Tank," I said.

"Glory has a four-year degree in biology and was accepted into medical school. She only attended for one semester before she had to quit and stay home," Tank said.

"Why did you have to quit?" Blades asked.

"Fuck that, she doesn't even look old enough to be out of high school," Guardian said. "No offense."

Glory glanced up at Tank, then squared her shoulders and faced the room again. "I graduated high school when I was fourteen, then finished my four-year degree in three years. I was seventeen when I was accepted into medical school. The reason I dropped out is personal, but considering why I'm here, I'll share it with you. I was walking across campus one night when two guys dragged me off into the bushes. They hit me several times, nearly knocking me out, then took turns raping me."

Her gaze scanned the room, stopping on each brother for a few seconds before moving on to the next. It was like she was daring them to say something. I saw several sympathized with her, and a few clearly wanted to hunt down the men who'd hurt her and kill them. I couldn't blame them. The world wouldn't miss a few more rapists. Hell, I wished we could round them all up and bury them.

"I have a daughter as a consequence of that night. No one found me for thirty-six hours, and by the time I was treated, it was too late for the morning-after pill to be as effective. They treated me for STDs and sent me on my way." She took a breath and her fingers clenched and unclenched at her sides. "My parents threw me out when I refused to have an abortion. Sienna, my daughter, is developmentally delayed but she's an angel. No matter how she was conceived, I'm lucky to be her mom."

"You dropped out to take care of your kid or because you were scared to be on campus?" Ripper asked.

"A little of both," she admitted. "I'm eighteen, in case anyone wondered. Almost nineteen. Tank heard about your project to help rape victims and thought of me. We met at the OB-GYN when I was there for a check-up during my pregnancy and I spilled my story to his wife."

I eyed my brother. He'd left that part out. "Anything I need to know, brother?"

Tank shook his head. "Got a vasectomy when the girls were about two years old. Those three are more than enough. We were just there for a routine thing. Emmie didn't want to go alone."

"You want to help as what? Medical staff?" Badger asked.

"After having been the victim of two rapists, I can understand where these women are emotionally and mentally," Glory said. "I have enough training to help with the basics, but you'd still need a licensed doctor or nurse practitioner. I'm CPR certified, and I've been taking some online nursing classes. I just haven't been able to do the hands-on part because of Sienna."

"She'll need a place to stay," I said. "Any objections to letting her use one of the apartments?"

"They only have one bedroom," Ripper said. "She needs more space if she has a daughter."

"Sienna isn't quite a year old," Glory said. "She's small enough we can easily share a room. We don't want to be any trouble."

Voices outside the door had Tank turning to peer into the hallway. He stepped out of the room a moment and returned with a pink bundle in his arms. He handed the kid over to Glory and I figured it must be Sienna.

"She's so small," Ripper said, "She's like a little doll."

Glory smiled. "She's my angel."

"You can use my house," Ripper said. "I'll stay at the clubhouse."

I shared a look with Badger. Neither of us had seen that coming. To give up his home and move back in here was sending a rather loud message. The way he eyed the little girl and her mom told me the Devil's Fury family might be growing again soon. Although, I didn't think Glory would give in all that easily.

"I'm not throwing you out of your house," Glory said.

"Fine. It's three bedrooms. You can have one and Sienna can have the other. We can be roommates until you get on your feet."

Glory opened her mouth like she might protest, but Tank leaned down and whispered something in her ear. Her cheeks turned pink and she nodded.

"She accepts," Tank said.

"Anything else?" Badger asked. "Any other surprises I need to know about?"

I knew that one was directed at me and I just smiled at him. Yeah, I'd pay for it later. It wasn't a good thing to spring shit on the Pres, especially in the middle of Church. I honestly hadn't planned it that way, but Tank had arrived in town just as Church was starting. I'd sent him a quick text telling him to go ahead and stop by with Glory so we could get things in motion.

"If that's all, everyone get the fuck out. Ripper, help Glory get set up at your place and let me know if they need anything."

I slapped Badger on the shoulder as I headed for the door. Glory kept casting glances at Ripper, and I wondered if the two might pair off at some point. I couldn't see Ripper with a kid, but what the fuck did I know? My brother, who looked more bear than human some days, had three little girls he adored. If Tank could handle three daughters, maybe Ripper could take on a single mom.

My brother followed me out and stopped next to his truck, which had a crib and a handful of boxes in the bed. I figured it must be Glory's stuff, which meant he'd need to haul it over to Ripper's place. The fact I didn't see any strange cars in the lot made me wonder if she'd ridden here with him. If that was the case, how did she plan to get around without a car?

"Ripper's house is that way," I said pointing to the right of the gate. "It's about half a mile down the road. Has some sort of flowering tree out front. Think Shella called it a dogwood. The old ladies had it planted there when Ripper patched in and got the keys to the house. Just look for a tree with white flowers."

Tank punched me in the arm. "I know what a dogwood is, fucker."

My brother might be a decade older than me, but he still had fists like fucking sledgehammers. I tried not to wince. If I bruised later, Shella would be pissed at him. Yeah, I'd hide behind my wife if I had to.

"Stop by the house when you're done. Too bad Emmie and the girls couldn't come with you."

"Next time," he said. "Or better yet, bring your ass to Alabama more often. The girls miss their Uncle Slash, and now you've given them an aunt. When I told them you'd gotten married, they squealed and nearly busted my eardrums."

My nieces were eight now, and I'd be willing to bet they were a handful. They were also adorable and had their daddy wrapped around their little fingers. I wondered what it would be like when my kids were born. Hell, I still didn't know what the second baby was, but part of me really hoped it was a girl.

I got on my bike and headed home just as Glory came out with Ripper. I knew Tank would make sure she was settled, and felt okay being alone with Ripper, before he came over. Didn't mean I had time for anything fun with Shella. I just had to convince *her* of that. I'd been gone from the house nearly an hour now, and I hadn't done more than kiss her before I left. No doubt her hands would be all over me the second I walked through the door.

Yeah, it sucked to be me.

I parked my bike next to her car and went inside. The door hadn't even shut all the way before I had an armful of Shella. She kissed me, her hands going for my belt.

"Shell." I set her away, but her fingers were still yanking on my belt buckle. "Butterfly, we can't."

She froze and looked up at me. "What?"

"Tank is here. He's dropping Glory off at Ripper's place, and then he'll be coming to the house. We don't have time right now."

She let out a frustrated growl, her nose wrinkling. Fuck but she was cute. And horny. Jesus! The woman couldn't seem to get enough. At twenty-one weeks pregnant, she seemed to have sex on her mind every second of the day. Thankfully, after a few orgasms, she usually fell asleep for an hour or two. I couldn't complain. I loved the fact she wanted me all the time, even if my dick could use a break every now and then. Her doctor had said it was just her hormones and the further along she got, the more it would taper off. Mostly because she'd be the size of a house and not feel up to it.

"Is he staying here?" she asked.

"I don't have a guest room set up right now, so no. Although, we probably should fix that, especially if you want him to bring Emmie and the girls sometime."

"We're having two babies," she reminded me. "We're going to need all the rooms upstairs that we've got."

"Then I'll make a guest suite of sorts out back. Something big enough for Tank and Emmie to have a bed, the girls to have a place to sleep, and a bathroom. Maybe a kitchenette."

She folded her arms. "With all that, they might as well have a house here."

I swatted her ass. "Watch the sass, butterfly. That love tap is nowhere near what you'll get if you keep it up."

I should have known better and kept my mouth shut. She lifted the hem of her dress and bent over, showing me her ass. Her very bare, not-wearing-panties, ass. Fuck me.

"Well?" she asked, wiggling her ass.

"You want the belt? Because I'm about to put a stripe across those white cheeks."

She gasped and looked at me over her shoulder. "You wouldn't!"

"Keep it up and see."

She lowered her dress and chewed on her bottom lip. "Maybe we could try it when Tank isn't going to be here? You never know. If you don't hit too hard with it, I might like it."

I adjusted myself, my dick going hard. "Behave."

She batted her eyes at me and grinned. Fuck it. I yanked a piece of paper from the drawer, scrawled a *come back in thirty* note on it, and taped it to the outside door. Then I locked up and carried my sassy wife upstairs to our room. I made quick work of stripping her bare and unfastening my pants, holding onto the belt.

"On the bed. Ass in the air." I made the belt snap in my hands and she hastened to obey.

No fucking way I'd take a chance on hurting her, so I gave her a light swat with the belt to see how she reacted. Not even hard enough to mark her skin. She tensed a moment but didn't so much as utter a sound. The next strike was a little harder. The one after left a pink mark across her ass and made her yelp.

"You going to sass me again?" I asked.

"Will you fuck the sass out of me if I do?"

I couldn't help but shake my head and laugh at her. Woman would be the death of me, but what a way to go. I spanked her with my hand until I felt the heat coming off her skin and it had pinked up nicely. Then I sank balls-deep inside her. I gripped a fistful of her hair and rode her hard.

"Yes! God, yes, don't stop!"

I leaned over her, bracing my weight and drove into her at a different angle. Her pussy gripped me tight as she screamed out my name. I felt the heat of her release and fought for control. I wasn't done with her. Not just yet.

I wrapped my arm around her waist and sat back on my knees, bringing her with me. Her ass settled on my lap, my cock still inside her. Reaching up to cup her breasts, I toyed with her nipples.

"Ride me, butterfly. Make us both come."

I tugged at her nipples and whispered filthy things in her ear. She became wild, slamming herself down, taking me deep. When she came a second time, I couldn't hold back anymore. I came inside her, holding her close.

She panted and looked at me over her shoulder. "I thought we didn't have time."

"I'm sure Tank is at the clubhouse drinking a beer. He'll be back."

She wiggled her ass and leaned back against me. "Is it wrong I wish we could stay like this? I love the way you feel inside me. Like we're two parts of one whole."

"We are, butterfly." I kissed her neck. "We are."

"I wish I'd never run away," she said softly. "Maybe we'd have been together all this time."

"Well, I did want to turn you over my knee a time or two when you were being a brat. It's possible that would have led us to where we are now."

"I do like it when you spank me."

I reached around and rubbed her clit. "I know."

"Oh. Oh! Talon, I..."

"When the babies get here, there's no sex until the doctor clears you. I'm going to wring as many orgasms from you as I can between now and then." I held her still, my arm clamped around her waist as I worked her clit. It only took a few seconds before she was coming again. "So fucking perfect."

"Not perfect," she murmured.

I placed my lips by her ear. "You are. You're perfect *for me*."

I'd never wanted a woman as much as I wanted Shella. I wanted her in my bed, sure, but I enjoyed the hell out of just spending time with her. Didn't matter if we were watching TV, eating dinner, or talking at the kitchen table. Every second with her was precious, and I looked forward to spending the rest of my life with her.

I placed a hand over her belly.

Her and our kids.

Patriot (Hades Abyss MC 6)

Harley Wylde

MaryAnne -- I was sixteen when I learned a hard lesson. No, it wasn't a lesson. It was worse. Kidnapped, tortured, abused in the worst of ways... I'd thought my life was over. Until the day my knight in shining armor came to save me. Patriot. Despite how scary he looks, he has to be the kindest man I've ever met. He not only rescues damsels in distress, but animals too. Under that hard exterior is a heart of gold. It doesn't matter that he's older than me. The more I get to know him, the harder I start to fall. But why would a man like him ever want someone like me? I'm dirty. Damaged. Broken beyond repair. Or am I? After all, Christmas is a time for miracles.

Patriot -- I've done my best to chase the fear and shadows from her eyes, show her she's safe. I've taken out nearly every man who ever hurt her, even if she doesn't know it. And the two who are still standing won't be for long. I want to see her smile. Make her laugh. What better time than Christmas to prove to her life is worth living? I'll make it the best she's ever had!

But there's only one thing I want under the tree this year... MaryAnne. She deserves better. I'm no angel. I've killed. Lied. Stolen. And worse. I tell myself repeatedly to keep my distance... until I can't. One taste and I know I'll never walk away. MaryAnne is mine! And if she won't listen to me, then maybe my whacky parrot can convince her. If there's one thing the African Grey excels at, it's talking when he shouldn't.

Prologue

MaryAnne -- 1 ½ Years Ago

"You'll be safe here," said the gruff biker as he handed me off to two orderlies.

The men gripped my arms and I tried not to fight them off. My skin crawled where they touched me. The Sadistic Saints kidnapped, tortured, and raped me before they sold me to a brothel. When my cousin's club, the Hades Abyss MC, found me, they assured me I'd be okay. I'd thought they were taking me to Sean, but instead I'd been brought here to The Dunbrooke Institute.

I couldn't speak. Inside, I was screaming for them not to leave me here. The men dragged me away and behind a secured door. I couldn't see the biker who'd brought me here, but I'd remember his name for a long time. *Brick*. I didn't think he meant to be cruel, but he'd abandoned me. I didn't like this place.

"Such a pretty little thing," one of the orderlies said, running his hand down my hair. "The doc is going to love her."

The other man chuckled. "I think we all will. Can't wait to have a taste."

No. No, no, no! I couldn't go through that again. I just couldn't.

I had no doubt what they meant. When they stripped me down and "helped" me shower, I knew I hadn't escaped hell. I'd only transferred to another level. These men would hurt me like the others had.

A man in a white lab coat stepped into the room before I'd been given clothes. I shivered, my arms wrapped around my torso. I felt exposed. Humiliated. And without hope. The man looked me over with a critical eye.

"What do we have?" the man asked.

"Seventeen-year-old girl, Dr. Jones. Some biker brought her here. Said he found her in a whorehouse."

A gleam lit the doctor's eyes. "Really? Well, then. It looks like we have ourselves a proven cash cow. Let's see how good she is."

One of the orderlies started stripping off his clothes, a leer on his face. I went hot, then ice cold. Fog crept across my brain and as he reached for me, his hand squeezing my ass, I went to the safe place inside my head. A dark room where I didn't feel pain and hopefully wouldn't remember all the vile things they did to me.

It was the only way I knew how to survive.

I didn't know how much time passed but I snapped back to reality when they submerged my body in icy water. I gasped and tried to claw my way out of the tub. They laughed and held me down, groping me.

"Oh, yeah. I'm going to like this one," one of them said.

"Leave her in the ice bath at least fifteen minutes," Dr. Jones said. "Then scrub her and put her in room 52K. I know exactly what we're going to do with patient 2763."

A number. They'd reduced me to a number.

What did it matter? MaryAnne Swenson had died the day the Sadistic Saints grabbed me and turned me into a whore. I was no one now. Nothing. A body for them to use as they saw fit. Maybe one day they'd kill me, then my suffering would be over. Until then, I'd escape inside my mind as often as I could.

Please, God. Send them back. Make them come get me. I can't stay here. I can't endure any more.

My prayers had gone unanswered for so long. I didn't think now would be any different. Yet somewhere deep inside, I still wanted someone to come rescue me. I'd already learned I couldn't save myself. Trying only caused more pain.

I only hoped if the Hades Abyss did return for me that there would still be some humanity left in me. I felt my mind slipping more and more every day. Soon, I'd only be a dried-up husk. Little more than a mindless puppet. If that happened, I hoped someone would end my suffering. I'd rather be dead than live like this another day.

* * *

Three Months Later

I'd been staying with Patriot for a few months now, and I still kept waiting for something bad to happen. No one had been mean to me, or tried to touch me since I'd come here. I wasn't sure I believed I was safe. Except with Patriot. He was the only one I trusted in this place. Even my cousin made me feel hesitant. It wasn't that I thought Sean would hurt me, but he'd changed and I didn't know this new version.

I stared at the pale yellow walls and delicate white curtains at the window. The room was soft and feminine, and a far cry from how it had looked when I first arrived. Patriot had worked hard to give me a place to call a safe haven. He'd painted the room himself and hung the curtains. I'd been too timid to ask for anything, so he'd also purchased bedding he thought I might like.

He'd treated me better than anyone ever had, even before I'd been kidnapped. I knew he probably wanted his home back. Even though he'd been unfailingly kind to me, I couldn't help but wonder if he only tolerated my presence. When I'd first arrived, Sean hadn't been in any sort of shape to take care of me, so Patriot had permitted me to stay with him. My cousin was back on his feet now, and yet I hadn't moved out.

I heard classic rock blaring out front and peered through my window down below. Patriot was on his back under the Bronco, his tools scattered around him and his jeans smeared with oil. I liked standing here, watching him. Maybe it made me a bit of a stalker, but there was something about him that drew me like a moth to a flame. I knew he was older than me, probably by quite a bit, but he was also handsome. I'd even go so far as to call him sexy, and I hadn't thought I'd ever feel that way about a man. Not after all I'd endured.

He slid out from under the Bronco and yanked his shirt over his head, tossing it aside. My breath caught at the perfection of his body. His arms and chest were inked and covered in muscle. The sun glinted on his reddish-brown hair, making it shine with copper tones. I sighed and wondered how he wasn't cold without his shirt. It was nearly December, and not exactly warm outside.

My phone rang, making me jump away from the window. I picked it up off the bed and saw it was my cousin.

"Hi, Sean." He growled softly and I winced. "Sorry. Galahad."

"It's been three months, MaryAnne. Last thing I need is you slipping up and calling me Sean in front of my brothers. It shows a lack of respect."

I sank to the floor, my back to the wall, and drew my knees to my chest. His tone of voice sent me back to a place I never wanted to go. My hand trembled as I held onto the phone. "Sorry. I didn't mean anything by it."

"I sometimes forget you're still a kid," he said. "Try to remember, okay? I'm not angry. Not really. You've been through hell and don't need me fussing at you."

The last thing I wanted was for anyone to call me a kid. I'd had to grow up fast after I'd been kidnapped. I'd met women ten years older than me who acted like they were still in high school.

"Why did you call?" I asked.

"Patriot isn't answering his phone. I needed to ask him something. Can you get him for me?"

I chewed on my lower lip. Yeah, I could technically walk out and hand my phone to him. I wasn't sure I was comfortable doing it. Taking a breath, I steadied my nerves and got up. Even though I had on fuzzy peppermint-striped socks that matched my red sweater and skinny jeans, I wasn't entirely sure I wanted to go out without shoes. Then again, it was the end of November in Mississippi. There was a chance it was in the seventies outside. I liked to be completely covered, head to toe, these days. Even having bare arms made me feel exposed.

I padded downstairs and went out the front door. The music was even louder as I approached Patriot. He'd slid back under the Bronco so that only his legs stuck out. I nudged his calf with my toes. His body went tight, and he slowly came out from under the vehicle. My throat went dry and my hand shook as I handed my phone to him. A frown marred his handsome face as he stood and took it.

"Who is this?" he demanded, keeping an eye on me. He listened a moment and his eyes narrowed. "What the fuck did you say to MaryAnne?"

I sucked in a breath. I'd noticed he was protective of me, but my heart always gave a little kick whenever he got that tone with someone. He didn't like it when anyone upset me, and it was only one of the reasons I'd started to fall a little in love with him. Except I'd recently turned seventeen and he was a grown man who could have any woman he wanted. Why would he want someone like me anyway? I knew he'd seen the videos of what happened at the hospital where they'd left me. Even if I ever felt I was ready to date, no one would ever want to touch me. Certainly no one who knew about my past, and I wasn't comfortable leaving the compound to start a new life elsewhere. It wasn't safe outside the gates.

He grunted and muttered something into the phone before disconnecting the call and handing the phone back to me. I took it and slipped it into my pocket, then shifted from foot to foot. He watched me, not moving or saying a word. Did he want me to leave? I backed up a step and he reached out, wrapping his fingers around my wrist only to release me just as quick.

"You have everything you need?" he asked.

I nodded, not trusting my voice.

"I'll be done out here in about a half hour. I'll need a shower, but when I'm done we can go grab a bite to eat. You feel up to going out somewhere?"

I hesitated. I loved spending time with him, but leaving the compound still frightened me a little. I knew they'd taken care of the rival club, and I'd heard the staff at the hospital were being picked off one by one. What I didn't know was whether or not I'd run into anyone who'd purchased time with me during my captivity. I wasn't sure I was brave enough to face any of those men.

Patriot moved a step closer and reached out, tugging a lock of my hair. "I'll keep you safe, Little Bit. Promise. No one will so much as breathe wrong in your direction. If they do, I'll gut them where they stand."

My lips twitched with a smile. I knew he'd do it too. He'd slammed the doctor against a concrete wall when he'd come to pick me up at the hospital. Granted, the man was a rapist and murderer. He'd deserved what he got and so much more.

"All right. I'll go."

He eyed me a moment, smiling when he saw my socks. "Not Christmas yet, MaryAnne."

"I like the bright colors. Makes me happy."

His gaze grew somber and he reached out slowly. His fingers skated over a lock of my hair. Anyone else tried to get this close, I'd have bolted. But Patriot wasn't just anyone. He'd saved me when no one else had bothered. I knew Titan, the President of the Hades Abyss Mississippi chapter, had sent him, but the way Patriot had knocked the doctor out and promised I'd be safe? It always made me swoon a little when I remembered how fierce he'd been. I'd been scared shitless at the time, but I knew now I could trust him with my life. Even then, I'd been drawn to him a little.

"I'll be okay," I said.

"I know you will." His lips quirked in a half-smile. "Strongest woman I know, Little Bit. Don't ever let anyone say different."

I didn't know how he could say such a thing. I wasn't strong. The men who'd taken me had nearly broken me. I might still be standing, but I didn't think I'd ever be close to the person I'd been before. That carefree girl was long gone. I'd seen the ugliness in the world, had it touch me, felt the darkness seeping into my soul. There were some things you didn't bounce back from.

No, I'd never be *that* MaryAnne again. I'd be someone new.

Chapter One

MaryAnne -- Present Day

I shifted from foot to foot as I stared at the clubhouse. Even though I was eighteen now, I knew I wasn't permitted inside. More for my safety than anything else. Well, that and I wasn't sure I wanted to see the club whores hanging on Patriot. I'd come to think of him as mine, and I hated the thought of him being with those women. He'd never given me even a hint that he might think of me as something other than a kid sister or pesky houseguest, but in my dreams, he belonged to me and I belonged to him.

I exhaled, my breath fogging the air. December in the south wasn't exactly freezing most of the time, but a cold snap had come through and it was now a chilly forty degrees outside. For a place that stayed over one hundred degrees in the summer, it might as well have been ten below zero. I clutched my leather jacket tighter and stomped my booted feet to warm up a little.

Music blasted from the building and I could hear the crowd inside. Not only was there a line of bikes across the front, but quite a few cars were parked in the lot too. I'd wanted to go to the clubhouse several times since Patriot had brought me here, to see what it looked like on a typical night, but I always chickened out. I knew they didn't want me inside, and Patriot would likely blow a gasket when he found out what I was about to do. This was the closest I'd come to actually going inside when a party was in full swing. I approached the building and put my hand to the door.

Come on, MaryAnne. Stop being a chicken.

I pushed my way inside and fought back a cough as I sucked in a lungful of smoke. I waved my hand in front of my face and surveyed the room. No one had noticed me yet. It wasn't like I was wearing a disguise. I went up to the bar and smiled at Riley. His eyebrows rose and he scanned the room before focusing on me again.

"Patriot know you're here?" he asked.

I sank my teeth into my bottom lip and shook my head. Was he going to make me leave? He looked around again, his muscles tensing. Riley took a step back and pulled a clear soda from one of the mini fridges, poured it into a glass, added grenadine and mixed it before he topped it with two cherries. He handed me the glass and I eyed it a moment.

"I'm not giving you alcohol," he said. "Why the hell did you come here tonight?"

I didn't know how to answer his question so I took a swallow of my drink and pretended I hadn't heard him. I felt heat along my back and a citrus scent filled my nose. I used the mirror behind the bar to see who it was and tried not to grimace when I saw Smoke practically on top of me. He braced an arm on the bar beside me and leaned in closer.

"Are you trying to piss off Patriot? Stop flirting with Riley and take your ass home."

My back straightened and I slowly turned my head to look at him. "I'm not here to flirt with Riley, or anyone else."

"Look around you, MaryAnne. What the fuck do you think women come here to do? Because it's not sit at the fucking bar drinking whatever the hell Riley gave you."

"It's a Shirley Temple," I said. At least, I thought that's what he'd made. I'd never looked up how you actually made one, but I'd read a book where the heroine only drank Shirley Temples.

"Girl, unless you want to be bent over a table and fucked, you need to leave."

I felt the blood drain from my face. A buzzing sound filled my ears and my hand shook, causing my drink to slosh all over the bar top. Riley cursed and leapt over it, heading into the crowd as darkness crept along the edges of my vision. I couldn't breathe. Everything started spinning, and I felt myself sway on the stool. It could have been seconds or minutes that passed. Time had no meaning.

I heard a door slam into the wall and everything around me went silent.

"What the fuck did you do?" Patriot roared.

I felt strong arms close around me and I cried out, tensing and clawing at whoever had grabbed me. Lips pressed close to my ear and the scent of leather and motor oil filled my nose, calming me a little.

"Easy, Little Bit. I've got you," Patriot said, his voice soft and low. "No one's going to hurt you."

"Fuck, man. I was only trying to get her to leave. I knew you'd be pissed to find her here," Smoke said. "She wouldn't listen to reason so I tried to scare her enough to send her running home."

"She was having a Goddamn panic attack. What did you say to her?" Patriot demanded.

"Nothing! Christ, I told her to look around, that women only came here for one reason. I knew she wasn't up for that. Hell, we all know it," Smoke said.

My heartrate slowed and I sucked in a lungful of air, then another. I leaned against Patriot as the world came into better focus and looked around. Riley was heading our way with Pretty Boy on his heels.

"I didn't know where you were," Riley said. "I went to the office and found Pretty Boy. The second she looked like she was going to pass out, I knew she needed to get out of here, but I didn't dare reach for her."

"And then I texted you because I knew you'd want to be here," Pretty Boy said.

Patriot turned me to face him and tipped my chin up. "What happened, Little Bit?"

"Nothing. I'm fine."

He narrowed his eyes. "You're not fucking fine. What did he say to you?"

Smoke started blustering but a quick glare from Patriot and Pretty Boy shut him up.

"He said staying meant being bent over a table and fucked." Saying the words made my hands clench and my stomach drop. I'd thought I'd healed, but maybe I was still every bit as broken as when Patriot had brought me here.

Patriot moved so fast, he was a blur as he spun away and landed a punch right across Smoke's jaw. Except he didn't stop. He went after him like a rabid beast. Pretty Boy, Brick, and Cache all tried to pull him off. It was like someone had flipped a switch inside him, and he wasn't going to stop until he'd made Smoke bleed all over the floors.

"Don't fucking talk to her again," Patriot said. "Don't even look at her."

Smoke worked his jaw back and forth, then spat blood on the floor. "Fine. But her ass has no business in the clubhouse on a night like this and you damn well know it. I was only trying to get her to fucking leave."

"She was sitting at the bar, that's it," Riley said in a subdued tone.

"I thought you were here," I said looking at Patriot. "I shouldn't have come. I thought... I thought I'd healed enough that I could handle walking in here, having a drink and... I don't know. But I was wrong. I'm not healed. I'm still broken."

A tear slipped down my cheek, then another.

Patriot wrapped his arms around me again. "No, you're not broken. You've come so far, MaryAnne. If you'd wanted to come to a party, even long enough to have a drink, you should have told me. I'd have brought you. We could have sat at a table or the bar together."

My cheeks warmed and I looked away, finding a spot on the wall rather fascinating. "You don't come here to babysit me."

Pretty Boy snorted. "He doesn't come here at all."

My gaze shot to him. "What?"

I felt Patriot tense, his arms tightened even more. It was a little like being hugged by a boa constrictor, except I knew he wasn't going to literally squeeze me to death. He didn't come to the clubhouse anymore? I'd thought the nights he left he'd come here to party, to be with the women I knew hung out with the club. If he hadn't been here all those times, then where had he gone?

Oh. My heart sank. It wasn't that he'd been leaving to party. He'd wanted time to himself. I'd invaded his house, a constant unwanted presence. He couldn't even be alone in his own home. I knew Sean didn't want me staying with him, but maybe I could figure something else out. I didn't have a job or money to rent a place in town, and I really didn't want to leave the compound.

"Whatever thought crossed your mind right now is probably the wrong conclusion," Pretty Boy said. "You look like someone killed your dog."

"Come on, Little Bit. Let's get you home," Patriot said, carrying me out of the clubhouse. I glanced at the door that still stood open and winced when I realized he'd slammed it so hard into the wall it had cracked the drywall.

I'd walked to the clubhouse since I didn't drive, and I'd planned to walk back. Patriot stopped at his bike, which I now realized hadn't been in the line of motorcycles in front of the clubhouse earlier. He'd left it in the middle of the lot when he'd come in to save me.

Patriot eased me down his body and swung his leg over the seat. "Get on, Little Bit."

I got onto the bike and placed my hands at his sides, gripping his leather cut. Patriot pried my fingers loose and pulled my arms around his waist until my hands settled over his belt buckle. My heart took off at a gallop and a weird feeling settled in the pit of my stomach. He took his time getting to the house, the motorcycle prowling the street at a near crawl. I wasn't sure if he was worried I'd been drinking and would fall off, or something was on his mind. Maybe he wasn't ready to go back home?

He pulled into the driveway and up under the carport. I got off the bike and backed up. When he shut off the engine, I felt like I should say something. He'd clearly had plans tonight, even if they hadn't included the party at the clubhouse. Didn't mean he hadn't been on a date. Oh, God. Was he seeing someone? Pain pierced me at the thought.

"You don't have to stay," I said. "I won't leave again."

At least, not until I'd packed and figured out where I was going. It was clear I was cramping his style and he needed some space. I backed up another step and kept going until I hit the side door. Patriot watched me, his gaze intent. I reached behind me for the knob and twisted it, letting myself into the house.

I'd no sooner shut the door than it flew open again. I whirled, my hand at my throat and pulse racing as I stared at him. Was he mad at me? Would he hurt me? He never had before, but I knew even the nicest looking man could have evil inside him.

"We need to have a talk, Little Bit," he said.

A small, gray puff ball raced into the room. Patriot hadn't named the little thing yet, but he'd rescued the kitten three weeks ago and now it seldom left his side. I'd noticed he had a tendency to bring home strays. Like me.

"If you needed your space, all you had to do was say so. I'll figure something out," I said.

He stalked forward, slamming the door shut behind him with a violent shove. I trembled, my feet rooted to the floor. It felt like my heart might pound out of my chest. He kept coming until his body pressed against mine. I took a step back, then another. He followed, matching my pace, until he'd backed me to the kitchen counter. He braced his arms on either side of me, leaning in close.

"Why the fuck do you think I want you out of this house?" he asked, his tone low and even with a hint of steel. "What have I ever done to make you think you're not welcome here?"

I licked my suddenly dry lips and forced myself to hold his gaze. "You needed time away from the house. Away from me. You shouldn't have to leave your home for some peace and quiet."

He closed his eyes, his nostrils flaring as he exhaled harshly. "Fuck."

The little kitten pawed at my feet and ankles before bounding around Patriot and then running from the room. I heard a bark and knew another of his strays hadn't liked being disturbed. For such a tough guy, he had a gentle touch when it came to injured animals. And people.

"I need a few days and I'll find a place to stay."

His eyes opened and he leaned in closer until his nose brushed against mine. My eyes nearly crossed, trying to hold his gaze. Before I knew what he was doing, his lips slammed against mine, his hand going to my hair. He grabbed a handful and held me still as he ravaged my mouth. I gripped the sides of his cut, holding on in case my legs gave out. It was my first real kiss, and it felt like I was floating, and burning at the same time.

He drew back, chest heaving, as he stared at me. My cheeks felt like they were on fire and my lips tingled. With anyone else, I'd have been terrified. But this was Patriot, the man who'd saved me, given me a place to live, taken care of me. And he'd kissed me.

"Fuck," he muttered again. "I shouldn't have done that."

He started to pull away, but I gripped him tighter and held on. My brain was foggy, and I wasn't sure I could speak yet. But I knew I didn't want him to go. I wasn't upset he'd kissed me. It was wonderful. *He* was wonderful.

"MaryAnne, I'm sorry. After everything you've been through, you don't need me taking advantage. Christ! I'm twelve years older than you." He ran a hand down his face and shook his head.

"Patriot, I didn't push you away, did I?"

"What are you saying, Little Bit?" he asked.

I felt my cheeks get warmer. "I liked it. I trust you, Patriot. There's no one else I'd want to kiss me."

"Ronan. Call me Ronan." He cupped my cheek. "If anyone should use my name, it's you. Maybe I'm a sick bastard for feeling this way, but there's always been something between us, a pull that I couldn't ignore anymore."

"Then don't. You said I'm not broken, so don't treat me like I am."

He pressed his lips to my forehead. "You deserve better than me, Little Bit."

"Why do you call me that?" I asked. "I'm not a child."

A smile ghosted across his lips. "It's not because of your age. You're a tiny little slip of a woman and seemed more like a phantom when I brought you here. Like a wisp."

"Wisp?" I asked.

"Will-o'-the-wisp. Little specters that roamed bogs and marshes. They appeared like little flickering flames. You reminded me of one. Here yet not, but I could see your fire hadn't burned out completely."

I smiled a little. "I can live with that."

Archimedes, a coon hound mix, barked as he chased the kitten. His nails scratched the floor as he raced by us. Patriot didn't even bat an eye at the chaos. The animals ran right back out and I heard a crash in the living room. Still he didn't budge.

"Why did you think I was at the clubhouse earlier?" he asked.

"I thought maybe you went there to hook-up with someone. I know the women there will sleep with anyone, or do anything you ask them to. You haven't brought anyone home since I came here." I shrugged.

"It seemed logical you would go there to have your needs met."

He slid his hand back and gripped my hair, tilting my head. "Let's get one thing straight, Little Bit. I haven't been with a woman in more than a year."

I felt my eyes go wide and he smirked at me. That meant... he'd been celibate since I'd come to live here? Even though he'd said he'd felt a pull toward me, I hadn't realized he'd given up women once I'd come here.

"Over a year?" I asked. I had a hard time believing a guy like him had gone so long without being with a woman.

"First time I went to the clubhouse after you came home with me, I had a club whore on her knees. The second she touched me, it felt wrong. I pushed her away. Haven't tried to be with anyone since."

"I was only seventeen," I said. "I would have never asked you to give up women. What if I'd panicked when you kissed me tonight? What if I could never give you what you want?"

"MaryAnne, I like spending time with you. Did I like kissing you? Hell yeah! And I'd love to do more, but only at your pace and when you're ready. Even if you'd never been able to give me more than your friendship, I'd have settled for that."

"You shouldn't have to," I said.

He kissed me again, soft and sweet. "I'll take whatever you can give me, Little Bit. I'm happy when I'm with you. Don't want anyone else."

His words made me melt a little and I cuddled closer to him, breathing in his scent. I made him happy? I smiled, realizing that what I'd been wanting was within my reach. The man I'd been falling for liked spending time with me, had kissed me, and wanted more.

Maybe he didn't see me as a stray he'd brought home, like all his wounded creatures, but I adored him every bit as much as they did.

Chapter Two

Patriot

I couldn't believe I'd kissed her! Or confessed that I'd wanted her for a while. Yeah, she'd been seventeen when I brought her here, and she'd needed to do a lot of healing, but even then I'd seen the beautiful woman she'd become. I would have never touched her when she was younger. It went against everything I believed in, but I hadn't lied about enjoying her company.

Whistling from the corner drew my attention. I grabbed a handful of sunflower seeds and added them to Hatter's bowl. The African Grey dove in, cracking open the seeds. "Mmm-mmm. So good."

I grinned at him. "You can have more later."

I focused on MaryAnne again. Having her in my arms was as close to heaven as I'd ever get. There was too much blood on my hands for me to ever stand before the pearly gates. I'd have to settle for having an angel in my life, the little wisp who had more power over me than she realized. I'd do anything for her. In fact, I had already. I knew there were times she felt like one of my critters. I'd seen the way she watched them and the looks she'd give me, wondering if I'd brought her home because she'd been wounded like them. Little did she know, she did have something in common with them. They were all survivors. All they needed -- fur, feathered, and human -- was a little love and a gentle touch.

Wizard and several of his hacker friends had managed to get the institute shut down, and they'd ruined the lives of the men and women who worked there. But it hadn't been enough for the savage beast lurking inside me. I'd wanted them to pay the ultimate price for what they'd done to my sweet MaryAnne.

I couldn't let her find out what I'd done. She was too good, too innocent even after all she'd suffered. There was light inside her. She'd thought she was broken, but they hadn't managed to destroy her. MaryAnne was stronger than she realized. I'd seen it the moment I carried her from that horrible place. If she only knew…

"You know what they did to me, what they made me do. And you still want me?" she asked, her voice nearly a whisper.

"None of that was your fault, Little Bit. What kind of man would I be if I held any of that against you? They victimized you, MaryAnne. Hurt you. Raped you. Tried to destroy you. But here you are, in my arms."

"I'm sorry I caused trouble at the clubhouse tonight."

"You didn't. Smoke should have kept his mouth shut. There was no harm in Riley giving you a drink at the bar. Everyone in the club knows not to touch you."

I'd be having words with Smoke later. Someone should have called to tell me MaryAnne was there. I'd have sat with her while she finished her drink and we'd have come home. It wouldn't have hurt anything for her to sit there for a bit. Unless seeing my brothers fucking the club whores would have been too much for her. She knew those women were there voluntarily, but it might have been a trigger for her.

"You should take a shower and get some sleep," I said.

MaryAnne nodded but held on tighter. Maybe one day she'd be in my bed, but I didn't see that happening yet. She'd responded to my kiss and hadn't regretted it. That was enough for now. A step in the right direction. I'd waited over a year for her. I could wait a few months more while she got used to being mine.

And yes, I was going to claim her. Hell, the club already knew how I felt. No one dared speak a cross word to her for fear I'd rip their spines out. I'd made it no secret she was under my protection. But more than that, they knew exactly why I'd stopped going to the clubhouse for the parties. I'd gotten some shit about it at first. It took a few months before they realized I was serious and backed off.

I lifted her into my arms and carried her upstairs. She didn't seem willing to release me anytime soon, but I could tell she was exhausted. I eased her down on the bed in her bedroom and helped her remove her jacket and boots. She looked so small. Defenseless. How any could have ever abused someone so sweet and innocent was beyond my comprehension. I knew evil was in the world, fought it all the damn time, but I hated that it had touched MaryAnne.

"The smoke from the clubhouse is clinging to you, Little Bit. Go wash off and get in bed. You've had a long day and I can tell you're tired."

She reached out her hand and I took it. "I don't want to be alone."

"I'll be down the hall like always."

MaryAnne shook her head. "No. That's too far. Please... hold me for a while? I know it's not fair to ask that of you, not when you want so much more, but I feel safe when I'm in your arms. I know you won't let anyone hurt me."

I nodded, knowing that while I might be giving her what she wanted, I'd enjoy the hell out of getting to hold her while she fell asleep. Might make me hard as a damn post, but I wouldn't make a move until I knew she was ready. Kissing her was one thing. Getting naked with her might be an issue.

"You're safe, MaryAnne. Take a shower. I'll be in my room when you're ready for bed. Just give me a shout down the hall."

I kissed her forehead and walked out.

When I got to my room, I pushed the door mostly shut and stripped out of my clothes, kicking my boots aside. She wasn't the only one who needed a shower. I set the water as hot as I could stand it, then stepped under the spray, letting my mind wander back to the first month she'd been in my house. The haunted look she'd had in her eyes, the way she'd flinched whenever someone got close. I'd been pissed as hell and decided to take my anger out on someone who deserved it.

Wizard had tracked down one of the orderlies who'd raped and tortured her. I shut my eyes and let the memory wash over me.

Bart Zimmer glared at me, his gaze full of hatred as he struggled against the duct tape holding him to the chair. There wasn't a point in taping his mouth shut. Besides, I was hoping he'd give me even more of an excuse to hurt him. Raping MaryAnne was enough reason for him to die, but I wanted to make him hurt first. Make him bleed.

I used the tip of my knife to clean my fingernails as I leaned against the table, ankles crossed and my posture as relaxed as I could make it. So far, he hadn't admitted shit, but it wouldn't take long to break him. I'd only been intimidating him so far. Once I started cutting, chopping off body parts, and having a bit of fun, he'd squeal like the pig he was.

"You ain't got shit on me," Bart said.

"That what you think? Let me guess. You're innocent of any wrongdoing. I've got the wrong man."

He nodded.

"Wrong. I saw the videos. I know exactly what you did to MaryAnne. Don't worry. You're the first, but you won't be the last. Every single man who dared to touch her will pay the ultimate price."

He paled a little and beads of sweat started to form on his brow. Good. Now he knew I meant business and he wasn't leaving this damn barn. Not alive at any rate.

"She screamed and begged for you to leave her alone. You got off on her pain and her fear. Now you get to see what it feels like. Except I won't be fucking you. Not my type. No, I have something else in mind." I moved as fast as a rattler, pressing down on his hand as I hacked off the index finger on his right hand. *"You didn't deserve to touch her."*

He screamed and begged for his life, pleaded with me to stop as I removed each of his fingers. I walked over to the burn barrel and lifted the hot poker. With a smile on my lips, I pressed the iron to his bleeding hand, cauterizing the wounds. Couldn't have him bleeding out before I was done with him.

The pussy passed out, so I waited. Gave him time to snap out of it. When I got tired of standing around, I tossed a bucket of icy water over his head, jolting him back to reality. The begging started again. Didn't matter. He could say whatever he wanted, promise me the entire world, and I wouldn't stop until he'd breathed his last. No one hurt Little Bit without paying for their sins.

Yeah, I was fucked. I already considered her mine, even if she was hands off and too damn young, and a little broken. If MaryAnne needed anything right now, it was a friend and a protector. I'd gladly take on both tasks. Making this asshole, and the others disappear, would ensure her safety. And if she ever asked about them, I'd let her know she had nothing to fear from them ever again.

I spent several hours removing pieces of Bart and keeping him from bleeding out. By the time I'd finished, I mostly had a pile of body parts and a torso to dispose of. I could have asked my brothers for help, but this was personal. I removed the corpse's hair and teeth, bagged it into five trash bags, and disposed of dear ol' Bart across several pig farms. Spreading him out, I knew the pigs would work through the remains in no time, leaving nothing behind.

A knock on the door brought me back to the present and I slicked my hair back from my face. Part of me wanted to tell her about the men I'd killed, let her know they'd never hurt her again. But I wasn't entirely sure how she'd react. She was a sweet girl, and I didn't know if she could handle the bloodshed, not to mention dismemberment, of my particular brand of justice.

"I'll be out in a minute," I yelled out. I finished my shower and quickly dried off, wrapping the towel around my waist. I hadn't thought to bring clothes into the bathroom with me.

I stepped into the bedroom and every muscle in my body locked up at the sight of MaryAnne sitting on the side of my bed. I'd thought she'd head back to her room to wait when she'd realized I was in the shower, but I'd been wrong. Her eyes went wide when she saw me wearing so little. I could go back in the bathroom and shut the door, ask her to leave, then come get my clothes. Or I could act like it wasn't a huge deal.

I decided to go with option two and went over to the dresser, pulled out a pair of sweatpants and slid them up my legs under the towel. Any other woman, I'd have dropped the towel to put them on. Last thing I wanted to do was scare MaryAnne. She'd seen me shirtless plenty of times, so I didn't bother pulling out a T-shirt. I knelt at her feet and reached for her clasped hands, enfolding them in mine.

Her pink pajamas were covered in kittens and coffee cups, and she had fuzzy pink socks on her feet. I fought back a smile at how damn adorable she was. The thermal top and stretchy pants didn't exactly hide her curves. Even covered from her collarbones to her ankles, she managed to be sexy without trying. I wouldn't tell her that. Not yet anyway. I'd noticed from the beginning, even in the heat of summer, she tried to cover as much of herself as she could.

"You ready to go lie down?" I asked.

"Can I stay in here with you tonight?"

Fuck. I couldn't exactly tell her no, but having her pressed up against me all night was going to give me a wicked case of blue balls. But for MaryAnne, I'd endure it. Nothing was more important to me than her well-being. If she needed to hold onto me tonight like a safety blanket, then so be it. I'd keep it to myself how much I would enjoy having her in my arms.

"Sure. You can stay here. Let me pull the covers down and you can get into bed. I want to do a walk-through downstairs before I call it a night. Need to put the animals to bed too."

I pressed a kiss to the top of her head, tugged the covers down, then walked out of the room. I went room by room on the first floor, making sure the windows and doors were locked. Before MaryAnne, I'd left everything unlocked all the time. Now that I had someone precious under my roof, I wasn't about to take any chances. Too much bad shit had happened over the years for me to think no one could slip past our defenses.

Once I knew the house was secure, had put the dog in his kennel, made sure the kitten had everything he needed, and covered the parrot's cage, I made my way upstairs. MaryAnne had remained on the edge of the bed but she stood as I entered the room. I shut the door and slowly moved closer, fearing if I moved too fast it would scare her. I motioned for her to slide into bed. She settled near the center of the bed, and I couldn't hold back my smile. Looked like she meant to stick close, and I was all right with that.

I flicked off the light and got into bed, pulling her into my arms. She snuggled close, her breath ghosting across my bare chest. A tension I hadn't realized I'd even felt suddenly released. Her scent filling my nose, her warmth pressing up against me, gave me a feeling of peace. It was like she was finally where she belonged.

"Do you think you'll kiss me again sometime?" she asked.

"I guess it depends. Do you want me to?"

She nodded. "I liked it. I've never felt that way before."

I tightened my hold on her and wished I could erase the past few years for her. I wondered what she'd been like before the Sadistic Saints had gotten their hands on her. Did she smile more? Had she been outgoing? I'd noticed she wasn't only quiet, but she had a tendency to try and blend into the background. It was like she wanted to be invisible.

I'd give anything to see her stop hiding from the world. I'd taken out most of the men from the hospital, and the club had already erased the Sadistic Saints from existence. Still, there were a few out there I hadn't been able to pin down yet. Not to mention the men they'd allowed to hurt my Little Bit, the ones who had paid for the use of her body. Wizard had tracked down anyone who'd been caught on camera, or left a paper trail. There was no way of knowing if there were others.

"I'll kiss you anytime you want. All you have to do is ask."

She lifted her face, her eyes wide. "Even now?"

I leaned in closer, my nose brushing hers. "You want a kiss right now?"

"Yes," she whispered.

I pressed my lips to hers, trying to keep things somewhat chaste. I wanted to devour her, to touch every inch of her body, but I held back. She wasn't ready for that yet. Might never be ready. I drew back and she gave a soft sigh.

"Such a sweet little angel," I murmured. "I think kissing you is my new favorite thing to do." Even in the darkness, I saw her cheeks flush.

"Maybe you should kiss me whenever you want?"

"Little Bit, don't even offer me that. I'd be kissing you all the time."

She was quiet a moment, then sighed again. "I think I might like that."

Well, fuck me. She wasn't supposed to agree with me. Now what the hell was I going to do? She didn't know what she was asking. If I kissed her any time I wanted, we'd never come up for air. Never tasted anything so sweet as MaryAnne.

Instead of responding, I kissed her again. Longer. Hotter. Wetter.

Yeah, I was fucked.

Chapter Three

MaryAnne

I heard a giggle outside and cautiously approached the living room window. Patriot had insisted on finishing his work on the Bronco today. I'd left him to it, but as I peered outside, I saw one of the club whores leaning against the car. Despite the fact her breath was frosting the air, she had a skirt so short if she bent over Patriot wouldn't have to wonder about what color her panties were. Assuming she wore any. She looked like the type who might go commando.

She flipped her blonde hair over her shoulder and giggled again at something he said. My hands curled into fists, my nails biting into my palms. *He's not yours. He can date or flirt with whomever he wants.* Or was he mine? He'd kissed me several times last night. Even said he hadn't been with anyone since I'd come to live with him. That had to mean something, didn't it?

The kettle whistled in the kitchen and I rushed to shut off the burner. I had two mugs on the counter with some cocoa mix. It wasn't as good as making it with milk and melted chocolate, but it was better than nothing. I filled the mugs and stirred them before topping each with a handful of marshmallows. I set them on the kitchen table.

I looked around the room as I took a deep breath. The dog and kitten dozed on a bed in the corner, and the bird eyed me. Probably wondered if I was going to give him a treat. He seemed to have Patriot wrapped around his feathers. *You're stalling.*

Gathering my courage, I went out to the front porch, folding my arms across my stomach to keep from shivering. My green fuzzy sweater was soft, but it wasn't doing much to keep out the frigid air.

"Patriot, the hot cocoa is ready," I called out.

He flashed me a smile. I went down the steps, thankful the ground was dry since I was only wearing socks. Green ones with little elves on them. Christmas had once been my favorite time of year. Last year, I'd tried to wear cheerful things in hopes they would make me smile. It only half worked. As I healed, I was finding joy in more things again. Like the holidays. I'd even carved a pumpkin this past Halloween. It hadn't looked all that amazing, but I'd had fun, and Patriot had made sure he lit the candle inside it every night. Until it had rotted and had to be tossed out.

"The grown-ups are talking," the blonde said, narrowing her gaze in my direction.

Patriot reached over, gripped my folded arms and tugged me against his body. He lowered his head and pressed a kiss to my lips. When his tongue flicked my bottom lip and I opened for him, he deepened the kiss, and I heard the blonde's shriek of outrage. As a fire settled in my belly, the world fell away. It felt like I was tumbling head over heels. Freefalling. Patriot gently bit my lip and drew back, a slight smile curving his lips.

Something cold and wet hit my face, my eyes going wide as whatever it was slid down my cheek under the neckline of my sweater. Patriot slowly turned to face the woman, fury blazing in his eyes.

"You have to the count of three to apologize to her and get the fuck out of my sight," he said.

The blonde folded her arms and tipped up her chin at a stubborn angle. "No. I won't stand here and watch you kiss her when we were having a conversation."

Patriot took a step and then another, his body nearly shaking with anger. When he reached her, he gripped her arm so tight she winced and tried to pull away. Patriot shook her like a rag doll.

"I don't owe you a damn thing. You're a fucking club whore. Easy pussy. I didn't invite you to my fucking house, and I damn sure won't let you insult MaryAnne."

I tugged my sweater away from my body and realized she'd thrown a slushie at me. Who the hell drank an icy beverage in the winter? I heard the pipes of a bike approaching and looked down the road. A slight smile spread across my lips when I realized it was Sean. No, Galahad. I didn't know how long it would take me to remember he had a new name. I'd been here long enough to learn it by now.

He came to a stop at the bottom of the driveway, eying Patriot and the club whore before his gaze swung over to me. It only took him a moment to figure out what happened, or at least the part where she'd thrown her drink at me. My cousin got off his bike and approached Patriot.

"Why the fuck is my cousin wearing your drink?" he asked the club whore.

She simpered and batted her eyelashes at him. Did that sort of thing really work? I'd always assumed it was a Hollywood thing only done in movies and on TV. When my cousin didn't relax even a little, and Patriot didn't seem to calm down either, I realized her antics weren't working on them.

"Bitch got mad I wasn't paying her enough attention when MaryAnne came out," Patriot said.

"He kissed her while he was talking to me!" The blonde stomped her foot and huffed out a breath. I hadn't seen her around before and wondered if she was new. It wasn't that I hung out with the club whores, or saw them much, but there were a few who tried to win over the bikers by cleaning up or offering to do laundry. But this one I hadn't seen around before, not even coming or going from the clubhouse.

Sean looked at Patriot and they seemed to do that silent communication thing I'd noticed most of the club seemed to do. Even the old ladies had their own version. I didn't think I'd ever be able to look at someone and talk to them without words.

"She needs to apologize to her," Patriot said.

"He called me easy pussy." The blonde looked spitting mad.

Sean snorted. "You are. A club whore is only good for spreading her legs, not running her damn mouth. You keep opening that pie hole and someone around here might shove something in there."

I pressed my lips together so I wouldn't laugh. She looked absolutely gobsmacked that he'd said such a thing to her. Anyone else and I've have been offended for them, and outraged. But Patriot had explained about the club whores and assured me they were there of their own free will. I knew she'd chosen this way of life, even if it did seem like she was here to land a permanent spot in Patriot's bed. How many of the others were hoping to end up with one of the bikers? All of them?

I almost felt sorry for them.

"She doesn't have to apologize," I said.

"Yes, she does," Patriot said, a little growl to his voice. "She insulted you. She's a fucking club whore and you're..."

"I'm what?" I asked. "Your unwanted houseguest? Galahad's cousin? I know you said you haven't been with anyone, and you kissed me, but... I don't know what exactly that means."

"You're mine," Patriot said, not even looking my way.

My heart flipped, then flopped as my stomach dropped to my toes. His? He thought I was his? Sure, we'd kissed a few times now. I'd slept in his arms. But... his? I glanced at my cousin, but he didn't seem the least bit surprised. Did the entire club know he thought I belonged to him?

The club whore squeaked as he gave her another rough shake. "Apologize now!"

"I'm sorry!" She struggled to break free. "I didn't know you had an old lady. I'm sorry and I won't do it again."

Patriot released her with a slight shove that sent her sprawling on her ass. Sean snickered and walked past her, not even offering to help her up. Both men approached me, and I felt like a deer being hunted by wolves. The urge to run was strong, but I held my ground.

"Yours?" I asked softly.

"I've been giving you time to heal," Patriot said. "And you can still take all the time you want, Little Bit. I haven't wanted another woman since you moved into my house, and I don't see that changing anytime soon. But yeah, you're mine and everyone around here knows it. If they don't, they're fucking stupid."

I wasn't sure what to say, so I decided to set all that aside for later. "The hot chocolate is cold by now."

His lips twitched like he was fighting not to smile. "Guess we'd better make more, right after you shower and change."

I nodded and hurried into the house, Patriot and Galahad on my heels. I went upstairs and grabbed a clean set of clothes in my bedroom before using the hall bathroom to rinse off and change. Thankfully, it hadn't gotten in my hair. I pulled the long tresses up into a messy knot on the top of my head while the shower warmed. When steam billowed out, I stepped under the spray and washed the sticky drink off my skin.

I tried to hurry, knowing both Patriot and Galahad were downstairs. I didn't know if my cousin had come to see me or Patriot, but I didn't want to miss his visit either way. After I dried off, I pulled on a soft red sweater. I paired it with green leggings that had a Santa print all over them, and my candy cane-striped fuzzy socks. I left my hair up, and briefly lamented my lack of makeup. I hadn't wanted any since Patriot had rescued me, but after seeing the way the club whores dressed and looked, I wouldn't have minded a little blush or lip gloss.

Then again, Patriot seemed to like me the way I was so maybe I didn't need any.

Archimedes must have followed me. He sprawled across the top of the stairs, watching the bathroom door as if he'd been waiting for me. I knew animals were sensitive and wondered if he'd felt the tension outside. I stopped a moment to scratch behind his ear. "Such a good boy."

He panted and stood. Hurrying down the stairs, I heard Patriot bellow from the kitchen. "Slow the fuck down, Little Bit, before you fall and bust your ass."

My cheeks flushed as I remembered the first time I'd raced down the stairs. My feet had gone out from under me and I'd slid the rest of the way down on my butt. I'd been bruised and sore for a few days, but mostly my pride had been hurt.

When I entered the kitchen, Patriot had three steaming cups on the table, and Galahad had already taken a seat. I picked up the bag of marshmallows on the counter and added extra to my cup before taking a seat. Patriot pulled out the chair between Sean and me, then sprawled in a way that I'd always found to be both casual and sexy. I didn't think he intended to make me drool a little.

"You know you need to officially claim her," Galahad said. "We may all know she's yours, but if you want her to have a property cut it has to go to the table."

Patriot flipped him off. "I've been in this club a lot longer than you, runt. I think I know how shit works. I was trying to give your cousin more time. If that fucking whore hadn't disrespected her, I wouldn't have said anything yet."

"I don't need time," I said, surprising both them and myself. "I mean, I don't know if I'm ready for… everything, but I liked being called yours. If there's anyone I trust, it's you, Patriot."

Two years ago, even one year ago, I'd have said I never wanted a man to touch me, much less kiss me or do anything else. But with Patriot, I wanted to be whole again. I wanted to be the kind of woman who greeted him with a kiss when he came home, the type who didn't only sleep in his arms all night but was ready for anything. I didn't know how I'd react if he tried to strip me naked and touch me. I could freak out, but I wouldn't know if I never tried. If anyone could get that close without sending me into a panic attack, it would be Patriot.

"You want me to make it official?" he asked. "Or do you want more time? Because I will wait as long as you need me to, Little Bit. I'd wait an eternity for you."

My heart melted at his words and I held back a sigh. He could be the sweetest man ever. Of course, I'd also seen him knock a man unconscious. Patriot had a protective streak a mild wide, at least when it came to me. How could I not love him?

"If you're sure you want to keep me, then you can make it official. I don't want you to find out that I'm more broken than you realized and regret your decision later."

He narrowed his eyes a moment, then glanced at Galahad. "Out. I need to have a conversation with your cousin, and you don't want to be here for it."

Sean didn't have to be told twice. He downed his cocoa and took off, the front door slamming in his wake. I fidgeted in my seat.

"I'm trying to be logical," I said. "It's not fair to you. If I can't give you what you want, what you need, then I don't want to be hanging around your neck like an albatross the rest of our lives. You deserve to be happy, Ronan."

"We already went over this. *You* make me happy, MaryAnne. I don't want anyone else. It doesn't matter if you never let me kiss you again, or if we never have sex. I like spending time with you, sharing my home with you. You've become my best friend since I brought you here."

"We can be friends without you claiming me," I pointed out.

"Do you not want me?" he asked. "Is that it? You don't want to belong to me? Because if that's the case, say so and I'll drop it. I'm not going to force you to do anything, MaryAnne. I'm sure as hell not going to make you be my old lady if it's not something you want."

"I do want that, more than anything, I'm just… just scared," I finished softly. "I don't want to disappoint you, Ronan. You mean everything to me, and I never want to be the one to cause you pain."

He leaned closer and kissed me, his lips whisper soft against mine. "Let me worry about the kind of pain I can handle, Little Bit. There's nothing you could say or do to me that would hurt worse than not having you in my life."

He deserved better than me, but I wasn't strong enough to push him away. I wanted to be with him every bit as much as he wanted to be with me. I wasn't sure it was in the same way. Yes, I wanted to know what it would feel like for him to touch me, wanted to see if I could handle being intimate with him. But I was also terrified that I'd fall apart, or worse. I didn't want to see pity in his eyes. I could handle a lot, but not that.

It was on the tip of my tongue to tell him how I felt, that I was falling fast and hard for him. Yet I held back. One day I'd say the words. When I felt stronger, less broken, and more certain of where I stood. He'd said he would claim me, make me his officially, but until I knew I could give him everything he needed and wanted, I'd forgo any confessions.

Chapter Four

Patriot

Christmas was getting closer. A permanent chill had settled in the air, and our small town had decorations up on Main Street. Most of the homes were strung with lights, and the shops were overflowing with people buying presents. I'd always preferred to do any shopping online, but this year was different. MaryAnne was going to be mine, my old lady, and I wanted to make this Christmas special.

Which was why I found myself at the mall three weeks before the holiday. The place was packed, and everyone was out for themselves. I'd watched two women who had to be at least eighty bicker over a sweater. Two men in the tool section had nearly come to blows over a socket wrench. It was like everyone had lost what little sense they'd had. Only good news was that most people gave me a wide berth.

I'd managed to buy MaryAnne a pink scarf and a matching peacoat, a silver bracelet with a heart charm, and a tablet with an SD card I'd been assured would hold thousands of books. The woman loved to read, and I was all for her finding pleasure wherever she could. As long as it wasn't with another man. I'd probably bought more than enough. Except last Christmas, I hadn't known her very well so I'd picked stuff like bubble bath, nail polish, and hair stuff. Or rather, I'd let Phoebe pick out those things, then I'd wrapped them and stuck them under the small tree.

Now that I knew how much she loved Christmas, I was determined to make this one the best she'd ever had. A six-foot tree was being delivered later tonight, and I'd picked up some lights and ornaments. An electronics shop caught my eye and I paused to check out the display. It gave me an idea. Several, in fact.

I stepped inside and went over to the counter. The man gave me a wary look, but didn't seem overly hostile. I was used to everyone assuming I was a criminal since I belonged to the Hades Abyss MC. They saw bikers wearing cuts with patches and figured we were all rapists and murderers. Granted, I'd slaughtered the men who'd hurt MaryAnne, and I'd gladly do it again, but I only took out the trash. Hell, I'd served my country and followed the rules for quite a while. I'd also learned sometimes those who deserved to burn were allowed to walk away. Now, I made sure those assholes paid the price for their crimes.

"How much for that one?" I asked, pointing to a small purple camera. He quoted me a price that seemed fair, so I paid for it and added it to the sacks in my hand. After several more stores in the mall, and a big box store on the way home, I'd made a dent in my bank account and hopefully guaranteed MaryAnne had a wonderful Christmas.

Hell, I'd even stopped at the pet store and bought a bag of treats and a bone for Archimedes, a new toy and some treats for Hatter, and a few toys for the kitten. Everyone in the house would have a gift.

Wrapping everything was another matter, and I didn't know where to hide it all where she wouldn't find it. So I stopped at Titan's house when I reached the compound. I knocked on his door and smiled when Delilah answered.

"I need a favor," I said. "I went shopping for Christmas gifts, except I don't have anywhere to hide them at home, and no idea how to wrap anything so that it doesn't look like it was mangled by a rabid badger."

She snorted, then laughed. "Bring it in. I went a bit overboard buying wrapping paper and bags, so I should have enough to take care of it. If not, I'll ask Titan to pick up a few more rolls."

"I heard that," the Pres yelled from somewhere inside the house. "I'm not buying another damn roll of Christmas paper. Make Patriot get his own shit. Fuck! Delilah, your son puked all over me, the couch, and the floor!"

I tried really damn hard not to laugh, but a snicker might have slipped out. Ever since Titan's son, Walker, had been born, the Pres had been a little out of sorts. It was clear he adored the kid, but he didn't handle puke well, and little Walker had a tendency to only throw up on his daddy. I personally thought it was hysterical. Although, the last time I'd laughed when it happened, Titan had smeared the puke on my cheek, which only made *me* throw up.

Delilah rolled her eyes and sighed. "Bring your stuff in and set it in the living room. If you happen to buy any wrapping paper in the next day or two, I'll gladly take another few rolls. If I don't use them this year, there's always next Christmas."

She walked off, presumably to save Titan from their kid, and I started hauling MaryAnne's presents into their house. When I'd finished, I shut their front door and headed home. Seeing exactly how much I'd bought for MaryAnne made me realize she'd probably want to do some shopping of her own, but I also knew she wouldn't take money from me outright. I'd have to be sneaky about it.

I sent Galahad a message. *If I give you an envelope of cash, will you give it to MaryAnne?*

He responded almost immediately. *Why can't you give it to her?*

Because I don't want her to know it's from me. She probably will want to shop for Christmas presents.

I got a thumbs-up in response and shoved my phone into my pocket before I went into my house. I didn't know exactly how much cash I had stashed in the small safe in my closet, but I knew I had at least a few thousand in there. I'd put a few hundred in an envelope and have Galahad give it to MaryAnne. She'd accept it from him easier since they were blood, even if he had been a dick to her on occasion.

I heard Christmas music playing when I walked in the door and smelled something sweet coming from the kitchen. I followed my nose and paused in the doorway, smiling as I saw MaryAnne dancing around the kitchen as she mixed something in a bowl. The kitten rolled on the floor with a paper towel, trying to shred it, while Archimedes stood at MaryAnne's side, eyeing the stove. *Jingle Bell Rock* played from the radio on the counter, and MaryAnne sang along. Even Hatter whistled a bit while he bobbed his head. Too fucking cute!

Her red sweater had reindeer covering it in a small print, and her dark jeans hugged her legs. She had another fuzzy pair of socks on that were red with white snowflakes. I'd never seen her happier than I had this holiday season. Her first Christmas here, I'd tried to make it special without going over the top. I'd gotten some smiles from her, but this year was different. She'd healed more and seemed less scared. Although, she still didn't venture outside the compound very often.

She poured the contents of the bowl into a pan, then rinsed the dish in the sink, completely oblivious to the fact I was watching her. The music was just loud enough she probably hadn't heard the front door. She shook her hips side to side as the song switched to *Last Christmas*. I loved seeing her like this, so carefree. She'd come a long way since I'd pulled her from the mental hospital.

"What are you making?" I asked, moving farther into the room.

She shrieked and dropped the mixing spoon, spinning to face me. "You scared me!"

Archimedes barked at me before pressing against MaryAnne's legs. Yeah, it seemed my woman had him wrapped around her finger too. She'd had me on my knees, ready to do anything for her, the moment I'd brought her home. She reached down and patted his head, and my heart warmed at the gesture. My rescues loved her, and she loved them back. I typically didn't keep the animals I brought home and tended while they healed, but this crew hadn't wanted to go anywhere.

"Sorry, Little Bit." I went to her, wrapping my arm around her waist and tugging her against me. I gave her a slow kiss, my lips brushing hers. "What's the occasion for all the baking?"

"I enjoy it. I know we can't eat all this, but I thought you could take some of it to the clubhouse for the single guys. I'm sure Phoebe and Delilah are making stuff for Kraken and Titan. And I'll give some to Galahad, since he's family. Well, blood-related family."

I pressed my nose to her hair and breathed her in. "You're such a sweetheart. I'm sure they'll love anything you want to send over."

"Have you..." She stopped and drew back a little. "Did you talk to the club about claiming me? Is that where you were?"

Shit. I hadn't thought to tell her I was going to the mall. I hadn't exactly wanted her to know I was buying presents for her. In the past, I'd never told her where I was going. Only that I'd be gone for a bit. But things had changed between us. She wasn't just staying in my house anymore.

"No, the club hasn't had Church yet. I went shopping for some presents." I kissed her forehead.

"Presents?" Her eyes went wide. "But I haven't gotten you anything!"

I cupped her cheek. "You're my gift, MaryAnne. But if you want to go shopping, you could always ask Phoebe or Delilah, or maybe check with your cousin. I don't want you going out alone."

"No worries. I don't want to leave unless either you or about four other Hades Abyss guys are with me. Even then, I'll be looking over my shoulder the entire time." Her lips twisted. "Guess I'm not that brave yet. The kitten seems to have more courage than me."

The floof in question was pouncing on Archimedes and biting at his ears. The coon mix gave an aggrieved sigh, but didn't try to retaliate. One swat with a paw, the kitten would go sailing. It wasn't more than eight weeks old and barely weighed two pounds.

"Little Bit, after all you've been through, you have every right to be overly cautious. Not a single person here will blame you for wanting extra protection when you leave the compound."

She pointed to the counter. "I have two tins of brownies and two of cookies ready to go. I also have a cake I was about to put into the oven, and there's another batch of brownies cooking too."

When she'd moved in, I'd been in the process of renovating my kitchen. With the thought of a family in the future, I'd put in a double oven. Of course, I'd have to tell her about my issue and inability to get her pregnant the normal way, but we'd cross that bridge when the time came. I'd only thought of the double oven because Phoebe had asked Kraken for one, and I'd figured my woman might enjoy having the same thing. I'd also purchased more appliances the last year than ever before. There was a toaster oven on the counter and a crock pot in the pantry, as well as anything else MaryAnne had mentioned would be nice to have.

"I have a live tree being delivered in the next hour. Think you'll be done baking in time to help me string lights and decorate?" I asked.

Her face lit up and she smiled so wide her cheeks had to hurt. "I can't wait!"

I kissed her again, then left her to her baking. While she finished up in the kitchen, I organized the ornaments and lights in the living room and shot off a text to Riley.

Pick up some wrapping paper and drop it by Titan's house.

I saw he'd read my message and knew it would get done. Riley had proven himself to be reliable, so far. I had a feeling both him and Morgan would be patching in before long. I didn't see the vote going any other way.

I hadn't thought to pick up any other decorations, or lights for the outside. I wondered if MaryAnne would want those things. As into the Christmas spirit as she seemed to be, I should have thought to bring home more stuff. Pulling my phone back out, I shot off another message to Riley.

Bring outside Christmas lights to my house, and clips to hang them.

I got a thumbs-up emoji which had me shaking my head. It bugged the shit out of me when they didn't respond with actual sentences, and everyone in the club knew it. I sometimes thought they sent some mix of emojis and broken sentences to aggravate me.

There was a knock at the door, and I opened it right as MaryAnne came out of the kitchen, wiping her hands on a towel. Morgan and Cache stood on the other side, my tree on the ground behind them.

"Where do you want this, Patriot?" Cache asked.

"Living room. There's an empty corner where I think it will fit."

They hauled it inside and I grabbed the base from my Bronco. I hadn't thought to bring it in yet. While they got the tree into the base and situated into the corner, I showed MaryAnne the different ornaments I'd picked up. They weren't anything fancy, but I'd hoped she'd like them. There were times she had a childlike wonder about her, so I'd grabbed a bunch of little animals, as well as the usual Christmas characters like Santa, the Grinch, and Frosty. The tree was going to be a hodgepodge of things, but I'd never understood those fancy trees where everything matched.

"They're perfect," MaryAnne said, leaning against my arm.

"We can always pick out more. This is your tree as much as it's mine. You should get to decide what we hang on it."

She brushed a kiss against my cheek and started digging through everything.

Cache cleared his throat. "Um, Patriot, you want us to help string the lights?"

I glanced at MaryAnne and realized as short as she was, she probably wouldn't be much help getting the lights around the fat tree. I'd picked one that was close to my height, but the base was easily two of me. It definitely would take more than one person to get the lights on it.

"Go ahead," I said, tossing them the boxes of lights. "Use all of them."

Morgan's eyebrows lifted. "There's about eight hundred lights here. Are you trying to spot the tree from the moon?"

MaryAnne snickered and I thought the humor in her eyes and the smile on her lips were the most beautiful sight I'd ever seen. She hadn't had much reason to smile over the last couple years, but I'd made it my goal to keep her as happy as I could. She deserved the best in life, and while I didn't kid myself by thinking I was the best, I did know I'd do anything for her. Even kill for her, which I'd done several times.

"String the damn lights, Prospect," I said with a bit of a growl.

"Aye, aye!" Morgan saluted and I couldn't contain my snort.

"I was in the Army, asshole. Not the fucking Navy."

Cache punched Morgan in the arm, and they got to work stringing the lights on the tree. The kitten had charged into the living room and now eyed the tree like it was his greatest challenge. I had a feeling I'd be pulling him from the branches until I threw the tree out. Good thing most of the ornaments I'd bought weren't breakable.

"We're missing something," I said. "Wait right here."

She cast me a nervous look before glancing at the two Prospects. I hurried from the room, knowing they wouldn't hurt her, and grabbed the radio from the kitchen. Archimedes lumbered after me, probably deciding he didn't want to be left out. He flopped in front of the couch and huffed as he laid his head on his paws. I plugged the radio in near the couch and Christmas songs filled the air.

"Can't decorate a tree without setting the mood," I said.

She moved closer and reached out, wrapping her hand around my arm. I felt the way she trembled and hated that she didn't feel safe in our own home. Cache and Morgan had always been careful around her. Hell, the entire club had walked on eggshells whenever MaryAnne was present, but it wasn't enough.

I leaned in closer and dropped my voice so only she would hear me. "They won't hurt you, Little Bit. You're safe here, even when I'm not in the room."

"Sorry," she mumbled.

"You don't have to apologize. I wish you felt safe. I'll do whatever it takes to ensure no one ever hurts you again."

She nodded and reached for the ornaments again. I kissed the top of her head. When the Prospects were finished, I stepped out front for a cigarette. I'd technically quit, but there were times I still indulged. As I blew the smoke out, I thought about all the men who'd hurt my sweet MaryAnne.

"Kurt Timms, do you know why you're here?" I asked.

He tightened his lips and stared at me, hatred blazing in his eyes. I slid the blade of the knife along his thigh, leaving a trail of blood. He screamed and thrashed in the chair. The duct tape I'd used to hold him down didn't give an inch.

"She's a little whore. The doctor said so! Said some club had used her up."

Wrong answer. I slammed the knife down into his thigh and twisted it. I yanked it free and worked on carving "rapist" into his chest. Kurt blubbered like a damn baby.

"She screamed. Begged. Pleaded with you not to hurt her." *I sliced a chunk of skin from over his ribs.* "I saw the videos. You knew damn well what you were doing, that she didn't want you to touch her. I also saw you get off on causing her pain, humiliating her."

I reached for the branding iron. It had three bars, a throwback to an old ranch in the area. Once it was nice and hot, I used it to mark the asshole's face. It burned through the flesh of his cheek.

When I'd finished with him, no one would ever recognize him. His teeth were gone, as were his hair and nails. Any tattoos had been burned off. I bagged him up and disposed of the body.

I pulled my phone from my pocket and pulled up my list. Using my finger, I marked off the name Kurt Timms. One by one, I'd take the fuckers out. Maybe after they were gone, MaryAnne's nightmares would be too.

I tossed my cigarette onto the ground and stomped it out with my boot. I went back inside and ran upstairs to brush my teeth and spray on some cologne, knowing from past experience that MaryAnne would have a flashback of some sort if she smelled the cigarette on my breath or clothes. It was a large part of why I'd stopped smoking. Every now and then, I still craved the nicotine.

When I got back to the living room, she'd hung a few ornaments on the tree. The kitten had already climbed up the bottom part of the tree and tried to swat her while remaining hidden. MaryAnne ignored him and reached for another ornament. I joined her, working on the top half where she couldn't reach. The next time she hung something on the tree, I snapped a quick picture. She probably didn't know how many I had of her on my phone. One day, I wanted to frame some of them and set them around the house. I wasn't sure she was ready for that yet.

From the kitchen, I heard Hatter whistling to the current song on the radio and knew he felt left out. I pressed a kiss to MaryAnne's temple and went to get the bird. I'd made sure his cage not only could roll easily, but also fit through the doorways. I wheeled him from the kitchen into the front entry and parked him outside the living room. He had a good view of everything and started bobbing up and down to the music while he fluttered his wings.

Couldn't decorate for Christmas without the entire family present. Even if more than half weren't human.

Chapter Five

MaryAnne

I didn't believe for one second the envelope of cash was actually from Sean. I loved my cousin, but he hadn't exactly been warm and fuzzy toward me since I'd come to live with Patriot. No, the money had to have come from Patriot. I didn't know why he hadn't given it to me himself, but he'd been right about me wanting to buy some presents. Not having my own money wasn't ideal, but I couldn't exactly go out and get a job. Well, I could. But I'd run the risk of freaking out and getting fired.

Phoebe smiled as I got into her car. "You ready to shop?"

I nodded. "I mostly want to shop for Patriot, but I'd like to get a present for Titan, since he's allowed me to live at the compound. And I should probably get a gift for my cousin."

"Trust me, my dad is happy to have you. Besides, I think if you left, Patriot would follow you. That man is completely smitten."

"Smitten?" I asked. "Does anyone use that word anymore?"

I heard the pipes of three bikes and noticed we were being followed by three patched members. It seemed Patriot had made sure I would feel safe, since he wouldn't be with me.

"They do if they read historical romances." Phoebe shrugged. "Seemed like an apt description. Has he said anything?"

"He wants to claim me. Said he'd bring it up in Church." I twisted my fingers in my lap. "I don't know why he'd want me. I don't think I can give him the kind of relationship he needs, but he insists that he doesn't care if we're ever intimate. It doesn't seem fair to him."

Phoebe cut her eyes my way. "You love him, don't you?"

"Yeah. I do."

"Then that's all that matters." Phoebe turned on the radio and started singing along with *Jingle Bells*.

Was she right?

The mall was packed, and we had to walk what felt like miles to reach the doors. Inside, Phoebe looped her arm through mine so we wouldn't get separated. She stopped at a leather store first, picking out a wallet for Kraken. I browsed but didn't really see anything that looked like something Patriot would want. There was a leather jacket I eyed, but once I saw the price tag I kept going. It cost more than what I'd been given.

Phoebe stopped next to me, looking at it. "You aren't buying it?"

"It costs more than I have, and I want to buy several presents today."

She pulled out her phone and started tapping on the screen. When it chimed a moment later, she showed it to me.

Can I use your credit card for MaryAnne to buy something for Patriot?

Sure.

I opened my mouth to protest, except Phoebe grabbed the jacket off the rack and practically ran to the register. I followed and felt myself pale when the clerk gave us the total.

"Four hundred, seventy-two dollars and thirty-three cents."

Phoebe handed over the card and smiled at me. "Don't worry. My dad wouldn't have said to do this if he hadn't meant it. Trust me. He won't even blink when he gets the bill. I've put way more on there in the past. Kraken hates that I have it, insists he can take care of me, but my dad wouldn't take no for an answer. Only time I use it is when I don't want Kraken to see what I've bought or how much I spent."

I'd have to make sure I thanked Titan. He had two kids, grandkids, and a wife to take care of. The last thing he needed was me holding my hand out asking him for money. My stomach knotted and twisted. It felt wrong.

Phoebe nudged me. "Hey. It's really okay."

I gave her a quick nod and followed her to the next store. In addition to the jacket, I bought Patriot a black sweater and a watch. Well, not just any watch. It was waterproof to fifty feet and did all sorts of cool things. If it hadn't been marked down seventy-five percent, I'd have never been able to afford it, and I refused to let Phoebe buy anything else of mine with Titan's credit card.

"I don't know what to get your dad," I said.

Phoebe pointed to a bookstore. "He likes to read, when he has the time. You could always give him a gift card, or pick up a new release. I'll tell Delilah what title you get so we can make sure Dad doesn't pick it up before he opens your gift."

"He paid for a four-hundred-dollar jacket and sent Patriot to bring me to the compound. A book doesn't seem like nearly enough."

"Come on. Let's see what they have."

She tugged me into the store, and we approached the new release rack. They had a signed copy of a hardback she insisted Titan would love, so I bought it for him. I still hadn't gotten anything for Sean, but I'd grown apart from my cousin and didn't know what he'd like. I finally decided on a gift card to his favorite fast-food place.

"How am I getting this stuff into the house without Patriot seeing it?" I asked.

"Let's stop at Target on the way back and get some stuff to wrap everything. I'll ask Kraken to get Patriot out of the house. We can wrap everything at your place, then I'll haul mine home. Besides, if I try to wrap with Ember underfoot, she'll end up seeing stuff she shouldn't. Not to mention she can't keep a secret."

We loaded our things into her car, then headed for Target. I checked the side-view mirror several times, ensuring our bodyguards were still there. Or rather mine, since Phoebe didn't seem to mind going around town on her own. I picked up the boxes I'd need, as well as two rolls of wrapping paper, then grabbed gift tags, and tape. I couldn't remember seeing scissors at the house, except the ones in the kitchen, so I picked up an inexpensive pair.

Phoebe got several rolls of paper and tags as well, then we made our way to the checkout. The lines were insanely long, and I found myself browsing the nearby items. I remembered seeing some baseball cards in one of Patriot's dresser drawers so I selected a few packs to put into a stocking, only to realize, we didn't have stockings. Thankfully, there were a handful on a display closer to the registers so I picked out one for each of us and hoped I could figure out where to hang them.

A bag of Christmas chocolates made it into my cart, as well as some peppermints. I found Patriot's favorite gum as we inched our way closer to the counter and added it to the cart for his stocking. Then tossed in an Apple gift card he could use with his phone. I hoped I had enough, since I'd bought more than I'd planned, but when I heard my total I breathed out a sigh of relief. I was able to pay for everything and had a little left over.

Phoebe checked out behind me, and then we put our stuff into her car, with help from Stone and Philly. Brick was on his phone, even though he scanned the parking lot at least twice while we loaded the car. Once we were on our way home, Phoebe cranked the Christmas music and we both sang along.

At the house, Brick helped us carry everything inside, after assuring me Patriot wasn't home. "I'll keep him busy."

I thanked him and started to spread everything out in the living room.

The kitten saw the wrapping paper and immediately pounced on it, sticking his little claws into the roll and leaving pinpricks. I didn't think Patriot would mind. I pulled off a section of ribbon and cut it, tossing it in front of the ball of fluff. It diverted his attention and allowed me to wrap gifts relatively undisturbed.

"You really need a name," I murmured, reaching out to stroke the kitten's ear.

Phoebe took one half of the room and I claimed the other. I didn't have as much to wrap as she did, so after I finished wrapping mine, I helped her finish up. If she'd already done part of her shopping, then Ember was going to be spoiled rotten. Even little Banner had a lot of gifts.

As I held the little bear dressed as Santa, my throat started to burn, and I realized I was close to crying. I pressed a hand to my stomach and wondered what it would be like to carry a baby. I didn't know for sure because I'd been too scared to ask, but I didn't think I could have children. It wasn't until that moment I realized Patriot hadn't said a word about kids. What if he wanted them some day? He'd said he wanted me, even if we never had sex, but he could change his mind.

"What's wrong?" Phoebe asked.

"Sorry. I … I realized I don't know if I can even have children. I was holding your son's bear and it hit me that I may never have the chance to pick out gifts for my own kids."

Phoebe's jaw dropped and her eyes went wide. "Wait. You don't know if you can have them? What about…"

"Patriot?" I asked.

She nodded.

"We didn't discuss kids. What if he wants a family and I can't give that to him?"

"Oh, MaryAnne," she said in a near whisper. "I'm so sorry. Wouldn't the doctor be able to tell you?"

I hadn't seen a doctor since Patriot had brought me here. Well, Bones had tended to me whenever I'd gotten sick, but I couldn't stand the thought of going to a clinic, or seeing anyone dressed in scrubs or a white lab coat. I didn't know if a fertility test was something Bones could do or not.

It wouldn't matter if I couldn't get over my fears and let Patriot do more than kiss me. If we never had sex, there wouldn't be kids anyway. I hated that he'd have to give up the chance to have a family. Maybe I should ask him to hold off on claiming me.

The front door opened, and Phoebe squealed, quickly wrapping the last of her presents. Patriot walked in, a bemused look on his face as he took in the mess we'd made. I'd put his presents under the tree, but it didn't look like much. He stepped over the rolls of wrapping paper, tape, and scraps, then knelt next to me.

"Hey, Little Bit. Have fun shopping?" he asked.

"Yes."

"You aren't supposed to be here!" Phoebe stood and folded her arms. "What if she hadn't been finished wrapping your gifts?"

"Need help loading your car?" he asked.

Phoebe smiled. "Did you just tell me to pack my shit and leave?"

He shrugged a shoulder. "Not in so many words. Don't need Kraken getting pissy, but yeah… I need to talk to my woman, preferably without an audience."

Phoebe rolled her eyes. "Fine. I can take a hint."

She started carrying everything out to her car and I heard the door shut after her third trip. Patriot cupped my cheek and leaned in to kiss me. He could be so sweet. I knew as part of the Hades Abyss he'd done his share of bad things. The men weren't saints by any means, but they did treat women right. Or at least the women they wanted to keep. Even though the club whores were here voluntarily, I still cringed a little whenever I saw the way the club talked to them. Although, Patriot had been nice enough to the one who came here, until she'd insulted me.

"So, it seems we need to have a talk," he said.

"You heard?" I asked, thinking of the conversation I'd been having with Phoebe.

"Yeah, I heard. Why didn't you ask me if I planned to have kids some day?" he asked.

I didn't like admitting there was something wrong with me. Hated it. Didn't change the fact I was damaged, mentally, emotionally, and physically. I had my share of scars, but for the first time, I wondered about any damage done to the inside of me.

"Little Bit, I'm going to say this once and only once. So listen up. I can't have kids. Not the regular way. I have some sperm frozen and on hold at a sperm bank. Had it done when I was eighteen before I enlisted, in case something went wrong. Got sick overseas with a bad infection that made me sterile. So if you can't carry a baby, don't feel like you failed me. Because you haven't. We can adopt. Or if you're able to get pregnant, you can still have my kid even if we have it the old-fashioned way. Well, sort of. In the sense you'd carry the baby and give birth."

I wasn't quite sure what to say to all that. I hadn't realized he wasn't able to have children. Some of the tension eased from my shoulders. I didn't feel like a failure knowing there was a chance we'd have never had kids together anyway. From what I'd seen on TV, getting artificially inseminated didn't always work.

"Any other objections to being mine?" he asked.

"No. I wanted to be yours, I... I didn't want to hold you back."

He pressed his forehead to mine. "Little Bit, you're the reason I wake up smiling every morning. No more doubts, all right?"

"Okay."

"I need to pick up your presents from Titan's house. Delilah was going to wrap them for me so they wouldn't look like a badger had mangled them. When I get back, we'll go out to eat."

"I could make something," I offered.

"Not a chance. We're celebrating."

"What?" I asked.

He kissed me hard and fast. "You being mine. I made it official while you were gone. Had Brick and the others with you text in their votes. It was unanimous. You're mine, Little Bit."

My heart warmed and I couldn't stop smiling. While he went to get my presents, I cleaned up my mess and changed my sweater. My hair was tumbling out of my clip so I ran a brush through it and decided to leave it down. It was a bit chilly outside today and I didn't think we'd go out on his bike, but if we did I'd make sure I had a ponytail holder in my pocket so I could pull my hair back.

I heard him moving around downstairs and rushed to the living room. He'd put so many presents under the tree I wondered if he'd bought out the mall. Archimedes and the kitten were nowhere to be seen, which meant they'd likely gone to the kitchen. I was surprised the paper and shiny ribbons hadn't attracted the kitten's attention like it had when I'd been wrapping gifts.

"Ronan, you got too much!" I protested.

"No, I didn't get nearly enough." He stood and pulled me into his arms. "It's our first Christmas together as an official 'us' and I wanted to make it memorable. Last year I did the bare minimum because I wasn't sure you were ready for more."

"You're so good to me," I said. "I don't know why Titan picked you that day, but I'm glad it was you who came to get me."

"Me too, Little Bit. I've been thankful every day that you've been a part of my life." I rubbed his thumb along my jaw. "I'd thought I was going to rescue a girl. It never occurred to me Titan had sent me after a young woman who would be perfect for me. Maybe we should get him a present."

"I already did. Phoebe helped me pick out a signed hardback for him. But if you have an idea for something else, we could always give him two presents. I told her a book didn't seem like much."

"I'll think of something. He's talked about getting a custom leather seat for his bike at a shop not too far from here. Maybe I'll pay the deposit on it and get them to contact him about what he wants." He kissed my forehead. "Now where do you want to eat? We can go anywhere."

"Well, it's Christmas. Almost. What about the buffet on Market Avenue? I heard they were going to have turkey, ham, dressing, bread pudding, and a bunch of holiday treats all month long."

"Then that's where we'll go."

He took my hand and led me out to the Bronco and helped me onto the seat. When he started it up, he turned up the heat and made sure the vents were pointed my way. With it being an older vehicle, it didn't blow hot or cold very hard, but I knew he loved driving it. And since it's what he'd brought to rescue me, I rather liked it too.

Chapter Six

Patriot

I couldn't remember a time I'd ever seen MaryAnne smile so much. Seeing the joy on her face, hearing her excited chatter as she talked about all things Christmas, and watching the look of rapture that crossed her face with every bite of her food made me wish the night would never end. All I wanted was for her to be happy, and at the moment, she was. I knew eventually another nightmare would creep up on her, but she hadn't had one in over a week. At least, not that I'd heard.

After dinner, I took her by the coffee shop for some hot chocolate, and then we drove around looking at Christmas lights while she sang along with the carols on the radio. One house in town had animated lights that matched the music on a particular radio station. We watched for at least ten minutes before I moved on so someone else could have a turn. It made me wish I'd thought to ask every brother at the compound to put lights up, just so MaryAnne could see them and smile.

At the house, she went straight upstairs, her steps slow as exhaustion hit her. I could see the fatigue in her eyes, but she'd struggled to keep going. I locked up and shut off all the lights, let Archimedes out one last time and put the animals to bed. When I'd finished, I headed up to my room, only to hesitate outside the guest room she'd been using. Now that she was officially mine, my room was now *our* room. I lifted my hand to knock and tell her as much. Until reality crashed in. She might never be ready to share a room with me, and the last thing I wanted was for her to think I was pushing her. Even though she'd wanted to sleep by me the other night, it didn't mean she wanted to do that all the time.

I went to my bedroom and shut the door before stripping off my boots and clothes. I started the shower, not bothering to turn the heat up too much. I'd gotten used to cold showers, especially the last six months, when MaryAnne had started to come alive. Stepping under the spray, I pulled the door closed and let the water beat down on my head. Goose bumps covered my skin. The cold didn't seem to bother my cock since it stood upright. Hiding my reaction from MaryAnne had gotten easier lately. Mostly because I knew she wasn't looking below my belt, so as long as I held myself a certain way, she didn't pay attention to the fact my cock was trying to escape my jeans.

I reached down and gripped my shaft, squeezing it at the base, willing my erection to go down. It never worked, but I always tried anyway. I slicked my palm with soap and started stroking my dick with long, hard tugs. Bracing my other hand on the wall, I closed my eyes and imagined MaryAnne was the one touching me. It didn't take long before I was coming. My heart pounded in my chest as cum splashed the tiled wall. Even after my release, my cock hadn't softened.

"Ronan."

My body locked up tight and I turned my head, opening my eyes. I'd hoped it was only my imagination, but no. MaryAnne was standing in the bathroom, staring at me with wide eyes. *Fuck*!

"You shouldn't be in here, MaryAnne."

She shifted from foot to foot, wringing her hands in front of her. "Since you said I was officially yours now, I thought... I mean... Do you want me to share the same room with you?"

"I've told you that I'll never ask for more than you're willing to give, Little Bit."

Her cheeks turned pink. "I liked sleeping in your arms."

Yeah, I'd liked that too. A little too much.

"I'm not sure you'd like it tonight." I looked down at my cock. If anything, it had gotten even harder with her standing so close.

"I've seen naked men before," she said. "I know what happens when a man gets turned-on. You won't shock me."

"Dammit, MaryAnne! You weren't given a choice! You have one now. I won't force you to be around me while I'm like this. You're not obligated to share my bed and feel my cock digging into you all night, because it's not going to get soft anytime soon. If anything, having you next to me will only make it worse."

She moved closer, pressing a hand to the glass door. "Were you picturing me while you…"

"Yeah. I was," I admitted, not wanting to lie to her.

"Then you should at least know what to picture. I know you saw me naked that first day, when you came to the hospital to get me, but you didn't look. Not really."

She reached for the hem of her shirt and I nearly choked on my tongue as she pulled it over her head and let it drop to the floor, then shimmied out of her pants. She wore plain white panties but fuck if they weren't sexy on her. She removed those too, then opened the shower door. She shivered as the cold water hit her and I reached for the knob, turning up the temperature.

"What are you doing?" I asked.

She held her arms out. "Look at me, Ronan. Really look. My body isn't perfect. What they did to me took its toll."

I knew I shouldn't look, but I couldn't seem to help myself. My gaze skimmed over her breasts. Plump with pretty pink nipples. As I looked closer, I saw what she'd meant about not being perfect. There were silvery lines that marred her skin. Scars, most likely from a knife. There were more across her stomach and all the way down to her pubic bone. When she turned, I saw the brand on her right ass cheek. I knew that symbol. I'd seen it on a finger I'd cut off in the last year.

I growled and reached for her, lightly touching the scarred, puckered flesh. "I wish I could kill him all over again."

Her back tensed and she looked at me over her shoulder. "What?"

I took a breath and knew I needed to tell her. Confess what I'd done. "I've spent the last year tracking down every man identified as one of your rapists. I've slaughtered them. Slowly. Made them suffer, beg, cry. The man who left this mark is gone. I saw that symbol on his ring when I cut his fingers off."

She turned to face me, her eyes wet with tears. "You've been tracking them down and killing them? All of them?"

"Any that were recognized with the software Wizard has. He used it on the videos the hospital had of you. They recorded a lot of what happened." I held her gaze. "I've done everything I can to wipe every last one of them from the earth. There are only two I haven't been able to kill because they live too far away. One moved to Montana and another out to California. I've put the word out I want their heads."

She threw herself against me, wrapping her arms around my waist. "I knew you were my knight in shining armor."

"Don't make me out to be something I'm not, Little Bit. I have blood on my hands. A lot of it. I've done bad things. But I will fucking die before I let anyone go unpunished who dared to cause you pain." I put my arms around her, holding her close. "I want you to feel safe, MaryAnne. To know you can leave the compound without fear any of those men will come for you."

"I always feel safe with you," she said in a voice so soft I nearly didn't hear her.

I didn't know why, especially since my dick hadn't softened yet and was now trapped between us. After everything they'd done to her, how could she stand here, naked and in my arms? I'd have thought removing her clothes would terrify her, much less being pressed against me without anything between us.

Maybe I didn't know as much about her as I'd thought. I'd known she was stronger than she realized, but perhaps her strength was greater than even *I* had discerned.

"If you want to shower, I'll get out. I meant what I said before. I don't expect anything of you, Little Bit. We can go at your pace, however slow that might be."

"What if I want to try? I want to be normal, Ronan. I'm tired of being scared, of only remembering pain when it comes to men. You've kissed me several times now. It didn't scare me. I liked it."

"It's not a good idea, MaryAnne. Not while we're both naked. Even I don't have that kind of control."

She reached up and cupped my cheek. "I think you do."

"You were wrong, you know? I still think you're beautiful. These scars..." I reached out and traced one of the silver lines across her breast. "They don't make you ugly. They show your strength. Your determination to survive."

Her nipple hardened and she sucked in a breath. I kept my gaze on her face, watching for her reaction, as I let my finger slide down, then lightly caress the pretty pink tip. She bit her lip, but her eyes darkened. Not from fear but from need. I cupped her breast and rolled her nipple between my fingers.

"Feel good?" I asked.

She nodded. Christ. I was going to hell. I knew I should get the fuck out and put some space between us, but I wanted to show her pleasure, to give her a good memory to associate with being touched.

"I do anything you don't like, or that scares you, I want to know. Understood?"

"I understand," she said.

I leaned down and kissed her, tasted her. Before I realized it, I'd backed her to the glass wall. She didn't protest. If anything, she leaned into me, silently asking for more. I cupped her ass with both hands and lifted her. MaryAnne wrapped her legs around my waist and her arms looped around my neck.

"We don't have to do this, Little Bit," I murmured before kissing her again.

"I know, but I think I need this as much as you." She blinked at me before giving me a hesitant smile. "I need to know I can enjoy being with you, that sex isn't painful. Take away my memories and give me new ones. Please, Ronan."

Fuck me. When she asked so sweetly, how could I tell her no?

"If you get scared..."

She silenced me with a kiss. "I won't."

I reached between us, rubbing her clit. Her lips parted and I saw the pulse in her throat start to race. It only took a few strokes before she cried out, hips bucking against me, as she came. The flare of surprise in her eyes, the startled expression on her face, was enough to tell me she'd never had an orgasm before.

"That's it, Little Bit. Come for me. Let go." I kept rubbing, not stopping until the last tremor had raked her small frame. While she was loose and wet, I positioned my cock against her pussy and eased inside, giving her time to tell me to stop or push me away. "Fuck, MaryAnne. You feel so damn good."

Her nails bit into my shoulders. "Don't stop."

I placed a hand on her hip and drove into her. She tipped her head back, her eyes narrowing to slits as she stared at me. Soft cries escaped her as I thrust into her tight pussy, over and over. I felt my balls draw up and knew I wouldn't last much longer. I rubbed her clit again, and when she found her release, I came inside her.

It had been too fucking long since I'd been with a woman. If it had been anyone in here with me other than MaryAnne, I'd have been embarrassed. I knew she wouldn't judge me.

My cock twitched and throbbed, but I wasn't ready to pull out. The way she tightened her hold on me, it seemed she was okay staying as we were for at least another minute or two. I smoothed her hair back from her face.

"You all right?"

"I'm perfect." She smiled. "Thank you, Ronan."

I shook my head. "Trust me, Little Bit. I'm the one who should be thanking you. And I know this is a little too late, but I'm clean. If you were wondering, you are too. Bones tested you for STDs when he examined you the first time."

The smile slipped from her face. "I hadn't thought of that."

"I only brought it up because we should have discussed it beforehand. If I weren't sterile, we'd have had that conversation too. Seeing as how we got that part out of the way…"

She cupped my cheek. "I don't care that you can't have kids, Ronan. Like you said. If I'm fertile, we can try the sperm you had frozen. If I'm not, or the artificial insemination doesn't work, we can adopt. Family doesn't have to be blood."

My cock started to soften, and I pulled out, letting MaryAnne slide down my body. I took my time washing her, letting my hands caress every inch of her soft skin. She leaned into me, like a little kitten seeking attention. How anyone could have ever hurt her wasn't something I could comprehend. I'd never met anyone sweeter.

"Ready for bed?" I asked. She nodded but something in her eyes made it seem like she didn't want to get out of the shower yet. "What is it, Little Bit?"

"Where am I supposed to sleep?"

I kissed her soft and slow. "Anywhere you want. You can keep your room, or you can share the bed with me. I told you… at your pace, MaryAnne."

"I'm yours. You said so."

"Yeah, Little Bit. You're mine. Sleeping in a different room won't change that."

She pressed her cheek to my chest. "I want to stay with you. I slept better the night you held me than I have in years."

"Me too." I wrapped her in my arms again and held her until the water started to cool. I shut off the shower, dried us both off, and led her into the bedroom. I handed her a T-shirt to sleep in. "You can move your clothes in here if you want to sleep here every night."

"Is there room?" she asked.

"I'll make room. You tell me what you need, and I'll make it happen."

She crawled into bed and I turned off the lights before joining her. She cuddled close and I breathed in her scent as I shut my eyes. It was like everything inside me settled. Having her here in my bed, lying against me, made it feel like everything was right in my world. MaryAnne had been mine since the day I pulled her from hell, but this was the first time she was where she belonged.

And if she changed her mind later, I wouldn't stand in her way. I knew she needed to feel like she had some sort of control over her life. As much as I wanted to pull a caveman act and tell her she wasn't fucking leaving my bed, I couldn't do that to her. It would crush her, possibly destroy her. I'd do anything to protect her, even if it was from my own needs.

Her breathing deepened and I knew she'd fallen asleep. I hoped she wouldn't have nightmares. If what we'd shared set her back, then I'd keep my dick in my pants until she could handle more. Even if it did give me blue balls. Wouldn't be the first time I'd had them since she came to live with me. Doubted it would be the last.

At least I no longer had to hide what I'd done. It hadn't felt right keeping it a secret. Now that she knew I'd killed the men who'd hurt her, maybe she wouldn't be so scared to leave the compound. Hopefully it wouldn't take long for someone to handle the last two men. I'd pay whatever price they asked, as long as those fuckers were dead when it was all said and done.

Anything to keep a smile on her face, to chase the shadows from her eyes, and give her the life she deserved. I wasn't ready to admit it out loud, but I knew damn well I didn't just like MaryAnne. I loved her.

Chapter Seven

MaryAnne

I stretched and tensed for a moment. A hot, heavy arm was draped over my waist and I felt a male body up against my back. A hard cock nestled in the crack of my ass. The room spun for a minute and I couldn't breathe. Panic beat at me until I remembered everything.

It was Ronan.

Not the men who'd hurt me. I wasn't being restrained. Nothing bad was going to happen.

I looked over my shoulder and smiled at how peaceful he looked. I was safe, with the man I'd fallen in love with. A biker who wouldn't let anyone hurt me ever again. He'd gotten rid of my demons, sent them to hell where they belonged. I'd never be able to repay him for what he'd done.

I eased out of bed, careful not to wake him. After I used the bathroom and went down the hall to brush my teeth, I went to my old room. I put on panties and my warm pajamas, along with a pair of fuzzy socks. As I pawed through the drawer, I realized I had at least a dozen pair or more. Every time I saw a pair, I had to have them. If I didn't slow down, I'd run out of space for them.

Once I was toasty warm, I hurried downstairs to make breakfast for Patriot. He always took care of me, and I tried to do the same for him when I could. Before I'd come here, I hadn't known how to cook. I still wasn't that great at it, but I was learning. I'd never been interested in things like making cookies or learning how to cook from scratch. Until the day I'd been snatched by the Sadistic Saints, I'd been too busy worrying about my next trip to the mall, who was dating which boy, or what I'd wear the next day to school.

Things were different now. I'd had to grow up fast, and the stuff I'd always thought was so crucial didn't matter anymore.

Before I got started, I let Archimedes outside and put down fresh water and food. I uncovered Hatter's cage and took out his bowls. His water bottle was still half-full so I left it alone. After I put his bird food into one dish, I stuck it back in his cage. The second dish I knew Patriot used for fruits and veggies. Hatter had his own storage tubs in the fridge. Today it looked like he'd be getting apples, grapes, and carrots. I sliced them up and dropped them into the dish before giving it to him.

"Mmm. So good."

I smiled and reached through the bars to stroke his head. "Eat up, Hatter."

I let Archimedes back in, then decided to get started on feeding the humans. I pulled out eggs, bacon, and a can of biscuits. I'd looked up how to make bacon in the oven after I saw someone make it that way in a movie, and now I preferred it baked over fried. I laid out the strips on a baking sheet while the oven preheated. I also preheated the toaster oven so I could make the biscuits at the same time.

After I had the bacon and biscuits cooking, I brewed a pot of coffee for Patriot. I took out some diced ham and shredded cheese to add to the eggs. Before I could get them started, I heard a knock at the front door. Archimedes stood and shook himself before leaving the kitchen. I heard a soft bark and hurried after him. Any other time, I'd have cowered and been afraid to open it, even knowing I should be safe here. Now I knew Patriot had killed all but two of the men who had hurt me. It made me realize I didn't have to hide anymore.

I answered the door, peering around the edge of it since I was in my pajamas. Archimedes pressed against me. Smoke stood there, hands in his pockets. He rocked back on his heels when he saw me.

"Patriot is still asleep," I said.

"Actually, I came to see you."

My hand tightened on the door. "Me? Why would you come here to see me?"

He raked a hand through his hair. "I wanted to apologize. I shouldn't have said what I did at the clubhouse. No one here would ever expect anything from you, MaryAnne. Even before Patriot officially made you his. It was a dick move and I'm sorry."

I opened the door a little wider. "You're sorry?"

He nodded. "Shouldn't have said it. The second I saw you, what I should have done was call Patriot, and make sure the club whores didn't bother you. I won't fuck up again, all right? You want to come drink at the clubhouse, I'll make sure the club whores keep their distance."

"Thank you." Not that I wanted to go there anytime soon. Well, not on a party night anyway. The days the clubhouse was for family only was another matter. I enjoyed going when Phoebe, Delilah, and the kids would be there.

"Right, so... I'm gonna go. I just needed to come say that. You need anything, let me know."

He backed away and I shut the door. Archimedes followed me into the kitchen and laid down near the table. The kitten immediately went over and started to chew on the poor dog, but Archimedes ignored him. I checked on the bacon and biscuits, then cracked the eggs into a bowl and beat them. I put in a dash of milk, a handful of diced ham, and a good bit of shredded cheese. I tried to be quiet as I dug the skillet out from the bottom cabinet, then set it on the burner to warm. By the time I'd finished the eggs and plated our breakfast, I heard Patriot coming down the stairs.

"Something smells wonderful," he said as he stepped into the kitchen.

"Wonderful!" Hatter said and fluttered his wings.

"I thought I'd make breakfast. It's not anything fancy."

He paused long enough to kiss my temple before going straight for the coffee. I smiled as he drained a cup, gulping it down, then poured a second one. I set the plates on the table along with forks. Patriot nearly collapsed onto a chair. It always took a few cups of coffee to get him going in the morning. I poured myself some juice before I sat down.

"You doing okay?" he asked. "After last night… I wasn't sure what to expect today."

"You worried I'd regret what happened?"

"Something like that."

"Eat your eggs before they get cold. I'm fine, Ronan. Better than." I smiled before I dug into my food. "Smoke stopped by. He wanted to apologize."

"Good. Means I don't have to kick his ass again."

"The first time was more than enough. You shouldn't beat on your brothers."

He grunted and kept eating.

"Do you think someone would take me to the store? I want to get some more baking supplies. I seem to do better at that than cooking most of the time. I'd also love some eggnog. It's nearly Christmas and I haven't had any yet."

"I can take you."

"Really? You don't have club business to handle?" I asked.

He paused, fork halfway to his mouth, and stared at me. After a moment, I squirmed and wished I hadn't said anything. Had I overstepped? Or come across as too eager for his company? I didn't have much experience with men. Not the right kind anyway. I'd never had a chance to date, or have a boyfriend.

"There's only one rule, Little Bit. I will tell you anything you want to know, as long as it isn't club business. But to answer your question, no, I don't have other obligations today."

I felt my cheeks warm. "Sorry."

"Not mad, Little Bit. But I need you to know that's one thing I won't discuss, even now that you're my old lady. Speaking of, you should have your property cut in the next day or two if all goes according to plan. It's been ordered."

"Like the ones Phoebe and Delilah have?"

He nodded. "Yep. Except yours will say *Property of Patriot*."

"I can't wait to see it."

He winked and finished off his food, then carried his plate to the sink. "Better get ready, Little Bit. I'll clean up in here. Won't take me but a minute to change."

I eyed his beard and bedhead. "Might want to use a comb or something too."

He looked at me over his shoulder. "You saying I look rough?"

Not exactly. More like extremely sexy. He looked like he'd recently gotten out of bed, which he had. Except any woman who saw him like this would be imagining what he might have been doing other than sleeping.

"Keep looking at me like that and we won't be going to the store," he said before facing the sink again.

Part of me wanted to see if he'd really take me back to bed. But the other part wasn't sure I was ready for something like that in the light of day. While my nightmares had mostly happened at night, it had felt like the darkness outside had somehow wrapped me in a cloak, made me braver. I couldn't explain how else I'd gotten the courage to do what I'd done. Removing my clothes in front of him, letting him touch me and so much more… it hadn't been easy, but with the sunlight streaming through the windows, I didn't feel as confident as I had in the shower.

I hurried upstairs and went to my old room. Last night, I'd said I wanted to move into Patriot's room. Waking up in his arms had been wonderful, after the initial scare of thinking someone else had pinned me down. I still wanted to move my things in there, but it would have to wait. I picked out a pair of jeans and another Christmas-themed sweater and socks. It didn't take me long to change. Since I'd showered last night with Patriot, I didn't bother taking another one.

After I ran a brush through my hair, I pulled it up into a bun. I ran my fingers down my neck as I turned my head one way, then another. I seemed so bare with no earrings or necklace. My jewelry was probably still in my room at home. I hadn't been able to face my family, except Sean. What little of it I had left. I knew it was wrong to push them away, but I wasn't the same girl they'd known before and they expected me to be. I'd been told more than once I'd bounce back, like they could only love me if I wasn't damaged by what had happened.

Sean had helped me make a break from them. No one called anymore, or tried to come see me. There were times I missed them. Until I remembered they didn't want the new me. They wanted the old MaryAnne, and I wasn't sure she existed. The innocence had been burned out of me. The people here had become my family. The Hades Abyss accepted me as I was.

"I'll help you move your stuff later," Patriot said, leaning against the bathroom doorframe.

He'd managed to tame his hair and beard, and he'd pulled on a gray long-sleeved shirt and jeans. He'd already put on his cut and seemed to be ready to go. Patriot looked down at my feet and smiled. I curled my toes and studied my socks. Green with Santa hats all over them.

"Cute, Little Bit, but I think you'll want some shoes."

"I'll grab some. Meet you downstairs?"

He nodded and pushed off the doorframe. "I'll get the Bronco going so it can start to warm up. There's a bite to the air today. Might want your coat."

"I'll get it."

He left, his steps heavy as he went down the stairs. I put on the ankle boots he'd bought me when I'd come to live here and grabbed the denim jacket lined with sheepskin. I rushed downstairs and out to the Bronco. Patriot opened my door and helped me onto the seat. I fastened my seatbelt while he walked around the front and got in.

"You want the grocery or one of the super stores?" he asked.

"I think the grocery is fine. If we go to one of the other places, it will be even more crowded. This close to the holidays it seems to be packed everywhere."

"Grocery won't be much better."

"Maybe not, but at least we won't be fighting people shopping for presents. Besides, they have some boxes up front where we can donate non-perishables. It would be nice to make sure someone else can have Christmas dinner."

He reached out and brushed his fingers along my cheek. "Heart of gold. My Little Bit is an angel come to earth."

"I wouldn't go that far, but I do want to make someone happy." I chewed on my lower lip. "Do you think... could we find a family who maybe can't give their kids a Christmas this year? I'd like to get a few toys to give them. Make sure they have a good holiday."

"Why don't we get the entire club involved and adopt a few families?" he asked.

"Even better! Think we can do it?"

He nodded. "Sure. We'll stop by one of the churches on the way to the store."

I watched him a minute. I wondered if he knew how amazing he was. Had anyone ever told him? He'd called me an angel, but he'd come and saved me, gave me a home and everything I could ever need, and now he was taking my idea and making it even better.

"Does anyone else know how big your heart is?" I asked.

He cut me a quick glance before focusing on the road again. "Don't go spreading that shit around. You'll ruin my rep. I'm a badass biker and don't you forget it."

I smiled. "All right. I'll keep your secret."

He pulled up to a small church on the outskirts of the rougher side of town. Patriot scanned the area before helping me out of the Bronco. With one hand at my waist, and the other free to most likely pull whatever weapons he had on him, he ushered me into the building. A man in dress slacks and button-down shirt greeted us with a smile.

"What can I do for you folks? Interested in joining the church? We can always use more youngsters in here," he said.

"We actually wanted to ask you about some opportunities to better a few lives this holiday season," Patriot said. "Assuming you don't have an issue with me being part of Hades Abyss."

"We're all God's children," the man said. "I'm Reverend Burson. Now what did you have in mind?"

Patriot nudged me and gave me a slight nod. "I know the local grocery takes up donations of food for families in need, but I wondered if there might be some families who were struggling to give their kids a Christmas this year. Even though there are programs out there to help with that sort of thing, I'm sure not everyone gets the assistance they need."

"Bless you, angel! You're the answer to my prayers!" The man lifted his hands. "It just so happens I have three families who come to this church who have fallen on hard times. Each has small children and I know their parents would be grateful for anything you'd like to donate."

Patriot rubbed his hand up and down my back and I leaned against his side. I was so glad he'd brought me here. With his help, maybe we could make a difference, no matter how small.

"Would you happen to have a list of toys those children might like to see under their trees this year? Or could you get one for us?" I asked.

"Well, I don't have anything right now, but I could have it for you within the next hour or two. But as for putting presents under the tree, I don't believe any of those families actually have a tree. It was on my list of things to accomplish. I thought I might be able to get some older fake trees donated, ones that aren't being used anymore."

"We'll do one better, Reverend. We'll pick up three new pre-lit trees and some ornaments for each. I don't want to go scaring anyone, and I know people around here don't always look too kindly on my club. We can bring everything here and you could arrange for them to get everything?" Patriot asked.

The man held up a finger. "You wait right there. Don't move, and certainly don't leave!"

He hurried off and I took the time to admire the inside of the church. Stained glass windows lined both sides of the sanctuary. Each was beautiful in its own way and filled the room with a sense of peace. I trailed my fingers over the back of a pew and tried to remember the last time I'd been to church. I breathed in and held it a moment before releasing the air in my lungs, and some of the tension. I didn't feel like I belonged here anymore, and yet I didn't exactly want to run away either.

The reverend came back, a piece of paper in his hand. "I spoke with all three families, and they were overjoyed. Each has experienced a hardship in the last few months and they've struggled. In fact, two of the mothers started crying. You've brought them a Christmas miracle."

He handed the paper to Patriot and I leaned over to read it along with him. Four boys and five girls were listed on the paper, along with their ages and the top three things on each of their wish lists. At the bottom, the reverend had included some information on the parents as well. A warmth filled me, as well as a sense of purpose. I hadn't been good for much of anything since Patriot brought me home, but this year I could do something that mattered. No, *we* could.

I hesitated only a moment. "Reverend, you said they've been struggling. Do they need help with other things? Like maybe groceries?"

His eyes lit up and he eagerly nodded. "They do indeed. They've gotten what they can from the food pantry, but as you can see there's a lot of kids on that list between the three couples. Not easy to feed that many mouths."

I looked up at Patriot and he winked at me. "Guess we better go shopping, Little Bit. We'll get the stuff you wanted to make your desserts and grab some items for these families too. If it's all right with the reverend, we'll bring the food by here, and then we'll go hunt down some trees and ornaments."

"I'll be waiting," Reverend Burson said.

Patriot and I went back out to the Bronco and drove straight to the grocery. We each grabbed a cart since we now planned to buy more than double the food. I got the baking supplies I needed, then focused on what to feed three families with children, stuff that wouldn't necessarily spoil easily. We grabbed several packages of fresh pork chops. I noticed the pork tenderloins didn't expire for nearly a month so I grabbed one of each flavor for all three families.

"What else you want to get them, Little Bit?" he asked.

"I don't want to spend all your money."

He tipped his head and studied me a minute, then pulled out his phone. He tapped the screen a few times, then put the phone on speaker with the volume turned down so the entire store wouldn't hear.

"I'm tired. My kid keeps puking on me. What the hell do you want?" Titan asked by way of greeting.

"Little Bit wants to adopt a few families for Christmas. They've fallen on hard times and need food and toys for the kids. Club interested in chipping in? She's worried she'll deplete my account if we tackle it by ourselves," Patriot said.

"I think it's safe to say the club would agree to help with such a worthy cause," Titan said. "I'll have Wizard shift some money into your account. You need more, let me know."

He apparently hung up since the phone went silent. Patriot held onto his phone and motioned for me to keep going.

I grabbed bags of frozen chicken breasts, knowing while they may not be the most nutritious thing in the world, it was better than letting those kids starve. And what kid didn't like chicken nuggets? I added two bags each for all three families. We circled around to another section and I loaded the carts up with bacon, sandwich meat, and even found some pre-sliced, pre-cooked hams that wouldn't expire for a long while. I added six to the cart.

And then it hit me. All this food might last them a week. Possibly they could stretch it two weeks. And then what? My shoulders sagged and my eyes pricked with tears as I thought about those poor children. Hungry. Probably scared. And their parents? I couldn't imagine the fear of wondering how to feed their kids, or keep a roof over their heads. I'd felt good about this, but it wasn't nearly enough. It might give them a slight helping hand, but... they needed more than this.

"What's wrong, Little Bit?" Patriot asked, his voice soft and low.

"What happens when they eat all this food? What about next week? Or the one after? This isn't a good enough solution, Ro -- Patriot. Yeah, it feels good to help them, but are we helping enough?"

"One day at a time, MaryAnne. We'll deliver the food, pick out trees and ornaments, and then we'll sit down and figure out the next step." He reached out to cup my cheek. "We'll help however we can. If it means that much to you, I'll find a way. Nice save, by the way."

"Thank you."

He pressed a quick kiss to my lips, then walked off with one of the carts. I caught up to him just as he grabbed several packages of cookies. While he stuffed his cart with those, I selected some crackers, then rushed over to the dairy section. I added milk for each family, two large blocks of cheese each, and even included packages of yogurt. If the kids didn't like it, maybe the parents would. Eggs, bread, and a bunch of canned vegetables and macaroni finished off our shopping carts.

We checked out and made sure everything got divided in a way that would make it simple for each family to collect their groceries, and I made sure my baking stuff didn't get mixed in. After Patriot paid and we'd loaded the Bronco, we drove back to the church with our haul. The reverend smiled so wide I thought his face might crack. We sorted the sacks into three groups and as we turned to leave, a man in worn jeans and a thin sweater stepped into the church.

"Is this them?" the man asked the reverend.

Reverend Burson nodded. "These are our very own angels. Folks, this is David Boscoe. His family is one of the ones on your list. I hope you don't mind, but he'd hoped to meet you."

"I'm Patriot and this is MaryAnne." My good-hearted biker shook the man's hand.

"I can't thank you enough for what you're doing," David said. "Ever since I lost my job, it's been a constant struggle to feed my family, keep the lights on, and not lose our home. I appreciate everything you're doing for us. You have no idea what a relief this is."

My throat grew tight with unshed tears. I didn't know why I was so emotional. For whatever reason, I felt compelled to help. Not only in the small way we had already, but I wanted to do more.

I tugged on Patriot's hand and he leaned down. "Ronan, I... I need to..."

"I got you, Little Bit." He kissed my forehead. "Mr. Boscoe, I know we're strangers, and I also know how hard it is to accept help even when you need it most. Would you let us help a little more? MaryAnne and I have so much more than we need, and my Little Bit here has the biggest heart I've ever seen. It's tearing her up, thinking about your kids not having a home, food, or any other basics needed to survive."

I licked my lips and looked up. "Mr. Boscoe, it wasn't so long ago I was in a bad place. Patriot saved me, and I've kind of been drifting this past year. Healing at my own pace, but this holiday season has been the best I've ever had. Everything seems brighter. Happier. I want to share some of that joy with other people. I've been blessed by having Patriot and his club in my life. I only wish other people could be so lucky."

Patriot pulled out his wallet and took out a chunk of cash. "Before you say no, think about your family. Use this however you see fit. If you're behind on the utilities, put it toward that. Use it for rent, or whatever. It's a gift with no strings attached. There's only a few hundred there, but maybe it will ease a little of your stress over the next few weeks."

The man's eyes got glassy and he nodded, his lips pressed together tightly. He accepted the money and sounded choked up when he spoke. "Thank you. So much. This will keep us in the house another month, give me some time to figure out what we're going to do next. You have no idea what a tremendous gift this is."

Impulsively, I reached out and hugged him. It was quick and I immediately stepped back to Patriot's side. It was the first time I'd hugged anyone who wasn't part of the club. The way Patriot curved his arm around my shoulders and gave me a slight squeeze told me he knew what it had cost me. I could also see the pride shining in his eyes when he looked down at me.

"We'll be back in a little while with something else for your family," Patriot said. "We heard your little ones don't have a Christmas tree this year, and we can't very well let them spend the holidays without a bit of cheer."

David nodded and I could tell he was close to crying.

"Come on. Let's get our shopping done," I said, nudging Patriot.

I was a woman on a mission.

Chapter Eight

Patriot

I couldn't have been prouder of MaryAnne. Not only for hugging that man, but everything she was trying to accomplish. She'd picked out three pre-lit trees and ornaments that wouldn't break easily, not wanting the little kids to get hurt. She was a complete wonder, and I was so fucking glad she was mine.

"Since we're here, why don't we see if they have any of the items on the lists? Although, if the families didn't have decorations, they may not have stuff to wrap the presents either. Better grab some wrapping paper and tape," I said.

"Did you ever check your bank account? What if we're spending too much?" MaryAnne asked. "I want to do some good, but not if it means spending all your money. Oh no! The animals! We've been gone so long already…"

I sent a text to one of the Prospects, asking them to let Archimedes out and check on everyone's food and water. Then I pulled up the banking app on my phone, checked my balance, and let out a whistle. It seemed Titan wasn't kidding about the club helping. I showed her the screen and her eyes went wide.

"The Pres had Wizard deposit ten thousand into my account, Little Bit. That means we get everything on their lists, maybe something for the parents too, and even give them some cash to help in the upcoming weeks. And that's after the expense of the food and all the other things we stuffed into these carts."

"That's so amazing!" She smiled and flung her arms around me, giving me a tight hug. "Thank you! I couldn't have done all this on my own."

"Anything for you, Little Bit. In fact, we can make this a yearly thing. Each December, we can check in with Reverend Burson and see if he has any families in need. And maybe a few times a year, we can drop off some non-perishable food at his church for anyone who needs it."

"You're the best." She kissed me. It was brief, but it was the sweetest kiss I'd ever had.

"Come on. Pick out some wrapping paper, I'll grab the tape, and then we can buy the presents for these families."

We ended up having so much stuff, we had to check out and go back in for more. Seeing her so happy, so carefree, made it all worthwhile. Not only were we going to make someone's Christmas a little brighter, but helping someone had given MaryAnne the last little push she needed to become whole again. I could see it in her eyes. The shadows were gone, leaving a vibrant, sweet woman I got to call my own.

We dropped everything by the church, along with an envelope of cash for each family, and a few hundred as a donation to Reverend Burson's church. I wasn't ready for the day to end just yet. I pulled into a parking spot outside the diner and led MaryAnne inside. It had been hours since we last ate, having missed lunch because of all our shopping, and I knew she had to be starving.

"I know you like their pie," I said. "Figured we should grab a bite to eat. If you're as worn out as I am, I know you don't feel like cooking when we get home."

"This is perfect."

We were seated in a booth near the window and given menus. After we placed our drink order, the woman scurried off. As many times as we'd been here, I didn't really need the menu but I decided to see if there was anything new. This time of year, they usually had some holiday specials.

"I think I want the chicken and stuffing sandwich," she said. "It looks interesting."

"Chicken, stuffing, and gravy on toasted bread. Does actually sound pretty damn good. Think I'll get the same."

A server rushed to our table with our drinks and set them down, a smile on her face. "My name's Beth and I'll be waiting on you today. Do you need more time?"

We told her our order and promised to save room for dessert. Although, I'd have much rather had MaryAnne's pie or cake than anything the diner had. My woman could bake like no one else. There'd been some burnt disasters along the way, as she taught herself how to follow recipes, but she'd become a pro. In my opinion anyway. And I knew my brothers damn sure liked it when she sent goodies over to the clubhouse for them. They'd devoured everything she'd made the other day.

She hadn't realized I'd shared with a few of them in the past. If I ate every cookie she baked, I'd be too wide to fit through our front door. So I ate my share and pilfered a few here and there to pass off to someone else. I'd never told her, not wanting to hurt her feelings. If I told her I couldn't eat them all, she'd probably think I didn't really like them, which was the furthest thing from the truth.

"Christmas is nearly here. I know we didn't do much last year. I didn't want to overwhelm you. Is there anything you'd like to do this year?" I asked.

"The Christmases I spent with my family, we'd go visit our distant relatives on Christmas Eve night, usually at my grandparents' house and later at an aunt's home. When we got back to our place, everyone got to open one present. Mine was usually a book and I'd spend the rest of the night reading." She smiled and leaned forward. "Christmas morning, my mother would get up before everyone else and make a breakfast spread. French toast casserole, small ham steaks and rolls, and another casserole which had ham, eggs, cheese, onions, and hash browns in it. The smell would always wake us up."

"And you'd sit at the table to eat together?" I asked, trying to imagine having something like that. My childhood had definitely been different from hers.

"Not exactly. Mom would put it all out on the dining room table, like a buffet. We'd grab a plate and get whatever we wanted, then find a spot in the living room. My dad would put on one of those Burl Ives animated movies like *Rudolph*. I think they were Claymation or something. Anyway, we'd watch it while we ate and after everyone finished and we'd taken our dishes to the kitchen, we'd claim a spot in the living room again and Mom would pass out the presents."

"That sounds pretty great," I said.

"It was. I miss those days sometimes, but I think..." She worried at her lower lip. "I think everything that happened changed me in a way that made me better. The MaryAnne from before wouldn't have thought about anyone else this time of year. I'd have been too busy trying to talk Mom or Dad into some expensive present or something. I'm not saying I'm glad I went through all the pain and humiliation, but I do think it had a positive effect on me as a person. I had to have ugliness and darkness touch me to realize what I had before."

I reached over and placed my hand over hers. "Little Bit, you were always remarkable. You just hadn't had time to grow into the woman you were supposed to be. You were still a kid when those bastards kidnapped you. The fact you survived, and came out even stronger than before, makes you one badass lady."

She gave me a slight smile. "Guess I'd have to be for someone like you to want to keep me. If anyone in this relationship is amazing, it's you."

I sighed and leaned back. Before I could say anything, our food arrived, and Beth topped off our drinks. I waited until she'd walked off before I decided to tell MaryAnne a little more about my past. We hadn't really discussed me much.

"I didn't have a home like yours. My dad was a drunk. A mean one. When I was eleven, he walked out and didn't come back. We found out two days later he'd been so plastered he'd stepped in front of a moving car. His wallet had been knocked so far away from him, it hadn't been found right away. As soon as he'd been identified, they knocked on our door to give us the news."

"Oh, Ronan."

I should have corrected her, since we weren't alone, but she'd said it soft enough no one had heard. I never told anyone about my past. I didn't want their pity -- or worse, having them think I used it as an excuse.

"Mom worked twice as hard, trying to pay the rent on our trailer and keep food on the table. Some weeks we didn't quite make it and went hungry. Others we had a little extra if she got nicer tips. I'd just turned eighteen when she passed away. Doctors said her heart gave out. I think she held on just long enough for me to officially be an adult."

"I'm so sorry."

I shrugged a shoulder. "Long time ago, Little Bit. Anyway, I joined the Army. Fulfilled the terms of my contract and decided I was tired of following orders. Drifted a bit until the Hades Abyss took me in. Our chapter is pretty new. I was with the original charter in Missouri until this one started up. I volunteered to come with Titan."

"The compound here seems too well put together to be so new," she said.

"It's new compared to the Missouri chapter. Titan has built it up a lot just in the last few years."

She eyed her sandwich, then picked up her knife and fork, cutting into it. I had to admit, picking it up wasn't an option. The chicken and stuffing spilled out of the sides and the gravy pooled under it. As we ate, I tried to think of ways to make Christmas feel more like the ones she'd had before. Neither of us would be going to visit family on Christmas Eve, but we could start our own tradition.

"I have an idea," I said.

She paused with her fork halfway to her mouth. "Does it involve more shopping?"

"Um. Sort of."

"It's either shopping or it isn't."

"It is, but I think we can do it from home and just have stuff delivered. I thought we could buy a handful of Christmas movies. On Christmas Eve, we could make a bunch of different finger foods to snack on all day and watch back-to-back movies. Then that night we can each open one present, just like you used to do with your family."

She set her fork down. "Really?"

I nodded. "I don't want you cooking all morning on Christmas, though. Maybe I could help you put one of those casseroles together the night before so you'd just have to pop it in the oven when we wake up. We can open presents while it warms up, or whenever you'd like."

She picked up her fork again and studied me. "Why are you being so nice to me? Not just now, but from the very beginning you've gone out of your way for me. Even when we were strangers."

"Because I've always known you were mine," I said. "Even when I didn't think of you in a sexual way, you were still mine to protect."

She ate a few more bites before she started pushing her food around her plate. "The two who got away. If no one finds them, do you think they'll come back here?"

"Are you asking if you're safe?"

She nodded. "I haven't been overly cautious today. Didn't look over my shoulder constantly because you said you'd taken care of all but two."

"I won't let them anywhere near you, Little Bit. I told you, they're states away. There are enough clubs out there who are outraged by what happened to you they'll be extra vigilant. Those men get anywhere near a member in those clubs and their days will be numbered."

We finished our meal, and had dessert, but MaryAnne had grown quiet. I worried those two remaining men were going to give her nightmares tonight. Unless something else was bothering her. The fact she wasn't telling me what was on her mind didn't sit right with me. I didn't want to push, but I wouldn't let her fret all night either. I'd give her until we reached the house. If she hadn't opened up by then, I'd find a way to get it out of her. I couldn't help if she didn't tell me what was wrong.

I paid for our meal and left Beth a good tip. With the holidays so close, I figured she could use some extra cash like most people. Being on her feet all day wasn't easy, and I knew people could be assholes and either leave no tip or shitty ones. Getting a decent tip had always made my mom smile. Now I tried to do that for others when I could, but especially close to Christmas.

I took MaryAnne's hand as we walked outside. She closed her fingers around mine and leaned her head against my arm. This little slip of a woman made me want to be a better man.

I unlocked the Bronco and helped her inside, reaching over to buckle her. I gave her a wink before I shut the door. The second before I turned, I saw the reflection of a man standing behind me and MaryAnne's eyes went wide. I ducked as he swung an iron bar at my head. It smashed into the glass, making MaryAnne scream as it sprayed across her. Little cuts dotted her fair skin. Seeing her bleed let loose the monster I tried to keep locked down tight.

With a roar, I spun to face the man and slammed my fist into his face. He swung the pipe at me, and I blocked it with my arm, snarling at the pain radiating up into my shoulder. I didn't think he'd broken it, but it would be bruised by morning. I went after him again, landing a punch to his ribs, one to his nose, then kicked his legs out from under him.

He sprawled on his back on the pavement. Hatred blazed in his eyes as he struggled to his feet. I didn't give him a chance to come after me again. I landed a right hook to his temple and he went down, knocked out cold. Sirens sounded in the distance and it wasn't long before red and blue lights came into view.

I opened the Bronco door and reached for MaryAnne. She shook so damn hard I thought I heard her teeth rattle. I unbuckled her and helped her down. I was trying to shake the glass from her clothes when two officers approached, guns out and pointed at me.

"Hands where I can see them," the older of the two said.

I slowly lifted my hands and turned to face them. "Just trying to get the glass off my woman. The asshole on the ground smashed a metal pipe into the window. She's been hurt."

Two of the diner employees rushed out, both leaping to my defense. I noticed one was Beth.

"He didn't do anything but defend himself and his wife!" Beth wrung her hands. "I called you. That guy came out of nowhere."

Wife. I liked the sound of that. I tried to look at MaryAnne to gauge her reaction. She took a step closer to me, but her eyes were huge and full of unshed tears. I wanted to hold her, but I didn't dare move in case either of the officers was a little trigger happy.

The older cop lowered his gun a fraction. "Self-defense?"

I nodded. "I was just having dinner with my wife. Came out and helped her into the Bronco. Soon as I closed the door, I saw his reflection. He swung at me and ended up busting out the window. The glass cut my wife. He swung at me again and caught my arm when I lifted it to block him from hitting my head."

The older one eyed me a moment. "Raise your sleeve. Nice and slow."

I lifted it and winced, noticing the skin had split open. Didn't look bad enough to need stitches, but it didn't exactly feel amazing. The older cop lowered his weapon the rest of the way and motioned for the younger one to do the same.

"Name's Officer Bowers, and this is Officer Jenkins. We'll get the guy into cuffs and put him in the car, but I'm going to need an official statement from you if we're going to hold him."

"I need to finish getting the glass off my wife's clothes, and she needs medical care."

"So do you," Officer Bowers said. He reached for the mic at his shoulder. "Dispatch, need a box at 223 Main. Two injured."

"Box?" MaryAnne asked.

"Ambulance," the officer said. "Looks like a box on wheels."

She smiled faintly and I started shaking the glass from her clothes again. Getting the window on the Bronco repaired wasn't going to be fun. Normally, I'd do it myself, but I might pay someone else this time around. Wouldn't be too hard for an auto glass place to track down one that would fit the big beast.

When the EMTs arrived, I had them check MaryAnne first. They cleaned and treated the wounds on her face and neck, which seemed to be superficial, then worked on my arm. I'd been right about not needing stitches, but they put some butterfly strips across it once it had been disinfected.

Officer Bowers came over with a wallet in his hand. "Says here the man's name is Walter Wilcox. Lives two towns over."

"Never heard of him," I said.

"He didn't say anything before he attacked?" Officer Bowers asked.

"No. Just appeared at my back and swung. I have no idea why he came after me. Never seen him before. I typically recognize anyone I've pissed off."

The officer chuckled. "Well, we'll haul him in and see what we can find out. On the off chance he isn't acting alone, might want to keep a close watch on your wife. And be careful."

I shook his hand and walked over to the Bronco. There was too much glass for her to sit in the front, so I folded the seat down and helped her into the back. "Sorry, Little Bit. Can't have you riding up here with all this glass."

"I just want to go home. Are you sure you're all right?"

I kissed her forehead. "I'm fine. Promise. I'm afraid it's going to be a bit cold since the window is gone. I'll get us home as quick as I can."

I'd have Wizard look into Walter Wilcox and see what he could find out. I didn't think this attack was about MaryAnne. I hadn't seen him in any of the videos, and she hadn't seemed to recognize him. This was either personal, or had something to do with the club. Unless it was a case of mistaken identity. Either way, I needed to know it was over now that he was being hauled off to jail, or I'd be looking over my shoulder every time I went out with MaryAnne.

I helped her into the house and held her hand, keeping her still a moment. "You know, Beth referred to you as my wife, and so did I. You didn't look too startled by it."

Her cheeks warmed. "Maybe it was wishful thinking."

I tipped her chin up. "You want to be my wife? You're already mine in any way that counts with the club, but if you want my name too, it's yours."

"You'd marry me?" she asked.

"Either the old-fashioned way, or I could ask Wizard to hack the county and state systems to make it happen. I'm good with whatever you want."

"I don't think I'd like a crowd of people at a wedding. If it's just us anyway, I don't see why we should go to the cost and trouble of standing in front of someone to say vows. Can you ask Wizard to do it?"

I nodded and pulled out my phone, putting it on speaker as it rang.

"Patriot, everything okay?" he asked. "Got an alert you had a chat with the police."

I snorted. Of course he had. Any time anyone in the club was linked to an incident in the police systems, he got a notice about it. Illegally, but still accurate.

"Some asshole smashed the Bronco window and tried to bash in my head. I'm fine, and MaryAnne is good. Got a few cuts, but she'll be okay."

Wizard whistled. "What do you need?"

"Two things. First, can you do whatever magic Wire has done in the past to make MaryAnne my wife?"

"I'd love to! Congratulations!"

"Thank you," Mary Anne said.

"What else?" Wizard asked.

"The man who attacked me is Walter Wilcox. I've never heard of him and didn't recognize his face. See if you can find out why he would come after me. I need to know it's safe for MaryAnne to leave the compound."

"I'm on it. I'll text when I have something."

I ended the call and shoved the phone back into my pocket. "Do I need to bring your baking stuff in tonight?"

She shook her head. "It's not anything that will ruin. Unless it rains."

Shit. I hadn't even thought of it raining, or maybe even snowing. "Give me a minute to put something over the window, and I'll go ahead and bring your stuff in. Why don't you head up and take a shower? Might feel better. Just be careful with those cuts."

She went up on her tiptoes to press her lips to mine. "Don't be long."

My dick went hard as steel. I ran my hand down my beard as she went upstairs. Fuck but she was sexy. And mine. Once Wizard did his thing, she'd be mine in all ways. I had to be the luckiest bastard alive.

I rushed through taping a trash bag over the busted window and left the sacks of her baking supplies in the kitchen on the counter. After I let Archimedes out, covered Hatter's cage, and settled the kitten, I let the dog back in and kenneled him before locking up. Taking the steps two at a time, I hurried to our room. The shower was still going. I stripped out of my clothes and boots, then went to join my almost-wife. And this time, I'd make sure I fucked her in the bedroom like I should have the first time instead of up against the shower wall.

Or maybe I'd do both.

Chapter Nine

MaryAnne

The moment I heard the shower door open, my nipples hardened. I could have rationalized it as being from the cool gust of air. I knew that wasn't it. No, my body responded to the nearness of Patriot. The door shut and his hands settled at my waist. I felt the heat of his body press against my back and I leaned into him.

"Should you get your arm wet?" I asked, thinking about the bandages holding his cut together.

"Probably not. But if you think I'm letting you shower alone, you're wrong. Couldn't pass up an opportunity to hold my sexy wife."

"Wife?" I asked. "Did Wizard message you?"

"No. But if he says he's going to get it done, he will. You might as well get used to being called MaryAnne Caffee."

"I like it." I tipped my head back and looked up at him. "I like everyone knowing I'm yours."

He traced his fingers down my cheek. "Do these hurt?"

I shook my head. "Not really. I think they're mostly scratches and will heal in a few days."

He kissed me, his tongue delving into my mouth, his hold tightening on me. I should have been scared. Terrified. I didn't have a single flashback. All I felt was pleasure. It was Patriot holding me, kissing me, and that made all the difference. I knew he'd never hurt me.

And I loved him.

"Not taking you in the shower right now," he murmured against my lips. "You deserve better... a bed and me taking my time."

"As long as it's you doing the taking, I don't care where we are. Well, maybe not somewhere out in public with other people watching, but in this house? It doesn't matter what room we're in."

He slid his palm across my belly and a little lower. His other hand settled at my shoulder and bent me at the waist. I slapped my hands against the glass wall so I wouldn't topple over.

"Should I take you now? Fast? Hard?" He worked his hand between my thighs and cupped my pussy. He stroked my clit with his thumb, and I couldn't hold back my whimper. It felt so good. *He* felt good. "Or maybe I should make you come a few times."

"Ronan, please."

He lifted me into his arms and spun so that he faced the opposite wall. He eased me down onto the built-in bench, then shoved my thighs apart, spreading me open.

"Hands above your head, and keep them there," he said. I lifted them over my head, crossing my wrists. He groaned, his eyes darkening as he stared at me. "Can you thrust those pretty breasts up? Offer those nipples to me."

My breasts grew heavy and my clit pulsed. I pushed my shoulders back and he dropped to his knees in front of me. Patriot slid his hands up my thighs, then back down. When he moved them up again, he used his thumbs to spread my pussy open. As much as I ached and wanted him to make me come, he just looked.

"So beautiful," he said. "And mine. All mine."

"Yes, I'm yours! Only yours."

His gaze clashed with mine. "That's right. No one will ever touch you, kiss you. Only my cock will stretch you wide, fill you with cum. You belong to me, and I belong to you."

"Please! I... I need..."

He leaned forward and took a nipple into his mouth. When he sucked on it, drawing hard on the tip, I cried out and my hips jerked. His thumbs grazed the sides of my clit, right as he gently bit down on my nipple. It was enough to make me come. I screamed out my release, my body bucking and tensing, every nerve ending coming alive. He slid his thumbs up and down, drawing out my climax.

Patriot switched to my other breast, giving the hard tip a nibble. He grazed my clit again and I trembled. "You... you're going to... I'm going to... to..."

He rubbed his thumb across my clit, pressing down tighter as he circled the little bud. I screamed out his name as I came again. A roaring filled my ears and it felt like the world had tipped sideways. I couldn't breathe, couldn't hear or see. Everything came back into focus a little at a time.

Patriot pulled my ass to the edge of the bench and bent down. He licked my clit before sucking on it. I felt a fullness and realized he'd slid his fingers inside me. He stroked them in and out while his tongue teased my clit. My arms started to slide down the wall and he growled, his gaze locked on mine.

"Keep your hands there."

I tried. I really did. When he made me come again, I couldn't help it. I reached for him, my fingers sliding into his hair. I rocked against his mouth, but he pried himself loose and sat back on his haunches. Something flashed in his eyes and before I knew what was happening, he'd lifted me and taken my place on the bench. I somehow ended up on my knees between his splayed thighs.

"Warned you, Little Bit. Think you can handle paying the price?" He ran his fingers through my hair, his touch gentle despite the hard edge to his words.

"What price?"

He gripped his cock and gave it a stroke. "Want those lips wrapped around me."

I took a steadying breath and placed my hands on his thighs, then lowered my head and swirled my tongue over the head of his cock. He groaned again and I took more of him into my mouth. I'd barely managed half of his length when I felt his fingers in my hair. He tugged on the strands, then I felt pressure against the back of my head and knew what he wanted.

I gave up control to him, something I'd feared doing. His murmured words of encouragement, and the fact I knew it was Patriot, kept me from going to a dark place. He forced more of his cock into my mouth. On his next thrust, he slid to the back of my throat and held still.

"Swallow," he said. "Swallow for me, Little Bit."

I did as he'd commanded, and it seemed to snap his control. He gripped my face between his palms and pumped into my mouth with hard, fast strokes. I felt his cock swell against my tongue and then spurt after spurt of his hot cum filled my mouth. I tried to take it all, but I felt some slide from the corners of my mouth.

Patriot pulled free, his chest heaving but his touch gentle. He smoothed his hand over my hair. "So good. Fuck, Little Bit. You're Goddamn amazing."

I wiped his cum from my chin and mouth. The soft expression in his eyes made me want to give him more. I liked pleasing him. It hadn't been scary, like I'd thought it might be.

"I think I owe you a few more orgasms," he said, standing and holding out his hand. "But let's move this to the bed."

My legs felt like rubber when I stood, and he helped me out of the shower. He briskly dried me with a towel before using it on himself, then it tossed it into the hamper. I followed him into the bedroom, where he tugged down the sheets and motioned for me to get on the bed.

He kissed me, slow and deep before drawing away. "Anyone else ever lick your pussy?"

I slowly shook my head. "No. I... I was a virgin when they took me. No one cared if I enjoyed what they did."

A shadow crossed his eyes a moment but cleared almost instantly. "I'll do better about bringing up past sexual experiences. Sometimes I forget for a moment how young you were... I'm sorry, Little Bit."

He toppled me to my back and pushed my thighs apart. Dropping to his knees beside the bed, he tugged my ass closer to the edge of the mattress. The first swipe of his tongue sent a shockwave of pleasure coursing through me. I'd read books where guys did this sort of thing, but experiencing it firsthand was another matter. His tongue was soft, wet, and hot... and wickedly talented. I moaned as he flicked it against my clit.

"Feels so amazing," I said.

Patriot took his time, bringing me right to the edge multiple times, yet never letting me come. It was both frustrating and exquisite torture. I loved every second of it and wanted more, but I also wanted an orgasm. Now that I'd experienced what it felt like, more than once, I was greedy and wanted lots more.

"Don't stop. Please, don't stop, Ronan."

He sucked at my clit until I saw stars. My toes curled from the intense pleasure, and I forgot to breathe for a moment. The weight of his body settled over me and I hugged his hips with my thighs.

"Is this okay?" he asked, his cock brushing against me.

"More than. You don't have to ask permission, Ronan. I want you every bit as much as you want me. I'm yours. As long as you don't cause me pain, I'll try anything you want. We won't know what will freak me out if we don't experiment a little."

"You're fucking amazing."

I felt the hard length of him enter me. He didn't slam home. No, he took his time. Every stroke was drawn out, and so perfect I nearly cried. The push and pull of his cock kept me on the edge of another orgasm. I dug my nails into his shoulders, never wanting the moment to end. I kept my gaze on his, watching as his eyes darkened.

"Make me come, Ronan, then take what you need."

I felt the vibration of his growl before I heard it. He did something with his hips, a slight twist on the next thrust that had my pussy clenching tight. It didn't take long before I was coming again. He drove into me, taking me hard and fast, his hips slapping against me.

"Yes! Yes! More!" I held on tighter as he seemed to lose control. When he came, he let out a roar, sounding more animal than human, his cock driving into me again and again, as his hot cum filled me up.

His chest heaved as he tried to catch his breath and I reached up to run my fingers over his beard.

Patriot turned his face to kiss my palm, and my heart warmed at the gesture. For a tough man, one who'd killed, he could be incredibly sweet.

"I didn't hurt you?" he asked.

"Not even a little."

"Let me catch my breath and we'll try again. Maybe a different position."

"If you want. Or you could just hold me. I'd be happy either way."

He kissed my cheek, my jaw, and finally my lips. "Love you, MaryAnne. Never loved a woman until you. And before you bring up my mom, she doesn't count. She gave birth to me. It's not the same thing."

I smiled and ran my fingers through his hair. "Love you so much it hurts, but in a good way."

He got off me, his cock sliding from my body. I felt his release leak out of me and didn't know if I should run clean up, or leave it. He took the matter out of my hands when he picked me up and settled me against the pillows. Patriot walked into the bathroom and I heard the sink running. After a moment, he returned with a wet rag. He gently cleaned between my legs, then tossed the rag back into the bathroom before getting into bed with me.

"Get some rest, Little Bit."

I sighed and closed my eyes, snuggling against him. When I heard his phone chime, and then go off again, I reluctantly let him go. Patriot rolled out of bed and went to retrieve his phone. His brow furrowed as he scrolled through the messages.

"Everything okay?" I asked.

"Yes and no. The man who attacked me doesn't have anything to do with your past. That's a blessing. Means no one is out for revenge because of the men

I've killed. But he does pose a problem. If he gets out of jail, he'll come for me again."

"Why? Or is it club business?" I asked.

"It is, but you're a small part of it. Remember the club whore I told to leave? The one who insulted you?"

I nodded.

"She's apparently married. To the man who attacked me. All we can figure is he saw my cut and decided to get even. No way of knowing if he wanted me specifically, or any member of the club. Although, I don't know why Blaire would say anything to him about me knocking her on her ass."

My jaw dropped and I didn't know what to say. Why would a married woman come here to be a club whore? Had she been sent to spy? Or was it something else?

"What happens now?" I asked.

"If he's released, I'll handle it. Either way, that bitch has a lot to answer for. I'll be back in a minute, Little Bit. Need to call Kraken and let him know what's up. I'll be to bed as soon as I've handled this. Can't have the club blindsided, and if the bitch is still hanging around, she needs to go. Immediately."

I couldn't have agreed more. I rolled to my side and snuggled into the pillow. Yawning so wide, I felt my jaw pop, I closed my eyes. I felt sleep tugging at me when the bed dipped, and Patriot pulled me into his arms.

"Kraken said he'd handle it." He kissed my neck, then my shoulder. "Let's get some rest so I can wear you out some more."

I couldn't help but smile. After I'd first been brought here, if anyone had told me I'd be lying in bed with a man, willingly, and looking forward to sex, I'd have told them they were fucking crazy. But Patriot wasn't just any man. He'd saved me, not only physically, but emotionally and mentally as well.

He may not have given me my life back, but he'd helped me create a new one. Given me a home. More than that, he'd given me his love, and had an infinite supply of patience. He'd never once pushed me to do more than I felt comfortable doing, whether it was leaving the compound or visiting with people. He understood me better than anyone.

The heat of his body curled around me made me feel safe. I didn't just want to be with him because of that, though. It was so much more. When I thought about the future, it was Patriot I saw by my side. Even before he'd claimed me, I'd always seen him as being part of my life. I'd just thought I didn't stand a chance of him seeing me as more than a kid. I was glad I'd been wrong.

It didn't matter how many presents were under the tree because the most important gift had been his love. This wasn't going to be just a good Christmas, but it was going to be an amazing one. All because of Patriot.

I only hoped one day he'd understand when I said I loved him, it was more than three little words. It meant everything.

Chapter Ten

Patriot

The club whore who'd thrown her drink at MaryAnne had been tossed from the club, but she hadn't gone quietly. Blaire Wilcox was more trouble than she was worth. She'd thrown a beer bottle at Kraken, kicked Brick in the nuts, and raked her nails across Gravel's face before we'd managed to toss her out the gates, right on her ass. She'd shrieked and cussed, promised she'd get even. Wasn't anything we hadn't heard before.

We just hadn't expected her to follow through. And that's where we fucked up.

We'd had two days of quiet before all hell broke loose. Not an avalanche exactly, more like a slow trickle of bad luck. A few bikes had flat tires when my brothers came out of the clubhouse after partying. We'd thought it was a coincidence until other things started to happen. We still hadn't figured out who had let the air out of the tires. It had to be someone who still had access to the Hades Abyss compound. Wizard had been going through video footage trying to get a look at the culprit.

Phoebe's car had had *whore* spray painted on the driver-side door when she'd gone to the store the next day, which had sent Kraken and Titan both on a rampage. Two nights after that, someone poured a gallon of bright pink paint across the driveway outside the gate and wrote *pussies* in it before it had dried. They'd been far enough from the gate, we not only hadn't seen or heard them, but they weren't caught on camera either. But I'd known it was Blaire who cut the fence line and destroyed my yard and outside Christmas lights when I found three slushie cups tossed into the grass nearby. Bitch hadn't been as smart as she'd thought. Her DNA was all over the straws, and her fingerprints had been on the outside of each cup.

It wasn't until Wizard ran her prints I realized we needed to start vetting the women we let into the compound. The webcam girls were one thing, but it wasn't enough. We needed to vet the club whores too. Blaire was wanted in three states for prostitution, robbery, and had spent a year locked up for possession with intent to distribute. And her husband wasn't much better.

MaryAnne sat at the table with a cup of hot cocoa, Christmas songs playing softly from the radio on the counter, as she stared into space. Hatter whistled along with *White Christmas*, while Archimedes lay out beside MaryAnne with his head on her foot. Even the kitten seemed subdued.

"You all right, Little Bit?" I asked.

"I'm fine. Just wish this mess with Blaire and her husband was over with. They haven't caught him yet?"

I shook my head. The day he'd been headed to court for his hearing, somehow Walter Wilcox had managed to escape custody. He was still at large, and most likely off somewhere with Blaire, plotting their next move. She wanted revenge because I'd chosen MaryAnne and then humiliated her, and her husband hadn't liked the idea of his wife spreading her legs for a bunch of bikers. Free of charge, of course. Had we been paying her, he likely wouldn't have minded, since he appeared to be her pimp.

"Come on, Little Bit. Let's go watch some movies and have some quality time together. Seems like with everything going on, we haven't had a lot of time to just relax and enjoy each other's company."

She stood and gave me a wan smile. "All right, but I'm not sure how Christmas-y I feel right now."

I took her hand and led her into the living room. I left the radio playing for Hatter, but Archimedes and the kitten followed us. The kitten climbed the couch and curled up in MaryAnne's lap. I watched her stroke the little ball of fur while I selected a movie.

"I think you should name him," I said. "He seems to like you best."

She toyed with his little ears. "He's always getting into trouble. What about Rascal?"

I nodded. "Sounds like a good name. How about it, kitty? You like the name Rascal?"

The kitten purred and rubbed his face against MaryAnne. I laughed and reached over to pet him.

"I think he likes it," she said.

"Seems that way. I had a feeling he wasn't leaving here. I know you try not to bond to the animals I bring home, but I saw the way you looked at him that first night. All wet from the rain and covered in fleas and blood. Little thing was half-starved and dying. You didn't see all that, though, did you?"

"No. He might have looked mostly dead, but I could tell he wasn't ready to give up."

"Like you," I said, taking her hand.

"You have a tendency to bring home wounded things. All your animals. Me. What's next?"

I rubbed the back of my neck. Since she'd brought it up, it was the perfect time to talk to her about something. I wasn't sure how the conversation would go. Either she'd be thrilled, scared, or just outright refuse. Only one way to know for certain, and I was about out of time.

"Since you brought it up… there is one other thing I'd like to bring home."

She turned a little to face me. "What?"

"Remember those families we helped? The ones from the church."

"What about them?" she asked.

"One of those families has a fifteen-year-old daughter. She wasn't raped, like you were, but she did fool around with a boy who was old enough to know better and she ended up pregnant."

MaryAnne's brow furrowed. "I don't understand where this is going."

I tightened my hold on her hand, hoping she'd hear me out. I loved her, and I'd be happy with just the two of us and the animals, but I knew she wanted more. She wanted a family, and honestly, I did too. I wanted it all, as long as MaryAnne was the one by my side.

"The girl can't keep the baby. The family can barely feed everyone as it is, and at fifteen, she's just not ready to be a mother. The boy who got her pregnant signed away his rights. They were going to put the baby up for adoption when it's born." I stroked her hand with my thumb. "It's a girl."

I saw the pulse in her throat pounding. "A baby girl? And they don't want her?"

"Not so much that they don't want her, but they want her to have a good life. One where she won't struggle and will have more opportunities." I cleared my throat. "Told them we might be interested in adopting her, but I'd have to talk to you first. Then all this other shit started happening and there hasn't been a good time to bring it up."

"A baby," she said softly. "And she'd be ours? They wouldn't try to take her back later?"

"No, Little Bit. They won't take her away from us. We'll sign papers, do everything legally. Or mostly.

I did tell them Wizard could help move things along faster and they seemed okay with that."

"Can we really adopt her?"

"If that's what you want. I know you wanted kids and since I know for sure I can't have any, and you were worried you can't, it seemed like a good opportunity. Not just for us, but it will give that baby a chance at a good life, and the girl can finish school without worrying about raising a kid."

Tears misted her eyes, and she flung her arms around my neck, dislodging Rascal from her lap. "Oh, Ronan! I can't think of anything I want more."

I hugged her tight. "Then I'll make some calls and let them know we'll take her. I'll have to get a room ready. Think the girl is due before Christmas."

"This is going to be the best Christmas ever."

"Not sure I can ever top this one. I get the woman I love and a daughter."

"That can't be all you want in life," she said.

Was it? I had brothers I knew would have my back no matter what. A woman I loved who wanted me as much as I wanted her. And we were going to adopt a baby girl. Toss in my rescues and life was close to perfect. Almost.

"I want the last two fuckers who hurt you to pay the price, and I'd like Walter and Blaire Wilcox out of our lives forever. Other than that, I can't say there's really anything else I want. I have everything I need already."

She pressed against me and I held her close. Yeah, I definitely had everything I needed already. Even if the adoption fell through, it wouldn't matter to me. I'd love the little girl like she was my own flesh and blood, and I knew MaryAnne wanted a baby, but as long as I had her I didn't need anything else.

"We should bring Hatter in here. Everyone else in the family is ready for a movie night," she said. "Don't you think he feels left out in the kitchen by himself?"

I smiled and kissed the top of her head. "Making sure my bird doesn't get depressed?"

"Just doesn't seem fair is all."

"I'll get Hatter. We'll see how well Rascal does with him. I haven't trimmed Hatter's flight feathers lately, so if the kitten goes for him, he can fly away."

"I'll get a movie going. Any requests?"

"Whatever you want, Little Bit."

I went to get Hatter from his cage. He ran up my arm and settled on my shoulder with a rustle of his feathers. When he started grooming my hair, I reached up and rubbed the top of his head. I carried him to the living room and sat on the couch next to MaryAnne. She immediately leaned into my side and clicked PLAY on the movie. *The Year Without a Santa Claus* started up. My girl was nothing if not predictable. She loved her animated holiday movies. Didn't matter if it was Christmas or Halloween.

Hatter moved from my shoulder to the back of the couch. So far, Rascal hadn't noticed him. Or just didn't care the bird was roaming free. Archimedes groaned and rolled to his side, stretching out more on the floor. Rascal batted the dog's ear before curling up next to him. The two had become fast friends.

I heard a scraping sound outside and my gaze strayed to the window. I didn't see any movement through the blinds, nor did I hear anything else. It was possible one of my brothers was out there, probably taking a smoke break. Philly lived on one side of me and Poison was on the other. When we'd been assigned our houses, I'd joked with Titan and asked if he was trying to keep all the P names together.

Honestly, I didn't mind having Philly and Poison as neighbors. Neither was overly loud, and I got along with them. Hell, I got along with everyone in the club, even if Smoke had overstepped with MaryAnne recently. And Galahad tended to get on my last nerve with the way he treated her. Or more accurately, the way he seemed to not give a rat's ass. I knew that wasn't the case. He'd about fallen apart when he'd found out she'd been taken, and he'd done some shit he shouldn't have.

Another scrape from a different area caught my attention again. What the fuck was going on out there?

"Little Bit, I need to step outside for a second. Stay inside, okay?"

She tipped her head. "Are you going out to smoke?"

"Need to check on something. It's warm in here and you aren't wearing shoes." I kissed her temple. "I'll be back in a minute."

I went to the door and slowly pulled it open. I didn't want to worry MaryAnne, so I didn't pull the gun I kept on me. Not until I'd gone outside. I stepped off the porch and made my way around the side of the house facing Philly's home. His lights were off, which didn't mean much. This time of night, he was most likely at the clubhouse.

I'd almost missed it, but there was a small footprint outside the house below the guest room window. Could have been MaryAnne's, except she didn't make a habit of hanging out on the side of the house. There was another outside the living room. This time, I knew for sure it wasn't MaryAnne's. The footprint faced the window, like someone had been trying to look through the blinds, or perhaps anticipated scaling up to the second floor.

"What the fuck?" I muttered. I looked around and didn't see anyone. No more scraping sounds.

I walked the perimeter and didn't see anything else out of the ordinary. I couldn't shake the feeling something was wrong, but fuck if I could figure out what it was. I glanced at Philly's house again. I squinted a little and studied his home, noticing the front door seemed to be partially open. It could have been a shadow, but I needed to make sure.

I approached his house, gun still gripped and ready. A quick glance at my place, showed the door was still shut. I didn't hear Archimedes barking, or any screams. I hoped that meant MaryAnne was still watching her movie. Using the toe of my boot, I nudged the door open. Even through the darkness, I could see the shadow of a body on the floor. The leather cut had me moving closer. *Shit!* I knelt next to the body, feeling for a pulse. It was there, and strong.

"Philly." I gave him a nudge. Something shiny caught my attention and I realized he was bleeding. It looked like someone had bashed the side of his head. I pulled my phone out and sent a text to Titan.

Someone knocked out Philly.

There wasn't a lot I could do for him at the moment. I checked his house, making sure no one else was there, then went outside to scan the area. Had the footprints outside my place happened before or after Philly had been attacked? On the other side of Philly was Brick's home. On the off chance he wasn't out partying, I checked his home. He was out cold too, but he hadn't even made it into his house. Whoever had taken him out had caught him getting off his bike, or getting on it. Either way, he was knocked out in the carport. Had they started here, then moved to Philly's place, then mine?

MaryAnne! I took off for my house, not bothering to stay quiet. I rushed through the door and froze when I saw Blaire pointing a knife at MaryAnne. Her eyes were wild and bloodshot, and it looked like she hadn't combed her hair in a few days.

"What the fuck are you doing?" I asked.

"It was supposed to be me!" Blaire yelled.

"What was?"

"Why couldn't one of you have picked me? I needed you! Do you know what it's like being married to Walter? He doesn't love me. The only thing he loves is money and power. He uses me." She sniffled, but I wasn't sure if she was about to cry or if she'd been doing coke. "He made me a whore."

I saw the pity and understanding that crossed MaryAnne's face. Yeah, my girl knew something about that. If Blaire had come to one of us, been honest, we might have been able to help her. She'd gone about everything the wrong way, and now she'd taken out two of my brothers and held a knife on my woman? Bitch was going down.

"So you thought breaking into my house, threatening my wife, and knocking out my brothers was going to help your cause?" I asked.

"Wife!" She shrieked and jabbed the knife at MaryAnne. "You bitch!"

MaryAnne tried to scramble away, but she wasn't fast enough. The knife sank into her thigh. I saw her face pale as she bit her lips. My beautiful, strong girl refused to cry or scream.

Before I could make my move, Archimedes growled from the corner of the room. He slunk along the wall, then darted toward Blaire. He bit down on her ankle, making her squeal like a fucking pig. Rascal decided to protect his family too and puffed up, hissing and spitting at Blaire before he sank his claws into her other leg. She flailed, screamed, and cussed as she toppled to the floor.

Hatter came out of nowhere. He flapped his wings as he dug his little claws into her scalp and pulled on her hair. "Bitch! Bitch! Kill her!"

MaryAnne's jaw dropped and her eyes went wide. I hadn't taught Hatter that one, so it made me wonder just what my sweet MaryAnne had been saying when she'd been alone with Hatter. "Something you want to share, Little Bit?"

"Get them off me!" Blaire yelled.

I nudged Rascal and Archimedes aside and waved off Hatter. Grabbing Blaire by the arms, I flipped her over and gripped her wrists at the small of her back. "Little Bit, get the cuffs out of the bedside table drawer."

"Out of... where?" MaryAnne's eyebrows rose to her hairline. "Something *you* want to share?"

"Stop being a smartass and get the cuffs, woman. Unless you want me letting this she-devil go?"

MaryAnne scurried off the couch, or tried to. She cried out and collapsed. I saw the bleeding seeping through her pants leg and cursed. I couldn't release the bitch on the ground to check on her. Riley ran into the house with two more brothers on his heels. I sent him upstairs for the cuffs and tried to keep an eye on MaryAnne. Riley tossed the cuffs to me and I put them on Blaire just as Kraken came through the door. I sat back on my haunches and looked over at him.

"Are you shitting me?" he asked. "A fucking club whore took out three of our brothers?"

"Three?" I asked.

"She got Poison, Philly, and Brick." Kraken nudged her with his boot. "What the fuck is your damage?"

"I think she's on something." I hurried to MaryAnne's side and helped her back onto the couch. Blood gushed through the tear in her pants. "Get me a fucking towel or something. Need to tie this off."

"Did her husband really make her a whore?" MaryAnne asked, her voice soft and low. I could tell it bothered her. In other circumstances, I'd have felt bad for Blaire.

"She's been arrested multiple times for prostitution," I said. "Don't you fucking feel sorry for her, Little Bit. Her situation is nothing like yours."

Riley hauled Blaire off the floor and shoved her toward Kraken. He got a good grip on her arm and started marching her out of the house. I got a better look at her face and knew I'd been right. She was on something. Probably more than one thing. I didn't know what the club would do to her, but she wasn't my problem right now. I needed to focus on MaryAnne.

"Bones is tending Poison, Philly, and Brick," Kraken said. "I'm taking this one out to the barn. Think we need to have a chat."

"Find out where her husband is. I'd prefer not to have any more surprises tonight."

"Um, Patriot," MaryAnne said, her voice sounding a little thin. "I think I'm bleeding a little too much."

"Fuck!" I swung my gaze back to her. "Little Bit, I need your pants off to see how bad this is."

"Take her to the hospital," Kraken said. "If she needs stitches, it would be better if Bones doesn't have to do it. Text Bones and see if he has anything to help with the bleeding until you can get her there."

I lifted MaryAnne into my arms. "Come on, Little Bit. Kraken's right. Need to get this wound checked out. Maybe the hospital will give you something for the pain."

I carried her out to the Bronco, only to remember the damn window hadn't been fixed yet. I kept walking, heading to the clubhouse. We'd have to use a club truck. And I needed to get the fucking Bronco working, especially if we were bringing a baby home. Or maybe I needed to buy something new.

I eased her onto the front seat of the first truck and ran inside to get the keys. The hospital was twenty minutes away, and I didn't like the amount of blood soaking into her pants and the rag I'd used as a tourniquet. MaryAnne looked too pale.

I stopped long enough to text Bones. *Anything to stop MaryAnne from bleeding? She got stabbed.*

He responded almost immediately. *I had some Celox but I'm out.*

I reached over to squeeze her hand as I broke every speed limit in town, trying to get her some help as fast as I could. I also needed to come up with a story because if they went looking for Blaire, it would cause problems for the club.

"Little Bit, when we get there, we're going to have to tell them something."

She didn't answer and I glanced her way. She'd slumped against the window and her eyes were closed. Panic clawed at me and I brushed my fingers over her wrist, searching for her pulse. I found it, but it wasn't nearly as strong as I'd have liked. I stopped the truck at the ER entrance. Getting out, I ran to her side and pulled her from the truck before hurrying inside. I hoped like fuck she'd only passed out from pain and not blood loss.

"My wife's been stabbed!" I yelled out, hoping to get some help quickly. A nurse ran over and started asking questions. "I-I don't know. It happened kind of fast. We were taking a walk in town and someone came at us. A woman."

I was fucking this up and sounded like a damn idiot. But it was MaryAnne, and she was bleeding entirely too much. If my story was full of holes, I'd deal with it later. I finished answering her questions and stayed by MaryAnne's side. I held her hand as they took her back to a curtained off area.

"Sir, we need to get her undressed and into a gown," a nurse said.

"I'll do it," I said. "She's my wife. I can't leave her."

The woman gave me an understanding smile and set a gown on the bed. "If you need help, just call out."

After she'd closed the curtain again, I worked at getting MaryAnne undressed and into the hospital gown. It wasn't easy since she hadn't woken yet. The wound looked worse than I'd thought, and blood still gushed from it. It wasn't near an artery, so I didn't know why it was still bleeding so bad.

I yelled out for help and the moment the nurse saw the wound she started barking out orders. MaryAnne was wheeled away from me, the medical staff running alongside her. The nurse who had been helping us stayed behind, keeping me from following.

"Sir, you have to go to the waiting room. Your wife needs surgery and you can't go with her."

Surgery? Had it really been so deep?

"I can't lose her," I said. Even in combat I'd never been this close to coming undone. MaryAnne was my everything. I'd have rather faced several thousand insurgents than even think of living the rest of my life without her.

The nurse briefly touched my arm. "We're going to do all we can for your wife, but in order for us to do our jobs right we need you to remain in the waiting room and try to keep calm. As soon as we know something, we'll come find you. Is there someone you can call to wait with you?"

I nodded and followed her back to the waiting room, where I collapsed into a chair. I pulled out my phone and sent off a quick text to Titan.

MaryAnne is in surgery. They sent me to the waiting room.

The Pres didn't answer right away, and I figured he was dealing with Blaire, or tracking down her husband. When he did answer, I felt a moment of relief.

Delilah is heading your way, along with Pretty Boy and Stone.

Chapter Eleven

Patriot

I got up and paced until I found the coffee. I poured myself a cup and leaned against the wall as I sipped at it. It gave me something to do, but it didn't slow down my mind. All I could think about was how still she'd been, how pale. If MaryAnne died, I'd personally send Blaire straight to hell, and her husband too.

My phone chimed and I checked it, seeing a message from Kraken.

Bitch is high as a fucking kite, but she's talking. She acted on her own tonight. Another club whore helped with the tire incident. She'll be dealt with too.

Great. That meant Walter was still out there, and possibly gunning for the club. All because his wife tried to whore herself out to us in hopes we'd save her. Or that's what I'd gathered from all the screeching she'd done tonight.

My phone went off again.

Wizard is tracking Walter. Just focus on your woman.

I pocketed my phone and tried to do as Kraken said. It wasn't like Walter would come into the hospital, guns blazing. Well, he might, but I didn't think he was entirely stupid. The man had managed to escape police custody. It either made him incredibly lucky, or smarter than I liked.

The doors opened and Delilah rushed in with my brothers following in her wake. She came straight for me and gave me a hug.

"I'm so sorry, Patriot. How is she? Have they said anything?" she asked as she pulled away.

"Nothing yet. Thanks for coming."

"Phoebe offered to watch Walker. Titan went to help Kraken."

Pretty Boy stared at her. "You know more than you should."

She glared at him. "I'm married to your President. While he doesn't share everything with me, he does try to tell me enough that I don't worry myself sick over him every time he walks out the door. If you have an issue with it, by all means, tell Titan. Just let me get popcorn first before the show starts."

Stone snickered and slung his arm around Delilah. "I knew I liked you."

She rolled her eyes and faced me again. "We're here for however long you need us. Let Titan and the others handle everything else. Just focus on MaryAnne. She needs you more than the club does right now."

"She's not wrong," Pretty Boy said.

I finished my coffee and poured another cup. I found a spot and sat down with Delilah next to me and my brothers sitting directly across from us. I appreciated the three of them coming. It felt like forever before a doctor came out. He scanned the waiting room.

"Family of MaryAnne Caffee."

I stood, along with Delilah and my brothers. The doctor came over.

"How is she?" I asked.

"Are you her husband?" I nodded. "Mr. Caffee, the wound to your wife's thigh wasn't just deep, but whoever stabbed her must have twisted the blade a little. We were able to stop the bleeding and put in stitches. I don't think she passed out from blood loss but more likely from the pain, which is a good thing. We didn't have to give her any blood."

"She's going to be okay?" I asked.

"She should heal just fine as long as she follows her aftercare instructions. We're going to keep her for a few days, make sure she's healing well. Once the anesthesia wears off, we'll put her in a room, and you'll be able to go sit with her. Are you going to stay the night?" he asked.

"Yeah. I'm not leaving until she can go with me. One night. Four. Doesn't matter. I'm staying by her side."

"I figured as much. I'll be sure to let the nurses know. Someone will come get you as soon as Mrs. Caffee is settled into a room."

"Thank you," Delilah said. "For everything."

The man flashed her a smile and hurried off. It felt like a weight lifted off me and I could breathe again. Pretty Boy patted my shoulder and wandered off a moment, pulling his phone from his pocket. I didn't know if he was giving everyone an update on MaryAnne, or doing something else.

"We'll make sure the two of you have whatever you need," Stone said. "If the hospital asks for payment, stall them. I have a feeling the club will step up for this one."

I hadn't even thought that far ahead. I vaguely remembered handing over a card when the nurse was asking me a shit ton of questions. I pulled out my wallet and noticed my bank card was missing. Must have grabbed it instead of a credit card. "I think I may have already paid and overdrawn my account. They have my bank card."

Stone cursed and rushed toward the triage desk. While he spoke with the woman, waving a hand in my direction a few times, I sat again and stretched my legs out. Delilah retook her seat and placed her hand on my arm. "I know Titan will handle the bill. If they've charged you, he'll reimburse you from club funds. MaryAnne got hurt because of a club whore. That's not on you."

"Thanks, Delilah. I wasn't even thinking. They kept asking me shit and all I could think about was MaryAnne bleeding to death before they helped her. I don't even remember everything I said or did when we got here."

Tension rose in the waiting room and I glanced toward the door in time to see two police officers stroll inside. They went straight to triage, where Stone was still trying to get my card back from the nurse. I had a feeling they were here for me. At the very least, they'd have questions about how MaryAnne got stabbed. I couldn't remember what the fuck I'd told the nurses. Now what was I going to do?

The officers headed my way, and I recognized one of them from the other night. Officer Bowers. Looked like he had a different partner this time. One who didn't seem to be quite as wet behind the ears. I wondered what had happened to the younger guy.

"We meet again," Officer Bowers said. "Care to take me through the events that led to your wife being stabbed? Because I have to say, you have the shittiest luck."

"Or he stabbed her himself," the other officer said.

Bowers gave him a glare. "Already made up your mind, Taylor? I'll make a note of that in my report."

The guy backed off, but the red tinge riding his cheeks told me he was pissed about it. Officer Taylor refused to look my way, staring at a spot over my head. Guess he wasn't as seasoned as I'd thought.

"The night is kind of a blur right now. My wife just got out of surgery and I'm still processing everything." I stood to speak to him. "There was a woman. I remember her eyes being bloodshot and she kept sniffling. I wondered if she'd been doing drugs."

Officer Bowers nodded. "The hospital said you were attacked in town. Why didn't you call 9-1-1?"

"I didn't think MaryAnne had time to wait for an ambulance. Even if someone had been available right away, it would have taken longer for them to reach us and get here than if I'd just put her in the truck and brought her myself. I had a towel in the backseat. I tied off the wound and got her here as fast as I could."

"Any idea who the woman was?" Officer Bowers asked.

And here's where it got tricky. If I said I didn't recognize her and they somehow later discovered it was Blaire Wilcox, there would be more questions. If I admitted who it was, they'd look for her, and then her husband would be connected to the club. So I decided on partial truths.

"Looked like a club whore. Some new woman. I haven't been to any club parties since MaryAnne moved in, so I haven't officially met her before. And everything happened so fast tonight, I could be wrong. Might have just been someone who looked similar."

"Got a name?" Officer Bowers asked.

"Something with a B. I don't really remember. Just know some of my brothers have talked about her."

Pretty Boy had heard everything and must have figured out what I was doing. He gave me a subtle chin lift and approached. "Her name is Blaire. Don't know her last name. Haven't had the displeasure of being with her, but she's been hanging around the club for at least a few months. I think. Just popped up one day out of nowhere, looking to have fun. Those women come and go so much it's hard to keep track."

"A description would be nice," Officer Bowers said.

"Average height. Blonde hair." Pretty Boy shrugged. "I can't really help beyond that. I can see if Stone knows her better. He might be able to tell you more."

The club Treasurer headed off in the direction of the triage desk, where Stone either wasn't having any luck with my card, or was getting lucky with the nurse. It could go either way. Despite his stoicism, the ladies loved him.

"You and your wife seem to be having a rough time," Officer Bowers said.

"Wrong place at the wrong time. I'm starting to think we should just stay in our house until after the holidays. This time of year makes me people crazy."

He chuckled. "No truer words were ever spoken."

"I heard the man who attacked us escaped custody. Y'all find him yet?" I asked.

Officer Bowers shook his head. "Thought we'd tracked him down, but when we got there, the place was empty. We're keeping an eye out. Although, since he attacked you once already, this could be a related incident. Woman might know him."

"True. I hadn't thought of that."

Stone and Pretty Boy came back. Stone handed my card to me and I put it back in my wallet.

"They hadn't charged your account yet," Stone said. "Pretty Boy talked to Titan. You don't need to worry about the bill."

"Thanks, brother." I rubbed at my forehead where a headache was building. "Wonder how much longer until I can see her. Shouldn't she have come out of it by now?"

Officer Bowers took a step back. "We'll head out for now, but give me a call if you think of anything else. Even something small might help us find the woman who attacked your wife."

He handed me a business card and walked off, his silent partner trailing after him. Pretty Boy, Stone, and Delilah all waited with me until a nurse came to take me to MaryAnne. They followed us up to her room, got a list of things we might need, and left. I tugged the recliner closer to the bed and reached for MaryAnne's hand.

"I'm here, Little Bit."

Her eyes slowly opened, and she gave me a slight smile. "Hey."

Her voice sounded scratchy and I reached for the cup on the tray by her bed. I pulled out an ice chip and held it to her lips. She took it and sucked on it. "You scared the shit out of me."

"Scared me too."

"They had to do surgery, but think you'll be okay. You have to stay a few days, though. They need to make sure you're healing right." She gave my hand a slight squeeze. I leaned over and kissed her forehead. "I asked Delilah to bring you a change of clothes for when you can go home. Something soft like your leggings. And my brothers will drop off some clothes for me too. I'm not leaving until you can."

"Get bored," she murmured.

"I won't be bored. I'll be with you." I winked at her. "Besides, I'm sure we can find some Christmas movies to watch. Want me to turn on the TV?"

She nodded and tried to focus on the screen across the room. I flipped on the TV and went through the channels until I found something I thought she might like. It was one of those sappy romantic Christmas movies. She only watched it a short while before she fell asleep. I angled the recliner so I could still hold her hand but lean the chair back too and see the TV. I let the movie keep playing, on the off chance she woke up before the ending.

Another started after the first one. While it wasn't my usual type of movie, this wasn't about me. It was about MaryAnne and what she needed or wanted. Even though she dozed off and on, I played things I knew she'd enjoy for the moments she was alert. She watched a bit of the second one before sleeping a little more. The nurse stopped by and assured me it was normal for her to doze off and on. My stomach rumbled but the cafeteria was closed. I shot off a text to Riley, hoping he was available.

Any chance I can get some food before my stomach eats itself?

He sent back a thumbs-up. *Be there in thirty.*

I didn't know what he was stopping to get, and I didn't much care. As long as it filled me up, nothing else mattered. MaryAnne woke again, her fingers lightly squeezing mine.

"There she is." I smiled. "You keep falling asleep. How do you feel?"

"Hurt," she said and licked her lips. I got her cup and handed her another ice chip. I wasn't sure when they'd give her more medication for the pain, or if that's what was in one of the IVs.

"Want me to find a nurse?" I asked.

She shook her head. "I'll be okay."

"The officer who came the other night stopped by. I told him about you getting attacked on our walk." I glanced at the open doorway, hoping she wasn't so loopy she couldn't take the hint. "Think it was a club whore, but I can't be sure."

She nodded and I knew she understood.

"Riley is bringing me some food, but you're at the mercy of the hospital staff right now. I have a feeling you need a special diet, at least the next few days. I don't think they'd appreciate me feeding you fries and a greasy burger, or ordering a pizza."

Her lips twitched and she smiled a little. "Pizza sounds good."

"Then our first night home that's what we'll do. Order whatever pizza you want."

"Ruining Christmas," she said, her throat still a little scratchy. I offered her another ice chip and kissed her brow.

"Little Bit, you could never ruin Christmas. It's far enough off we should make it home from the hospital in plenty of time. Need to get you healed up a bit first."

"How's everyone?" she asked.

I felt like an ass for not even checking on my brothers, but I knew they were in good hands with Bones. I shot off a text to him asking about Philly, Poison, and Brick, then showed her the response.

Too hardheaded to die. They'll be fine.

She smiled and laughed a little only to wince. I'd imagine any jostling she did would pull at the stitches and cause pain for at least a few days. We watched the movie until Riley arrived. He handed me a sack from the diner, and I pulled out a container with a big ass burger and what looked like a double side of fries. He'd even gotten me a bottle of soda from somewhere.

"Thanks, man. Didn't want to leave her, but my stomach was demanding to be fed."

"No worries." Riley reached over to take MaryAnne's other hand. He glanced down at the IV needle stuck in the back of it. "Glad you're doing okay. You had everyone worried."

"Worried me too," she said.

"She was under anesthesia and seems to be a bit groggy still. She's dozed off a few times since I've been in here with her." I shoved a few fries in my mouth and nearly swallowed them without chewing I was so hungry. I chased them down with some of the soda. "Would you make sure the animals are okay? Keep them fed and watered while I'm gone?"

Riley nodded. "I have no fucking clue how to take care of your bird, though. Damn thing about took off my fingers when I put him back in his cage."

I smiled, remembering how even Hatter had tried to save MaryAnne. Hatter, Archimedes, and Rascal all going after Blaire had ensured their place in our home forever. Of course, I'd already planned to keep them, but they'd more than earned a spot in the family.

"There's some containers in the fridge with fruits and veggies. Cut up a little of each for Hatter and give him a handful of his bird food. You'll have to wash his bowls each morning too."

"Where do you keep the cat food and dog food?" he asked. "And the bird food."

"Everything is in the bottom cabinet near Hatter's cage. Archimedes is used to going out every morning, at least once during the day, and again before I head to bed at night. If I had a fenced yard, you could leave him out for a bit. It's cold but not cold enough he couldn't run around for an hour."

"Don't worry about your furred and feathered family members. We'll see they have everything they need," Riley said.

"They saved me," MaryAnne said. "They attacked Blaire."

Riley grinned wide. "Then they deserve the very best. I'll get extra treats for them. I don't want to tire you out, and I'm sure your man over there would rather have you to himself. Y'all call or text if you need anything."

Riley waved and headed out. I finished my food and took MaryAnne's hand again while we watched TV. Eventually, we both fell asleep. Didn't help much. The nurses were in and out about every hour or two checking on her. I wasn't sure who was crankier the next day. Me or her. Either way, I'd be glad when I could take her home. I fucking hated hospitals.

Chapter Twelve

MaryAnne

Eight miserable days of nurses constantly checking on me. My wound had bled through the stitches the first two days and set back my recovery, which meant more time in that horrible room. I knew they were doing their job and wanted me to heal. I wasn't really upset with them, but the constant in and out at night when I'd tried to sleep had annoyed me after the first night. Not to mention the food was terrible. It didn't have much of a taste, and I'd had to force myself to eat it. But now I was free!

A nurse wheeled me out to the truck. Patriot had pulled it up outside the hospital doors. I was more than ready to get out of this place. The doctor had been impressed with how well I was healing once they'd stopped the bleeding. I'd felt like telling him after all I'd been through, one little stab wound was no big deal.

Patriot lifted me into his arms and set me down on the passenger seat. He reached across and buckled me in before shutting the door. The nurse gave me a wave before heading back into the building. Patriot had Christmas music playing on the radio and I reached over to turn it up a little. Now that I was outside again, and no longer confined to the bed, I felt in the holiday spirit once more.

"Ready to go home?" Patriot asked as he got behind the wheel.

"So ready!"

He grinned and leaned over to kiss me. "Missed sleeping next to you, Little Bit."

He wasn't the only one. Even though he'd been in a recliner next to my hospital bed, it hadn't been the same. Getting to hold his hand and having him wrap his arms around me were two very different things.

"Let's go see what Archimedes, Rascal, and Hatter have been up to. I bet they'll be happy to see you."

"And you," I said.

I sang along to the carols on the radio, feeling more like myself. My leg still hurt if I put weight on it, and I knew I couldn't overdo it. But at least I'd get to go home. There was a huge difference in being in my own home, around my own things, with our furry family members, and being in the hospital on that hard bed with the smell of antiseptic burning my nose.

The gates to the compound opened and Shay waved as we pulled through. The clubhouse looked packed for the middle of the day and a strange feeling settled in my stomach when Patriot pulled into a spot out front of the building.

"I thought we were going home?" I asked.

"We are. Have to make one little stop. You can sit at a table and have a soda. I won't be but a minute."

Before I could protest, he got out of the truck and walked around to my side. He carried me into the clubhouse and when I saw everyone there, even the old ladies and kids, my jaw dropped. Someone had put a tree up near the bar and strung lights all over the place.

"What's going on?" I asked.

"I have a surprise for you. The day you went to the hospital, someone else did too."

My brow furrowed. How was that a good thing? I looked around the room, trying to figure out who else had been hurt. Philly had a bruise at his temple and a black eye. He gave me a slight wave and I smiled back.

Had he been in the hospital too? Was this a welcome home type of thing?

Footsteps drew my attention and everything in me went still. A young girl and an older man approached. A small wrapped bundle lay in her arms. My gaze shot to Patriot and he hunkered down next to me. "Ready to meet our daughter? She was born the night you were hurt. They kept her a few days to make sure she was all right since she was a week early."

Tears blurred my vision as I looked back at the girl with that sweet baby in her arms. "Are you sure?"

The man, who I figured was her father, gave me a nod. "We're sure. Your generosity to strangers, giving our family and others a wonderful Christmas, proved to us you have a good heart. My daughter and I prayed with Reverend Burson. We're certain the baby belongs with you and your husband."

I held my hands out and the girl placed the baby in my arms. She was so tiny, and so perfect! I felt the tears slip down my cheeks as I ran my fingers over her. "Thank you. Thank you so much. We will love her and give her the best life we can."

The man nodded and the young girl smiled. "We've signed the papers. The baby is yours. All we ask is that you don't tell her she's adopted unless it becomes necessary. There's no reason to cause the child pain over thinking her mother didn't want her."

"I understand," I said.

The girl leaned over to give me a hug and whispered in my ear. "Thank you for giving her a home."

I cried some more as they left, and I stared at the miracle in my arms. Patriot ran his hand over her hair. It was nearly the same shade as his. Our daughter opened her eyes and blinked at me.

"Delilah and Phoebe put together the things we'd need the first few nights," he said. "I know we never got a chance to pick out nursery furniture or get the room set up the way you wanted it, but we can redecorate later if you don't like it."

"I don't care. We have a daughter! Isn't she wonderful?"

Patriot kissed my temple. "She's gorgeous."

"Her hair has so many shades of red and brown. It looks like yours."

"What do you want to call her? The birth certificate hasn't been sent in yet. They were waiting to see what we wanted to name her."

"I bet her hair looks like fire in the sunlight," I said. "What about calling her Blaze?"

Patriot bit down into his bottom lip and I saw the humor flashing in his eyes. "Blaze? Are you trying to give us a rough road? Sounds like the perfect name for a hellion."

"If she's anything like her daddy, she'll have the spirit to match her hair."

Patriot kissed me again. Soft and slow. "Love you, Little Bit. We can name her whatever you want. I think Blaze will be perfect."

"Blaze Cara Caffee," I said softly. "I already love you more than anything."

"Best get your wife and daughter home," Wizard said. "As soon as you both sign these."

He set some papers on the table, and I saw other signatures. I didn't bother reading anything. I knew Wizard wouldn't have us sign something we shouldn't. Patriot and I both scrawled our names on the documents, then bundled Blaze up and took her home. We'd need a baby seat, but since the house wasn't very far down from the clubhouse, I kept her in my arms and Patriot drove at a crawl.

Archimedes met us at the door with a happy *woof*. Patriot stopped to scratch behind his ears and greeted Rascal and Hatter. The animals seemed curious over Blaze, but I didn't let them get too close. Mostly because I wasn't ready to share her yet. Even Patriot hadn't tried to take her from me.

He led me upstairs and showed me the nursery. They'd put it next to our room, and someone had painted the walls a pale lavender. A white crib, changing table, small dresser, and rocking chair had been put together, and the crib even had bedding. The room was bare except those things, which meant we still got the chance to decorate it the way we wanted.

"I don't want to put her down," I admitted.

"Little Bit, you walked to the truck carrying her, and walked into the house and up the stairs. You need to get off your leg before you end up hurting yourself." He shook his head when I kept staring at our new daughter. "Hold on tight."

I gave a squeak as he lifted me into his arms, with Blaze clutched in mine. He carried us downstairs and set me on the couch. Patriot put on an animated Christmas movie and stepped out of the room. I heard him letting Archimedes out the back door, and then he sounded like he was talking to Hatter.

"Welcome home, Blaze. You're going to be loved so much," I said to the baby in my arms. She yawned and closed her eyes.

"There's formula and bottles in the kitchen," Patriot said as he set a cup of hot cocoa on the table next to the couch. "Looks like someone bought a bottle warmer too. It's plugged in on the counter."

"They thought of everything," I said.

"Phoebe said she put some outfits in the dresser upstairs. She washed everything so it's ready for Blaze to wear. They wanted to give us a few days to settle in with her, and give you more recovery time, so there should be enough for at least three or four days of clothing changes."

"We have an amazing family, don't we?" I asked.

"We do. Those men and their women would do anything for us, same as we'd do anything for them. And they'd give their lives to protect the kids in this club, including Blaze."

I reached for my cocoa, then hesitated. What if I spilled any on Blaze? It would be hot enough to burn her delicate skin. Patriot reached over and plucked her from my arms.

"Hey!"

He smiled. "Sorry, Little Bit. You can't hold onto her forever. I get a turn too. Drink your cocoa and we'll watch the movie. You can have her back in a little while."

I sipped my drink and leaned against his arm. As much as I loved the movie, my gaze kept straying to our daughter. I couldn't believe how beautiful she was. And she was ours! My vision blurred again, and I knew I was close to crying. It seemed like everything I'd wanted was within my grasp. Patriot had married me, loved me, and now we had a baby.

"Our lives are perfect, aren't they?" I asked.

"Yeah, Little Bit. They are. Might have had a rough road to get here, and I have no doubt more shit will head our way, but we have a remarkable future ahead of us. All three of us."

"What about Blaire's husband? What if he comes after us? And what about her?" I asked.

"Blaire has been handled. I didn't ask Kraken for the specifics, but he's assured me she won't be a problem. As for Walter, I should have told you. Officer Bowers let me know they found Walter Wilcox. He'd holed up with some friends. They have him in custody again. Even if they go searching for his wife, they won't find her. Wizard will make sure it looks like she left town."

"So no Blaire and no Walter," I said. "What's left?"

He pulled out his phone and showed me the screen. "Well, in about ten more hours it will be Christmas Eve. I think what's left is our first family Christmas, and a lot of happy memories to make."

"I don't know how you were still single. You're pretty amazing," I said.

He kissed me again. "Had to wait on the right woman to show up."

When he said things like that, I completely melted. It wasn't fair. He wasn't only sexy and smart, but he had to be the kindest man I'd ever met. And so protective! I didn't know why Titan had asked Patriot to come get me that day, instead of one of the others, but I was glad. Without him, I'd have remained lost and never become the woman I was today. He'd healed me, but more importantly, he'd loved me and shown me I was worthy of a man like him.

"I think she's asleep," I said. "Why don't we put her to bed?"

He stood and went to the stairs, pausing to wait for me. I moved slowly as I climbed to the second floor. I let him put Blaze to bed and made my way to our room. I'd kill for a real shower. The nurse had put a waterproof bandage over my stitches before I left so I could get good and clean when I got home. I stripped out of my clothes and let the water warm. Steam billowed from the space and I stepped under the spray.

"I'll never get tired of this view."

I looked over my shoulder and saw Patriot removing his boots and clothes, his gaze locked on my body. "Neither will I."

The man was a work of art. Between his tattoos and his muscles, I would gladly stare at him all day. He stepped into the shower and I reached out, my hands pressing to his chest. I traced the ink and pressed a kiss over his heart.

"I can't seem to resist the temptation of you all naked and wet," he said. "I told myself last time I would wait until we made it to the bed. I'm not even going to bother lying to myself anymore."

"Then don't wait."

He skimmed his hands over my hips. "What about your leg?"

"Guess you better find a way to not pull my stitches. Think you're up for the challenge?"

"Oh, yeah." He smirked and rubbed his cock against me. "Definitely up for it."

"That was so terrible it was kind of funny."

He rubbed his nose against mine. "I aim to please. Speaking of… you ready to scream my name?"

"Do your worst."

He nudged me toward the bench, then sat and tugged me onto his lap, my legs on either side of his thighs. "This okay? Not hurting you?"

"It's good. It would be better if I was coming already."

He swatted my ass. "Impertinent wench. I'm getting there."

I leaned back, thrusting my breasts up and he latched onto a nipple, giving it a gentle nip before sucking on it. I threaded my fingers into his hair and held on, letting the sensations wash over me. "Don't stop. Please don't stop."

I felt his hand against my belly, and then his fingers rubbed against my clit. I cried out, tugging on his hair as I arched into him. I should have been embarrassed over how fast I came. Patriot didn't seem to care. He didn't slow down, just kept rubbing and sucking until I'd come two more times.

"Lift up, Little Bit. I'll do the work, but I think this position will put the least amount of strain on you."

I went up higher on my knees, then lowered myself onto his cock. I moaned as he filled me up, the stitches pulling a little. Patriot gripped my hips, taking almost all my weight, and thrust up hard and fast. I cried out and clutched at his shoulders. "Ronan! God, feels so good."

"Not God, Little Bit. It's only me."

He took me like a man possessed. His grunts and my cries filled the space. The world spun around me as I came so hard I forgot to breathe. I felt the hot spurts of his release, then he gathered me against his chest.

"Fuck! Every time with you is more amazing than the last," he said.

"Because we're perfect for each other," I said. "You're the other half of my soul, Ronan."

He kissed me, his lips devouring mine. "Love you, Little Bit. So fucking much."

"Love you too."

"Let's clean up and head to bed. As much as I want you again, I don't want to put a strain on your leg and tear your stitches. Only a few more days and you can take them out. Bones will do it if you want him to."

"I'll gladly let him do it."

"Come on. Before you tempt me again."

I lifted myself off him and stood on shaky legs. Only Patriot had the power to reduce me to a puddle of goo. I hoped that never changed, not even after we'd been together twenty years. He washed me with a tenderness I wouldn't have expected from such a big, badass biker. But I knew that inside, at least with me, he was a big teddy bear.

By the time we'd finished, and he'd dried me off, I was yawning and ready for a nap. It was still too early for bed, but I knew the baby wouldn't sleep forever. If the movies and books were right, I'd need to sleep while I could. Patriot helped me into my pajamas, then he crawled into bed next to me.

"Sweet dreams, Little Bit," he murmured.

"Always," I said. And it was true. Other than my first night as being his and sleeping in his arms, I hadn't had any more incidents of waking up not knowing where I was. I now knew it was Patriot holding me each morning. He'd not only destroyed my demons in real life, but he'd chased away the monsters lurking in my head as well. Patriot had saved me in every way possible and give me the greatest gift ever -- a family.

Epilogue

Patriot -- Christmas Day

Blaze slept in her new bouncy seat while MaryAnne and I opened our presents. For a newborn, she was a rather great kid. She slept at least six hours at a time, and hardly ever fussed. If she stayed this easygoing, I'd be amazed. Something told me we were in for one hell of a ride when she became a teenager.

MaryAnne opened the small box and her eyes went wide. "Ronan."

"Put them on. My wife deserves to have something pretty on her hand, something that tells everyone she's taken."

She removed the wedding set from the box and slid the bands onto her finger. "They're beautiful. Thank you!"

I'd opened all but one of my gifts, and I'd loved everything she'd picked out. It seemed my woman knew me rather well. As I opened the last package and pulled out a leather jacket, the love I felt for her swelled even more. "MaryAnne..."

"It looked like something you'd like, and it will not only keep you warm but it will protect you if you're in an accident on the bike."

"Love you, Little Bit."

She finished opening her presents, excitement flashing in her eyes with each gift. But the glances she cast toward Blaze told me our daughter was even better than anything I'd put under the tree. I had to agree. She and MaryAnne were my true gifts this year. As long as I had them, I didn't need anything else.

The front door opened and heavy steps came our way. Galahad entered the room with a few boxes in his arms. He'd reached out yesterday, taking me by surprise. Even though he was MaryAnne's cousin, he'd been a bit harsh with her at times. I'd worried their relationship would always be strained, but it seemed he'd pulled his head out of his ass. Finally.

"Sean!" She stood quickly, then winced. "Sorry. I meant Galahad."

He looked at me before focusing on her. "We're all family. It's fine. I come bearing gifts."

He passed a box to me, one to MaryAnne, then set one next to Blaze's bouncy seat. MaryAnne toyed with hers and seemed reluctant to open it. I knew what held her back. "Hey, Little Bit. Grab that envelope on the bottom branch of the tree."

She picked it up, saw her cousin's road name on the front, and handed it to him. I winked at her, hoping to set her at ease. Galahad opened the card and pulled out the Harley Davidson and restaurant gift cards inside with a wide smile.

"This is awesome. Thanks, guys."

"Welcome," I said.

Thank you, MaryAnne mouthed to me. I gave her a quick nod and she tore into her present. It was an oval-shaped locket with the word *Mom* engraved on the front.

"Oh, Sean. It's beautiful! I love it."

"Figured you could have a picture taken of Blaze and put it in there. Maybe get a family shot for the other side."

I opened mine and pulled out a *Ride or Die* long-sleeved tee with a skeleton riding a Harley on the back. "Thanks, brother. This is great."

"Why don't you help Blaze with hers?" Galahad asked MaryAnne.

She reached for the present and opened it. It was a large box with several gifts inside. A floor mat with toys that would dangle over her when she lay on her back, a silver keepsake rattle with her name on it, and a soft purple blanket. It looked like Blaze had melted Galahad's heart and he was ready to help spoil her. MaryAnne thanked him and set the box aside.

"Want to stick around for a while? I think MaryAnne is going to put some holiday movies on the rest of the day, and she has a small feast she'll be making in a bit. Although, she cooked some of it yesterday so she just has to warm it up."

"You okay with that?" he asked her.

"Of course. You're my family, Sean. The entire club is now, but you're my blood. You're always welcome here."

He swallowed audibly and stood, going over to give her a hug. "Love you, MaryAnne. Sorry I've been a dick lately."

"It's okay. I forgive you." She smiled. "But don't do it again, or I'll be sure to send Blaze to your house whenever she throws tantrums for the next eighteen years."

He held up his hands. "Whoa. No need to threaten violence."

MaryAnne stood and I tugged her down onto my lap. "Merry Christmas, Little Bit."

"Merry Christmas." She kissed me, her lips barely touching mine before she pulled away. "Thank you, Ronan. You've made all my dreams come true."

Her body tensed and her eyes went wide. I knew she'd just realized she'd said my actual name when we weren't alone. But as Galahad had pointed out, we were family. And not only in the brotherhood sense. If I didn't make an issue of it, maybe she'd realize I wasn't mad.

"No, Little Bit. You have more dreams ahead of you, but I'll gladly stand by your side while you achieve each and every one. Because you're an incredible woman. Beautiful, smart, determined… and you're mine."

"Um, if the two of you are going to keep up with the mushy love crap, I may take my chances at the clubhouse."

I narrowed my eyes at Galahad. "Shut it or you're on baby duty."

"Nope. I'm good." He leaned back in his seat and crossed his ankles. "Let the movie watching begin. Anything except changing diapers."

"Wuss," MaryAnne muttered and I snickered.

"Pick a movie, Little Bit. Let's start making those family holiday memories. The first of many."

With my wife in my lap, our daughter nearby, and Galahad lounging on our couch, it was a happy Christmas. I had the family I'd always craved, and the love of the only woman I'd ever wanted. She was my everything, my entire world, and I knew I'd do anything to keep her safe and happy. Whatever it took, I'd keep the monsters away from my girls, because I'd rather die than see either of them hurt.

I'd always heard Christmas was the time of miracles. It seemed they were right, because I'd gotten mine, and I'd cherish them for the rest of my life.

Harley Wylde

Harley Wylde is the International Bestselling Author of the Dixie Reapers MC, Devil's Boneyard MC, and Hades Abyss MC series.

When Harley's writing, her motto is the hotter the better -- off-the-charts sex, commanding men, and the women who can't deny them. If you want men who talk dirty, are sexy as hell, and take what they want, then you've come to the right place. She doesn't shy away from the dangers and nastiness in the world, bringing those realities to the pages of her books, but always gives her characters a happily-ever-after and makes sure the bad guys get what they deserve.

The times Harley isn't writing, she's thinking up naughty things to do to her husband, drinking copious amounts of Starbucks, and reading. She loves to read and devours a book a day, sometimes more. She's also fond of TV shows and movies from the 1980s, as well as paranormal shows from the 1990s to today, even though she'd much rather be reading or writing.

Harley at Changeling: changelingpress.com/harley-wylde-a-196

Changeling Press E-Books

More Sci-Fi, Fantasy, Paranormal, and BDSM adventures available in e-book format for immediate download at ChangelingPress.com -- Werewolves, Vampires, Dragons, Shapeshifters and more -- Erotic Tales from the edge of your imagination.

What are E-Books?

E-books, or electronic books, are books designed to be read in digital format -- on your desktop or laptop computer, notebook, tablet, Smart Phone, or any electronic e-book reader.

Where can I get Changeling Press E-Books?

Changeling Press e-books are available at ChangelingPress.com, Amazon, Apple Books, Barnes & Noble, and Kobo/Walmart.

ChangelingPress.com